"Farrah Rochon delivers the feel-good read of the summer."

—*Entertainment Weekly*

"Doggone delightful rom-com."

—*Publishers Weekly*, starred review

"Everything Farrah Rochon writes is an utter joy to read!"

—Ali Hazelwood, *New York Times* bestselling author

MORE PRAISE FOR FARRAH ROCHON

"Rochon is incisively funny, gifted at winging between laugh-out-loud scenarios, crackling banter, and pointed social commentary." —*Entertainment Weekly*

"Rochon is a romance master who adeptly writes interesting and dynamic characters." —*Kirkus*

"Rochon's books are always witty, hot, and engaging."

—BuzzFeed

"Farrah Rochon is one of the absolute best romance writers today. Period."

—Kristan Higgins, *New York Times* bestselling author

"Farrah Rochon writes intensely real characters with flaws and gifts in equal measure."

—Nalini Singh, *New York Times* bestselling author

Pugs
&
Kisses

OTHER BOOKS BY FARRAH ROCHON

Pardon My Frenchie

The Boyfriend Project

The Dating Playbook

The Hookup Plan

FARRAH ROCHON

FOREVER

NEW YORK BOSTON

Forever
Hachette Book Group
1290 Avenue of the Americas, New York, NY 10104
read-forever.com
@readforeverpub

First Edition: July 2025

Forever is an imprint of Grand Central Publishing. The Forever name and logo are registered trademarks of Hachette Book Group, Inc.

Print book interior design by Marie Mundaca

Library of Congress Cataloging-in-Publication Data has been applied for.

Names: Rochon, Farrah, author.
Title: Pugs and kisses / Farrah Rochon.
Description: First edition. | New York : Forever, 2025.
Identifiers: LCCN 2025001334 | ISBN 9781538739167 (trade paperback) | ISBN 9781538739174 (ebook)
Subjects: LCSH: Veterinarians—Fiction. | Animal shelters—Fiction. | LCGFT: Romance fiction. | Novels.
Classification: LCC PS3618.O346 P84 2025 | DDC 813/.6—dc23/eng/20250127
LC record available at https://lccn.loc.gov/2025001334

ISBN: 9781538739167 (trade paperback), 9781538739174 (ebook)

Printed in the United States of America

LSC

Printing 1, 2025

For the team at Riverlands Animal Hospital and all who do the honorable work of taking care of animals. A heartfelt thank-you for all that you do.

CONTENT WARNING

This story mentions the death of a pet, so please proceed with caution and care if reading about the loss of a fur baby is difficult for you. There are also mentions of infidelity and strained parental relationships.

CHAPTER ONE

Dumbstruck and unable to speak, Evie Williams stared into the open doorway of her bedroom, her brain tripping and stumbling as it tried to process the sight before her.

Everything looked and sounded familiar—the sunlight gleaming off the polished footboard of her mahogany sleigh bed, the melodic tick of the ceiling fan as it spun on its highest setting. Even the perfume she'd spritzed herself with before leaving this morning—Jo Malone Peony & Blush Suede—still lingered in the air.

And yet, everything was different. She knew with mind-numbing certainty that her world, as of this moment, would never be the same.

This could not *be happening.*

The words tumbled around in her head, over and over and over again. This could *not* be happening. There had to be an explanation.

Evie tilted her head to the side and continued to stare, trying to make sense of the senseless. The dark green satin sheets she'd washed yesterday partially shielded a perfectly tanned ass that pumped up and down in rhythm to guttural grunts. She knew that ass intimately. She'd seen it this morning, when her fiancé had walked from the shower to his closet while she stood at their bathroom mirror getting ready for work.

An impassioned cry rang out as a pair of shapely legs wrapped around Cameron's waist. Manicured nails clutched his back. They were painted a bright pink that Evie would never have chosen to wear in a million years.

The sight of that garish nail polish gave rise to another bout of confusion. The color was the antithesis of her own style. The man she knew better than any other would never bring a woman who painted her nails such an obnoxious color into their bed, would he? Cam had his faults, but he would never cheat on her, despite what she could clearly see happening with her own eyes.

This could not be happening*!*

She had to get out of here. Maybe if she left the house, then came back, this alternative universe she now found herself in will have righted itself.

Evie backed out of the doorway. Time slowed to the pace of a garden snail as she turned and made her way up the hallway, past the open-concept living room and kitchen, and out the front door. It felt as if her body were moving through molasses, the movements seeming to belong to someone else. Her hands fumbled with the house key as she locked the front door behind her and headed for her car.

She had experienced this particular sensation only a few times before, but it had been enough to recognize it as her body's response to shock. She needed time to process what she had just witnessed before she could deal with it.

Evie opened her car door but then stopped with her fingers on the handle. Her head snapped up.

"What is there to process?" she asked the slanted reflection staring back at her in the driver's side window.

She knew exactly what was happening. Cameron was in their bed, making love to another woman. The same bed where he'd made love to her last night.

The sickening feeling in the pit of her stomach morphed into a searing rage.

Evie slammed the car door shut and rushed back up the walkway leading to the house. This time her fingers were steady as she slipped the key in the lock and opened the front door. She marched through the foyer, her blood pounding to an angry beat in her veins.

She'd just entered the living room when a buck-naked Cameron sauntered out of the kitchen with a bottle of water, his toned six-pack abs gleaming and semi-flaccid penis bobbing as he walked. He ran a hand through his dark blond hair and brought the bottle to his mouth.

His steps faltered the moment he saw her.

"Ev... Evie!" he said, choking on the water. He glanced toward their bedroom. "Ev, what are... Why aren't you at... ah... at Ashanti's? Is everything okay?"

No! she wanted to shout at him. *No, Cameron! Everything is not okay!*

But the words would not come. Evie could only stand there. She stared in disbelief at the man she'd planned to spend the rest of her life with. Those plans were gone now, shattered by his callous disregard for their relationship.

"Evie," Cameron demanded in an irritated voice. "What are you doing here?"

"This is my house," Evie finally answered, both surprised and pleased at the calmness she managed to maintain. "Am I not allowed to visit my own house in the middle of the day?" She crossed her arms over her chest. "A better question is, what are *you* doing in my house in the middle of the day, Cameron?"

Instead of answering, he said, "You're supposed to be at work."

"So are you," she pointed out. "But you're standing in the middle of my kitchen without any clothes on. Why is that?"

"Stop calling it yours," Cameron snapped. "I pay half the bills here."

For the briefest second, Evie's eyes flashed to the knife block sitting on the kitchen counter next to the Keurig. But the satisfaction she would get from chopping Cameron's dick off wasn't worth the jail time.

He could keep his dick. She didn't want it anymore.

"Are you going to answer my question?" Evie asked. "Why are you standing here naked in the middle of the day, Cameron?"

"I can already tell you're jumping to conclusions," he said. He set the water bottle on the counter and held his hands up. "I only came home to take a shower. The Rousseaus' rottweiler got caught up in some barbwire. He was filthy when they brought him in and my scrubs were a mess by the time I finished examining him."

It was no easy feat to stop her jaw from falling to the floor. Was he attempting to lie his way out of this? Seriously? For some reason that made her more upset than when she first walked up to her bedroom and caught sight of his bare ass in her bed.

Evie didn't say anything as she lifted her phone from her back pocket.

"Are you calling the practice to check up on my story?" Cameron asked. "You don't trust me?"

She managed to hold in the hysterical laugh that nearly escaped. Evie swiped across the screen. Her fingers shook, a clear indication that the calm she'd managed to maintain so far was on the brink of dissolving.

She held up the phone. She was just far enough away that he wouldn't be able to make out what was on the screen.

"Unless you want the video I recorded of you fucking your little side piece posted on every social media site I can think of, you will get out of my house right now."

She was bluffing, of course. She had been too shocked to even think to record him, but she didn't need video. Just the threat would be enough to send Cameron scurrying. If Charles Broussard II caught even a whiff of scandal, he would snatch his veterinary practice away, leaving his youngest son to fend for himself. Cameron wouldn't survive a month without the practice he'd inherited.

"Cam?" came a feminine voice from the direction of the bedroom.

Evie froze.

"Okay, Ev," Cameron said, glancing toward the hallway. "Don't blow this out of proportion."

"You have five minutes to get out of my house," Evie told her fiancé.

Ex-fiancé.

"Evie, be reasonable."

"You can come back for the rest of your things later," she said. She had to strain to get the words past the lump of emotion that had suddenly lodged in her throat. The weight of this moment, of what it meant for how her life would progress from this point forward, overwhelmed her.

Cameron took a step toward her. "Come on, Ev. You're being ridiculous."

"Don't you dare come near me!" Evie's hand shot out in front of her, holding him back. "I told you to leave."

"Ev—"

"Cameron, get the fuck out of my house!" Evie screamed.

He snapped back. The surprise on his face mirrored what she felt inside. She'd never shouted at him like that before.

"Cam?" the voice called again. A moment later, the blonde with the hot-pink nails walked into the kitchen wrapped up in Evie's favorite sheets.

Great. Now she would have to burn them. That son of a bitch was buying her another set.

"Oh . . . no," the woman said. "You're the girlfriend, aren't you?"

"Get out of my house," Evie said again. If she had to say those words one more time, she would not be responsible for the actions that followed.

Cameron and his—what was she? His mistress? His girlfriend? An escort he'd hired?—hustled toward the hallway leading to the back bedrooms.

Evie folded her arms over her stomach and sucked in several deep breaths. Every square inch of her skin hummed with an irritating, prickly tingle, as if someone were jabbing her with a thousand tiny pins. She would have to google the stages of emotional shock to figure out exactly where this complex mash-up of tension, anger, and disbelief landed on the spectrum.

When would the numbness set in? That's what she wanted right now. Give her the bliss that came with not feeling anything.

At least ten minutes passed before Cameron emerged from the hallway. He wore the blue Vineyard Vines sweater she'd bought him for his birthday last month, along with khakis. It was his typical attire on Wednesdays when he taught a class at Tulane University.

That's where he should be right now. If she was in a steadier state of mind, she would have remembered that bit of information when he'd tried to feed her his bullshit story about the Rousseaus' rottweiler.

He must have canceled his class today. Was this the first time he'd canceled so that he could engage in midday activities that didn't require clothing? How long had this been going on?

His mistress, ironically, was the one wearing medical scrubs. The pants were pink and the top had little balloons on it.

For the second time, Cameron's steps faltered when he saw Evie. "You're still here?"

"This is *my* house!" Evie reminded him, her yell echoing off the pitched ceiling.

The blonde looked between Evie and Cameron. "My shift starts in a few hours," she said before hurrying past Evie and out the side kitchen door.

And, just like that, a huge piece of the puzzle fell into place.

"The broken tibia," Evie said.

"What?" Cameron asked.

Last Halloween, Angelique James had arrived at the veterinary clinic with her son Mychal and Spanky, their Jack Russell terrier. The dog had gotten into the Halloween candy before the family had the chance to welcome any trick-or-treaters. While they were still waiting to be seen, one of the vet techs brought the Edwards's bullmastiff into the lobby, and at the sight of the huge dog, Mychal had run like the hounds of hell were at his heels. He'd slipped on the tiled floor and let out a cry that Evie could still hear to this day.

Cameron had embodied Superman, the character he'd dressed up as for the holiday, swooping in and carting Mychal and his mother to the emergency room at Children's Hospital. The eight-year-old had broken his tibia. And, to Cameron's relief, his mother had not considered suing the veterinary practice.

"You met her when you brought Mychal James to the ER last Halloween," Evie told him. "Was she his nurse?"

"Ev—"

She put her hand up. "I don't care. Just leave." That painful lump had returned to her throat, and it pissed her off.

Cameron dropped his head back and sighed up at the ceiling. The condescending sound had her reconsidering jail time. Maybe it *was* worth it.

"Where am I supposed to go?" Cameron asked.

"Do you think I give a fuck?" Evie yelled. A dull ache began to throb at her temples. She rubbed them with her thumbs. "I'm sure your little girlfriend has a nice enough bed. Go there."

The bastard had the audacity to look annoyed. With her! As if *she* had somehow inconvenienced *him* by catching him in bed with another woman.

Evie had never had to fight so hard against the urge to commit bodily harm.

Without another word, Cameron grabbed the keys to his Mercedes S-Class and left through the same side door his girlfriend had used.

Only now did it occur to Evie that she hadn't seen his car parked on the street. Finding a spot in this neighborhood could get dicey in the evenings, but there was ample parking during the middle of the day. If his trip home had been as innocent as he'd claimed, there would be no reason for him not to park in front of the house.

"That cheating son of a bitch must have parked on one of the other streets and walked."

She didn't care enough to follow him and find out.

An oppressive exhaustion came over her. Evie stood in the middle of the open-plan living area, unsure of what to do next. It all looked the same, but everything felt different. Tainted. She hated feeling this way about a place she loved so much.

She'd bought the house from her grandmother three years ago, when she and Cameron were going through one of their "off" periods. There had been three of those during their ten-year relationship. She had moved out of Cam's one-bedroom condo with a vow never to take him back. With her grandmother's blessing, Evie had gutted this house, renovating nearly every inch.

She sometimes regretted the decision to renovate, but not today. She didn't want memories of what had just transpired to mar the sweet memories she had of this house back when Rita Mayeaux still lived here.

Her grandmother would have cut Cameron's dick off. No question about it.

Evie closed her eyes tight and covered her face with her hands.

Cameron was right; she shouldn't even be here. She should be at her friend Ashanti Wright's doggy daycare, Barkingham Palace, where Evie worked as the in-house veterinarian several afternoons a week. But she knew she wouldn't be able to continue with her workday—not in the state she was in. She couldn't even remember what she had come home to pick up; to examine anyone's pet in her current condition would be tantamount to professional negligence.

There was one thing she must do. And *right* now.

She stalked out of the kitchen and into her bedroom. She plopped her hands on her hips and stared at the scene of Cameron's betrayal. Maybe if she washed the sheets in really hot water and added an entire bottle of laundry sanitizer they would be okay?

"No, they won't," Evie said.

She stripped the sheets from the bed and carried them outside to the ninety-six-gallon trash receptacle. Garbage collection had taken place this morning. If she had been paying close enough attention, it would have registered that the garbage bin was in its spot next to the side steps and not at the curb where she'd dragged it before leaving this morning. Cameron must have brought it in prior to screwing the nurse.

There were always signs. She just hadn't looked close enough.

As she made her way back inside the house, Evie's steps faltered as reality set in. Her world had changed. It had cracked and shattered right here on her grandmother's polished hardwood floors, the one thing she had not stripped from the house.

She dropped to the floor and sat cross-legged, burying her face in her hands and fighting against the onslaught of emotions that threatened to suffocate her.

What was she supposed to do now? There was no way she could continue working at the practice. It provided access to too many sharp objects, and as of an hour ago, she had developed a penchant for violence she hadn't thought herself capable of.

But where else can you go?

She had only ever worked at Maple Street Animal Clinic, the veterinary practice Cameron's father had opened forty years ago and, after retiring, had passed on to his youngest son. Evie had joined Cam at the practice the week after *she* finished vet school. She had continued to work there even after their last breakup. It had been a delicate, two-month-long exercise of walking on eggshells while around each other and engaging in perfunctory conversion when warranted.

But that wouldn't work this time. There was no way she could practice alongside Cameron. Not after this. He'd crossed her red line. He knew infidelity was the one thing she could never, ever forgive.

Evie threw her head back and screamed at the ceiling.

"My God, Cam, how could you do this to me?"

She'd put more of herself into this relationship than he deserved. Putting her own reputation on the line when a patient sued him for negligence, even though she was never sure if she believed his account of what happened that day. Forgiving him when she learned he'd racked up over a hundred thousand dollars in credit card debt—and helping him pay it off. Always making concessions for what *he* wanted to do, where *he* wanted to travel, how *he* wanted to live!

And how had he repaid her? By fucking another woman in their bed.

Evie pressed her fist to her lips. The anger and hurt tightening her chest made it difficult to breathe.

"How could you hurt me like this, Cameron?" she whispered.

She doubted she would ever get an answer. Not that the answer mattered. She was done.

CHAPTER TWO

Evie pointed the remote at the television and fast-forwarded to the beginning of the scene in *Jerry Maguire* where Dorothy and Jerry decide their relationship is no longer working. She snuggled more securely underneath the crochet blanket she'd dragged from the closet and looked on as, with aching sadness, Renée Zellweger told Tom Cruise that it was her fault for believing she was in love enough for the both of them.

Evie tried to summon a tear—she always cried at this part—but she couldn't manage a drop, not even when Dorothy cradled Jerry's head and pressed a kiss to the top of it.

"Thank goodness," Evie sighed.

Her muscles relaxed with the welcomed relief of realizing she had finally achieved that sweet nirvana she'd been striving for since she put Cameron out of the house yesterday: Numbness. Blessed, beautiful numbness.

She stopped the movie just before Jerry showed up at

Dorothy's house for the famous grovel scene and went in search of another movie with a meaty breakup. Maybe Marcus and Angela's in *Boomerang*? Or what about Allie and Noah's in *The Notebook*? The breakup scene when they were teenagers, not the second one when they were adults. If she didn't stop the movie in time and had to witness that passionate kiss in the rain between Rachel McAdams and Ryan Gosling, she may spontaneously combust. That would ruin her grandmother's beautiful blanket.

"Oh, this is a good one," Evie said. She waited for the opening credits of *La La Land* to start, then skipped to the scene where Sebastian showed up late to Mia's play.

"Asshole," Evie whispered.

The past twenty-four hours had consisted of watching the breakup scene of every romantic movie she could find. But only the breakup; she refused to watch the couple get back together. She wasn't in the mood for that bullshit, happily-ever-after propaganda. Happily-ever-afters were for fairy tales. In the real world, even when you gave your everything to a relationship, it wasn't enough.

Evie rubbed her breastbone with her fist. It had to be indigestion causing the sudden sting there because she'd just established that she no longer felt any emotion at all. She'd attained the numbness stage of the grieving process, and she would cling to it for as long as possible.

Her cell phone started dancing across the coffee table. Evie reached for it, intending to decline the call, but when she noticed her best friend Ashanti's name—this was the fourth time she'd called today—she decided she'd better answer.

"Hello," Evie croaked, muting the television.

"Girl, where in the heck have you been? Why aren't you answering your phone? Do I need to send a search party out looking for you?"

"I'm sorry," Evie said. "I had my phone on silent." She pushed herself up from her prone position on the sofa and pulled one leg underneath her. "What's up?"

"I'm the one who should be asking *you* that question. Wait—are you sick?" Ashanti asked. "You sound horrible."

Evie jumped on the excuse. "Yeah," she said, punctuating her lie with a cough.

"Is it COVID?" Ashanti asked.

"I don't think so."

"Well, did Cam stay home to take care of you? Is he monitoring your temperature? Is he diffusing eucalyptus?"

"Cam isn't here. I sent him away." The words shot another jab of pain straight to Evie's chest, proving she did indeed still have some feelings left in her bones. "I'm not sure if I'm contagious and I don't want him to get sick."

Another lie. She would hold a celebratory breakdance performance in the middle of Jackson Square if Cameron came down with the worst case of food poisoning known to man, complete with explosive diarrhea. But she wasn't ready to talk about what happened yesterday, even with her best friend.

"Girl, I'm coming over," Ashanti said. "I'll wear a mask."

"No!" Evie shouted. She added another fake cough that turned into a fit of real ones. That's what she got for lying. She rested her head in her upturned palm and released a weary breath. "I'll be fine, Shanti. I just need rest."

"Are you sure about that? Didn't you tell me years ago that you once suffered from asthma?"

"I haven't had an asthma attack since I was in kindergarten," Evie said, then reiterated, "I'll be fine. I promise to check in with you tonight."

"Nope. In an hour. And then every hour after."

Evie rolled her eyes. "Exactly how am I supposed to get any rest if I have to check in every hour?"

There was a pause, then an exasperated, "Fine. *I'll* call *you* later tonight. You get one missed call, Ev. If I call a second time and you don't pick up, I'm coming with the fire department and we're tearing down the door."

"You know where I keep my spare key," Evie reminded her.

"Duh. The fire department thing was for dramatic effect," Ashanti said.

"Bye, Shanti," Evie said.

"Call me if you need anything," Ashanti said. "Love you, girl."

"Love you too."

Evie set the phone on the table and, for the first time since last night, when she'd cried into the pillow in the guest room, felt tears welling in her eyes. She held them back because the time for crying was over, even if they were happy tears.

Looking back on the maelstrom of emotions she'd battled over the past twenty-four hours, gratitude had not been one of them. But just a few minutes on the phone with one of her best friends reminded Evie of just how blessed she was when it came to the people who *truly* cared about her.

She picked up the remote and switched from *La La Land* to her problematic fave, *Love & Basketball.* Instead of stopping the movie after Monica and Quincy's college breakup, she let it continue to play through Monica's stint with the international women's basketball league in Barcelona and to her eventual return to Los Angeles.

Just as the opening notes of Meshell Ndegeocello's soulful "Fool of Me" began to stream from the surround-sound speakers, the front doorbell rang.

"Ugh. Why?" Evie said as she pushed up from the sofa. If this was yet another person inquiring about her interest in selling her house, she would scream.

She made a mental note to order a doorbell camera. Cameron had never wanted one, had said they were too invasive. After yesterday's revelation, Evie realized it was more than likely because having the camera would have made it easier to catch him during one of his daytime trysts.

Goodness, she felt like a fool.

She opened the door and found a brown paper grocery bag on the front step. The top was folded over and stapled together.

"What the—" Evie said, hefting up the bag.

"Grocery delivery," a young guy with shoulder-length dreads called from the sidewalk. "The person who ordered it"—he glanced at his phone—"Ashanti Wright, said you may be contagious, so I didn't want to get too close. Hope you feel better. Have a good one." He waved, then hopped onto a bicycle that he'd propped against her neighbor's Little Free Library and pedaled toward Napoleon Avenue.

Evie brought the grocery bag into the kitchen. The moment she opened it, the tears she'd managed to suppress for much of the day began streaming down her face.

She pulled out yellow daisies wrapped in cellophane first. Next were several magazines, a COVID test, saltine crackers, and chicken noodle soup from the deli of the grocery store a few blocks away.

She grabbed her phone and texted Ashanti.

I truly love you.

A moment later, she received a reply.

Love you too. Feel better. Three ellipses pulsed on the screen before another text followed. **I know you love the spicy lentil soup, but I thought chicken noodle was better given the circumstances.**

Evie replied with several thumbs-up and heart emojis. She felt even worse for lying to Ashanti, but maybe she wasn't lying after all. She *had* felt sick since the moment she walked in on Cameron and that nurse. And just the thought of cuddling up on the sofa with a bowl of that soup and this month's edition of *Essence* magazine made her feel better.

Maybe the magazine could help with ignoring the other thing that had been bothering her for much of the day: the massive guilt over abandoning her patients at the practice.

When Gwyneth, the front office manager who had been at the clinic since Cameron's dad opened it forty years ago, had called to ask why she hadn't shown up for the scheduled tooth extraction on the Ruffins' Boston terrier, Evie hadn't even thought to come up with the excuse of being sick. She'd told Gwyn straight up that she was leaving the practice, without providing any further explanation.

It had been an awful thing to do, but who could blame her?

Still, her patients shouldn't have to suffer because of her shitty mood and her ex-fiancé's even shittier behavior.

"They won't suffer," she reassured herself.

Gwyn was superb at her job. Evie had no doubt she'd rescheduled the two procedures she'd had slated for today. Cameron would make sure the dogs were okay, if only for the sake of the clinic's reputation.

None of that lessened the guilt she felt. Those were her patients, and she'd let them down.

This isn't your fault. It's Cameron's!

She would remind herself of that fact every hour until it finally sunk in.

Evie transferred some soup into a bowl and ate at the kitchen island while flipping through the magazine. The meal was exactly what her soul needed. By the time she placed the empty bowl into the dishwasher, she was ready to do something more than just wallow on her couch watching rom-com breakup scenes. She needed to find something that would lift her out of this funk.

She clamped her hands on her hips and stared at the emptiness surrounding her. One thing was clear: She wasn't getting out of this funk if she didn't leave this house.

But where could she go? The one thing that brought her the most joy—being surrounded by animals—was out of her reach. She could *not* go to the clinic. She would scratch Cameron's eyes out the moment she saw him. She couldn't go to either of Barkingham Palace's locations because she'd told Ashanti she was sick. Where was a girl to go to get some puppy love in her life?

Not even a second later, the answer popped into her mind. "Duh, Evie! Of course!"

The Sanctuary.

It was the perfect compromise. Not only was she guaranteed some quality doggy time, but also helping at the animal rescue would soothe a bit of the sting from her guilt.

Decision made, she put the container of leftover soup in the refrigerator and went into her bedroom to change.

She'd first volunteered at the animal nonprofit when she was in veterinary school and had continued volunteering several years after graduation. But when Ashanti asked her to become the in-house veterinarian at Barkingham Palace, Evie had had to cut back on her volunteer hours. They were now nonexistent. With a start, she realized she hadn't been to The Sanctuary in over a year.

Evie peeled off the leggings and baggy T-shirt she'd been wearing since yesterday and hopped in the shower. After changing into jeans and a lightweight sweater, she headed for the animal rescue.

The Sanctuary was located near the Audubon Zoo, less than four miles from her house in the city's Broadmoor neighborhood. Yet, because of afternoon traffic, it still took nearly twenty minutes to get there.

Evie smiled the moment she entered the nondescript building and spotted The Sanctuary's office manager, Odessa Carter, sitting behind the reception desk.

"Hey there, stranger," Evie greeted.

Odessa's head popped up. "Evie!" She pushed back from the desk and rounded it, her arms open wide.

Evie hesitated a second before remembering that she actually was not sick and therefore did not have to worry about infecting Odessa with her make-believe illness.

"It's so good to see you, honey," the office manager said. "It's been a while."

"I know," Evie said. "Life has been lifeing." She gestured to Odessa's short, natural 'fro. "I love the hair." It had been dyed platinum blond and looked gorgeous with her dark brown skin.

"I gotta keep things fresh," Odessa said. "Are you here to volunteer?"

Evie nodded. "I finally have some free time." Understatement of the millennium.

"Well, we can always use a hand here. Doc is at lunch right now, but I know he would be grateful if you could finish up the vaccinations he started this morning."

"How is Doc?" Evie asked as she followed Odessa into one of the rescue's three treatment rooms. There hadn't been much updating—make that *any* updating—since she was a student volunteer. The dingy yellow-green paint was peeling in several places and the stainless-steel worktables were dull and scratched.

"As hardheaded as ever," Odessa answered. "I don't even try to tell that man anything these days. He's just gonna do what he wants anyway."

"Hardheadedness is one of Doc's most endearing qualities," Evie said with a laugh.

Odessa huffed.

Before retiring last year, Dr. Frederick Landry had been the senior-most faculty member at LSU Veterinary School. One of his reasons for opening The Sanctuary—in addition to alleviating some of the strain on the city's underfunded animal control services—was to establish a student mentorship program for those considering a career in the veterinary sciences.

Evie went through the paperwork that had been abandoned on the table—Doc was just old-school enough to want everything printed, even though Odessa had convinced him to convert to an electronic system a few years ago—and collected the vials for the DHPP and Bordetella vaccines. She prefilled a dozen syringes and lined them up for easy access.

She made her way to the animal pens and felt an instant dopamine rush at the sight of the dogs. They went into a frenzy when they saw her.

Evie burst out laughing. Why hadn't she thought to come here sooner?

By the time she'd vaccinated the first three dogs, all adorable sibling mutts who, according to Odessa, had been found wandering the neighborhood together, much of the melancholy she'd been wrestling with since yesterday had dissipated. This is what being around dogs did for her. It had been that way since she'd found a stray while riding her bicycle in the park on her seventh birthday.

Evie smiled. She hadn't thought about Popsicle in years. He was the first of six dogs she'd had while growing up, all strays. Her tendency to find and rescue the scruffiest dogs in all of creation drove her mother up the wall, but those were the ones she gravitated toward.

Evie brought the siblings back to their shared pen and retrieved the next dog on the list.

"Aren't you a cutie," Evie said, picking up the fawn-colored dog. His dominant breed was clearly pug, but he was mixed with something else.

"Hey, Odessa, any idea what the pug is mixed with? Looks like maybe a beagle?" Evie called.

"That's what Doc thinks he's mixed with too," Odessa answered as she came into the room. "He was surrendered by his owner last week. The guy got him from a breeder as a gift for his girlfriend, but she wanted a miniature purebred pug and the breeder wouldn't give him a refund." She rubbed the dog behind the ear. "This one is a sweetie."

"Does he have a name?" Evie asked.

"He didn't come with one. He looks like an Oliver to me. Or maybe a Sam."

"You know I hate when dogs have people names," Evie said. As she scratched the top of his head, she took in his coloring. His light brown coat reminded her of Butterball, the Pomeranian she'd rescued in the eighth grade. But the dark brown face and ears were hallmarks of a pug.

"This brown spot on the top of his head is pretty unique," Evie said. "What if we call him Waffles?"

Odessa plopped a hand on her hip. "So you'd rather name a dog after breakfast than after one of the greatest singers of all time, Sam Cooke?"

"No offense to Sam Cooke, but Waffles is the perfect name for this cutie." Evie pointed to him. "Check out the shape of the dark brown spot on his head. It looks like a splash of syrup.

"You're a cute little stack of waffles, aren't you?" She rubbed her nose to his as she continued the head scratch.

"If you say so," Odessa said, leaving the room.

"You like the name, don't you?"

He tilted his head to the side and looked at her like she'd just grown a third eye in the middle of her forehead.

"It'll grow on you," Evie said. "Now, I'm sorry for what I'm about to do, but it's for your own good," she whispered to Waffles a second before administering the vaccine. "Good boy! You took that like a pro."

She pressed a kiss to the top of his head.

"I wish I could take you home," Evie said.

She missed having a dog in the house. She hadn't had one since she and Cameron moved in together, because Cam never wanted a dog. He always said he got his fill at work; he didn't need any pets in his home.

That should have been her first glaringly red flag. What veterinarian didn't want to own their own pet?

"There were *so* many signs, Waffles," Evie said. The dog barked.

She laughed. "Look at that, you're already answering to your name. I told you it would grow on you."

She really wished she could bring this cutie home with her.

Evie jolted, her head rearing back. "Wait a minute," she said. "I *can* take you home. Who's there to stop me?"

She snuggled Waffles against her chest and walked to the lobby.

"Odessa?" Evie called. "Draw up the paperwork. I'm taking this one home."

"Just because you gave him a name? Well, heck, girl, go on and name the rest of them."

She chuckled. "One is enough for now," she said, nuzzling Waffles's neck. "I think this little cutie is exactly what I need."

Just then, the door to The Sanctuary opened and Evie heard Doc Landry's jovial laugh coming from just over her shoulder.

"Evie Williams, is that you?" Doc said.

"It is!" Evie turned.

And her heart stopped.

"Well, if this isn't perfect timing," Doc said, his cheery voice taking on a muted quality as it battled with the sudden chaos that had erupted in her head. "Look who's in town."

He pointed to the tall, dark-skinned, outrageously handsome man who'd come in behind him. A man dressed in tailored navy slacks and an expensive-looking powder-blue sweater. A man she had not come face-to-face with in eight years.

"Bryson," Evie whispered.

Bryson Mitchell.

The other man who'd broken her heart.

CHAPTER THREE

It had been a long time since something had taken Bryson Mitchell's breath away in such stunning fashion, but that's exactly what happened the moment he saw Evie Williams standing in front of him. It felt as if someone had reached into both lungs and yanked every bit of air from them.

"Evie," Bryson said.

He hadn't spoken her name in years. Just the feel of it on his lips sent an energized tremor catapulting through him. He was coping with an avalanche of emotions at the moment: shock, excitement, longing, regret.

More longing. Even more regret.

"Bryson," she said, her voice soft, polite. Apathetic. "Hello."

"Is that the world-famous veterinary surgeon?" Odessa Carter rounded the desk and captured Bryson in a bear hug.

"I don't know if 'world famous' is accurate, but you got the other part right," Bryson said, pressing a kiss to her temple.

"Oh, don't you come around here being all humble," Odessa said, giving him a playful tap on the arm. "Weren't you just in Rome speaking at some fancy conference?"

Bryson glanced at Evie. That impassive expression was still there.

"It was Milan," Bryson said to Odessa. "And I was only there for the food."

"Nonsense." Odessa gave him another slap. "You were there because everyone wants you as their keynote speaker."

"You haven't changed a bit, Odessa," Bryson told her with a laugh.

"Neither have you. You still don't like bragging on yourself."

Barking broke out from somewhere beyond the lobby, and Odessa threw up her hands. "Let me go check on these dogs before they tear this place apart."

"Well, you may not like bragging on yourself, but I brag on you enough for the both of us," Doc Landry said. "In fact, I just sent the write-up on you from *Today's Veterinary Business* to an old colleague of mine." He patted his pockets, then looked around at the floor. "Dammit," he said, snapping his fingers. "I left my phone in my car again. I'll be back in a minute."

And just like that, Bryson found himself alone with Evie Williams for the first time in eight years.

An awkward silence fell over the lobby and his clothes suddenly felt too tight, too itchy. That long-forgotten sensation of feeling uncomfortable in his own skin had made an unwelcome return. It shouldn't surprise him. He'd turned into a tongue-tied mess the first time he'd met her.

Bryson jammed his hands into his pockets and squeezed

his fists tight, trying to relieve the tension in his muscles and the knot that had formed in his stomach.

Evie glanced his way, then quickly averted her eyes to focus on the dog in her arms. Rubbing her thumb on the crinkly spot between the dog's eyes, she said, "So, how are you, Bryson?"

"Alive," he answered with a grin. But the smile died on his lips when she didn't return it.

His reply had been a running joke between them back when they both volunteered at The Sanctuary. Whether it was after a late night of studying or, on the rare occasion, partying, they always answered the morning greeting in the same way. Given the rigor of Louisiana State University's Veterinary Medicine program, they'd felt lucky just to live to see another day.

Maybe she'd forgotten about their silly greeting. Or, more than likely, she was uninterested in tiptoeing down even the most innocuous parts of memory lane where he was concerned.

"What about you?" Bryson asked. "How are you doing, Ev?"

"Fine," she answered with the cordiality of someone speaking to a complete stranger about the weather.

After all these years with zero contact, they *were* strangers. They had only spent one summer together. But they'd shared so much in those months, it was hard to imagine they would ever find themselves in a place where they could barely speak two sentences to each other, where this cloud of unease hung over them.

That regret-filled knot tightened in the pit of Bryson's stomach.

Both he and Evie turned at the sound of Doc opening the front door. Its squeaky hinges screamed for a shot of WD-40.

"How have things been going, Doc?" Evie asked.

"Good, good," his mentor answered with the exuberant gaiety Bryson always associated with him. True to form, Doc seemed oblivious to the tension hovering in the air.

"It's been a long time since you've dropped by," Doc continued. "I gather things have been busy over on Maple Street?"

Bryson flinched at the mention of Maple Street. One of the reasons he'd pushed thoughts of Evie out of his mind these past eight years is because the thought of her working at Maple Street Animal Hospital with her boyfriend—no doubt her husband now—made him sick to his stomach. Literally. He would need to find the nearest trash can if anyone so much as mentioned that asshole's name.

"Things are always busy there," Evie answered. "And at Barkingham Palace."

"I bet they are. That boarding place has been all over the news." Doc turned to Bryson. "Remind me to show you the video with the poodle and the French bulldog. What's their names again, Evie?"

"Duchess and Puddin'," Bryson answered at the same time she did.

Evie looked over at him, her brows arched high over eyes that were even more beautiful than he remembered.

"I should have known you'd seen that video," Doc said. "I watched it over and over for a week. Couldn't help myself."

Bryson doubted there was a single person in the country who hadn't seen the footage of those two dogs that went viral last year. He didn't realize Evie worked at the pet daycare center where it had been taken. Interesting.

There was so much he didn't know about her, which was

a damn shame. At one time his every thought had been consumed by this woman.

"That daycare—what's the name? Barkingham Palace?—it seems pretty popular," Bryson said.

"It is," Evie answered. "I'm lucky to work there." She turned her attention to Doc and, in a voice coated with ten times more warmth, said, "I had some free time on my hands and decided to drop in and see how things are going at The Sanctuary, but now I'm convinced fate brought me here." She smiled a genuine smile and kissed the dog's head. "As I just informed Odessa, I'm taking this little one home with me."

"She already named him," Odessa said, coming back into the lobby. "Waffles. I think Sam is a better name, but what do I know?"

"This one has been a bit skittish," Doc said as he gave the dog a head scratch. "But I think he'll warm up to you in no time."

"He already has," Evie said.

Bryson stood there with his hands in his pockets, feeling awkward as hell as Evie and Doc chatted about her new dog. Should he remind Doc that he'd followed him back to The Sanctuary after their lunch for a reason, or should he slowly back away and follow up with his mentor later?

He could smash through the wall like the Kool-Aid Man and he doubted anyone would notice.

"I've been meaning to ask, where are the students?" Evie said. "There hasn't been a single volunteer since I arrived hours ago."

"Uh, we can get into that later," Doc said. "Besides, I only had a few vaccinations to administer. I didn't really need any volunteers today."

"It was more than just a few vaccinations," Evie said. "That's what I've been doing all afternoon. I'll finish them up before I leave."

Doc waved her off. "Don't worry about those. I'll get to them later. I have two of my best volunteers here. This is a time for visiting, not vaccinating." He clamped a hand on Bryson's shoulder and his other on Evie's. "Now that I think about it, we can do both. Since I've got you two here, I might as well put you to work. It'll be like old times."

Bryson noticed the way Evie stiffened, her shoulders going rigid in a clear sign that she'd rather do anything but revisit old times.

"Uh, Doc, I have to—" Bryson started.

"You can spare a half hour to help out," Doc said. It wasn't posed as a question. "Come on, you two. Let's bring this little reunion to the treatment room."

Doc started for the rear of the building, not looking back to see if either of them had followed. There was no reason to doubt they would. As happy-go-lucky as he appeared, Bryson was willing to bet that not one of Doc's former students would dare defy him.

He motioned to Evie to go ahead of him. "After you."

"Thank you," she said, her voice lacking any of the warmth it held when she spoke to Doc or Odessa.

Was he surprised by her chilly reception? No.

Did it hurt? Fuck yes.

Would he give anything—the shirt off his back, his favorite coffee mug, his signed copy of S. A. Cosby's *Razorblade*

Tears—to have Evie greet him with even an ounce of the excitement he'd felt upon first seeing her?

Again, fuck yes.

But it wasn't meant to be. Not that he could blame her. *He* was the one who'd messed up eight years ago. She didn't owe him so much as a smile.

It doesn't look as if you'll get one either.

The stomach knot tightened.

Bryson followed her into the treatment room where they used to perform routine spays and neuters back when they volunteered here. He wasn't sure what he expected after nearly a decade, but it wasn't for this room to look exactly the way it had all those years ago.

Same faded posters of the canine muscular and skeletal systems. Same corkboard with various business cards and takeout menus tacked to it.

He squinted. Those couldn't possibly be the same menus that had been there eight years ago, could they? The room was like a time capsule.

What were the odds that the first time he returned to this place that had one of the biggest impacts on his life, he would find himself here with Evie, the woman who'd had one of the biggest impacts on his life? The universe had jokes.

Bryson knew when he'd made the decision to return home that he would eventually run into her. New Orleans was a big city compared to the little dot on the map where he'd grown up, but it was still small. And the veterinary community was even smaller. It was inevitable their paths would cross.

But after only three days home? Couldn't he get a full

week to settle in before having to face the one person from his past who could send his emotions into a tailspin?

Was it kismet? Fate? There had to be something more than coincidence at play. Visiting The Sanctuary hadn't even been part of today's plans. He'd only followed Doc back here after their lunch because his mentor had insisted on giving Bryson a lapel pin to wear at his speaking engagement on Saturday. What were the chances that Evie would be at The Sanctuary when it was apparent that she hadn't visited in a while either?

Doc kept up most of the conversation as they all worked as a team, examining the dogs, then vaccinating, then soothing. Bryson fought his mind's treacherous urge to journey back to those afternoons when he and Evie were here as vet students, with their mentor stepping in only occasionally to supervise.

Doc was always too wrapped up in grading coursework or handling the many fires that would arise in his role as the faculty head. It left way too much time for Bryson and Evie to get into the kind of things they definitely should not have been getting into while on the job.

He could *not* let his thoughts wander into that territory. Not right now. Not at all.

It was a long time ago. He was a different person. And he could only imagine that Evie had changed over the past eight years in ways he couldn't even fathom. Bryson wasn't sure he would ever find out. Based on the reception he'd received so far, he doubted there would be any reminiscing about the good times over a cup of coffee.

"—before Milan, Bryson?"

His head jerked back at the sound of his name being called.

"What was that?" Bryson asked.

"Where was it that you spoke before Milan?" Doc asked. "Was it Amsterdam?"

"Uh, no. Austria," Bryson said.

"That's it! I knew it was one of those places I've never been but always wanted to go. You ever been to Austria, Evie?" Doc asked.

"I can barely make it north of Canal Street," Evie answered. "My life is tied to this area of the city." She rubbed the head of a Chihuahua mix. "It must be nice to see the world and collect a paycheck for it."

Bryson was pretty sure that was a dig at him, but because he couldn't be sure, he said, "I never get to see much outside of the conference hotel when I travel for these things. It's exhausting, if I'm being honest. I plan to cut back drastically on the number of speaking engagements I accept."

"Well, I'm glad you finally accepted the LVMA's invitation to speak," Doc said.

Bryson had turned down the Louisiana Veterinary Medical Association at least a dozen times over the years. He'd always had a conflict, but he doubted he would have accepted even if he'd had space in his schedule. He hadn't been ready to come back to New Orleans. This time, the timing had worked perfectly with his plans to finally return home.

"Evie, did you know Bryson was speaking at the LVMA's quarterly meeting?" Doc asked. "I'm assuming you'll be there. You don't want to miss his talk about how 3D printing is the wave of the future in veterinary medicine." Doc waved a hand at Bryson. "I personally think you young folks are out of your minds with this 3D stuff, but if anyone can convince me otherwise, it's you."

"I . . . ah . . . I'm not sure if I'll make the meeting this quarter," Evie said.

"But you always go to the meeting. It's the only place I see you these days," Doc said.

"I know, and I'm sorry about that, Doc. I just have a lot going on right now," she said. She looked as uncomfortable as a person could possibly look while trying to pretend they were not uncomfortable.

The tightness in Bryson's throat made it difficult to swallow. She'd probably had every intention of attending the quarterly meeting up until discovering that he would be the speaker.

"Ah, that's too bad," Doc said. "It's sure to be a great discussion." He snapped his fingers. "The lapel pin! That's why I brought you here, Bryson. Why didn't you remind me? I'll be right back."

"Doc—" Bryson called, but Doc had already taken off. And if his office was anything like Bryson remembered, his mentor would have to search under mountains of paperwork to find that lapel pin.

He regarded Evie, taking in the rigidity of her shoulders and the tightness in her jaw. Her discomfort was too obvious for him to deny it or to pretend it was anything but his presence causing it.

It would be better for both of them if he got out of here.

"Can you let Doc know that I had to leave?" Bryson said. "I need to go over my presentation for Saturday."

He could give that presentation on the spot and not miss a beat, but it was the easiest excuse he could come up with.

"Sure," she said, her attention still on the Chihuahua.

Bryson studied the crown of her head, willing her to turn.

To give him even the slightest indication that there was a possibility they could regain the friendship they once shared. He knew better than to expect *more* than friendship, but now that he was back in New Orleans, now that he'd seen her again, the thought of not seeing her—of having to avoid her—was like a punch to the gut.

But she didn't turn.

His throat had to work overtime to swallow past the painful lump that had suddenly formed.

You did it to yourself.

"It was good to see you, Ev," Bryson said, because he couldn't just walk away, no matter how much his brain told him he should.

She looked over at him. Her lips twitching in what, if he squinted and tilted his head to the side, could feasibly be called a smile.

"Good luck on Saturday," she answered.

Ouch.

He guessed it was too much of a stretch for her to say it was good to see him too.

You did it to yourself.

CHAPTER FOUR

Delightfully chaotic.

That was the best way to describe the atmosphere at Barkingham Palace on any given day. Evie had smiled more in the two hours since she'd entered through the freshly painted doors of the pet daycare's newest location than she had in the past two days.

Since arriving, she'd witnessed a cocker spaniel and a bichon frise engaged in a fierce tug-of-war over a stuffed Baby Yoda, a long-haired Chihuahua executing a perfect backflip in exchange for a doggy treat, and she was certain her favorite corgi, Franny, had said the word *store*. Or maybe it had been *stove*. Either way, the dog had talked.

This was the kind of mayhem she needed in her life—not the kind Cameron had wreaked.

Not to mention what seeing Bryson Mitchell had done to her.

She paused for a moment, giving her brain time to adjust to the cosmic shift that took place whenever she so much as thought his name. The intense reaction that went through her the moment she turned around and saw Bryson standing behind Doc Landry yesterday had been involuntary. And inevitable. How could her body *not* react to seeing him again after all this time?

Over the years, she had tried to convince herself that she had created an unrealistic memory of him, but that was not the case. At all. Bryson Mitchell was still one of the finest men to ever walk the planet. Smooth, dark brown skin. A smile so bright it made her want to put on sunshades. A cut jawline that fit perfectly in the palm of her hand. Lips that...

Don't go there!

She would not think about his lips and all the places they could and *did* go.

He still had that tall, svelte physique he'd had as a basketball player at LSU, but his chest and shoulders had filled out even more over these past eight years. The way the lightweight sweater had contoured to his pecs left an imprint on her mind, one that refused to leave no matter how many times she tried to blink it away.

Had she opened an umbrella indoors? Walked under a ladder? Encountering the only other man who'd managed to break her heart within hours of having her heart broken by the man she'd been engaged to marry was next-level bad luck. Maybe it was karma for hitting that pothole on Poydras Avenue last month and splashing a woman waiting to cross the street. She'd felt horrible, but that had been the Public Works Department's fault, not hers.

"Whatever it is, you'd better fix it," Evie whispered.

She had been lucky to get through that hour-long encounter with Bryson without having the emotional meltdown she'd desperately needed. She didn't want to chance anything else happening that would send her over the edge.

As she used her penlight to examine the ear canal of a Maltese new to Barkingham Palace, her nerves began to settle. She relished being able to lose herself in the familiarity of doing her job. It was therapeutic. No, it was *necessary.*

If she really was done with the clinic on Maple Street—and she was; there's no way she could go back—she would have to find a full-time job soon. For one thing, she could use a steady paycheck, but she needed the comfort of being around animals more than she needed the money. Hopefully she could convince her patients from Cameron's practice to follow her wherever she landed.

He would be *so* pissed. It's exactly what he deserved.

There was a soft knock a second before the door opened and Ashanti slipped inside the exam room. She was dressed in Barkingham Palace's signature purple polo shirt and wore her skinny micro-braids down around her shoulders.

"How is Cassiopeia's ear?" Ashanti asked. "Is it infected?"

"Slightly," Evie answered. "I have some drops at—" She paused. She no longer had a practice from which she could simply pick up medication. "I'll prescribe some drops. It won't take long to clear this up."

"Gentamicin and clotrimazole?" Ashanti asked.

Evie welcomed the grin that tilted up the corner of her mouth. "You've still got it, my friend."

Ashanti licked her finger and tapped herself on the ass while making a sizzling sound. "At least all of that schooling didn't go to waste."

Before her best friend became the owner and operator of the most popular doggy daycare in the Gulf Coast region, she had been a fourth year alongside Evie at LSU's School of Veterinary Medicine. In fact, it was Ashanti who had convinced Evie to become a vet.

As determined as she had been to save every stray as a child, Evie had been on track to follow in the footsteps of the other members of her immediate family and go to medical school. It's what the Williamses did. But when her bubbly, freckle-faced roommate discovered that Evie had always dreamed of working with animals—which, let's face it, were so much better than people—Ashanti urged her to go for it.

The day she'd decided to finally tell her parents that she was changing her major to veterinary medicine was seared into Evie's mind. Her father thought she was joking, but once it became clear that she was not, it was her mother who'd lost it. She still hadn't forgiven Evie for undermining her dream of being a dynamic mother/daughter cardiologist duo.

Evie was grateful they hadn't gone into full controlling-parents mode and refused to pay for her schooling unless she majored in the field they chose for her. But, even if they had, she would have found a way to pay for vet school on her own. Because once she'd made the decision, it was as if someone had flipped on a light—one of those cool lights that cast rainbows and stars on the ceilings and walls. She'd suddenly felt excited about her future instead of simply accepting of it.

The only thing that would have been better was going into practice with Ashanti as they'd always planned. And maybe they would have if Ashanti had not been forced to quit vet school to raise her twin sisters after losing both her parents. She knew her friend was more than satisfied with how things were going with the daycare, but Evie still found herself asking, *What if?* Especially over the past forty-eight hours.

"How are you feeling?" Ashanti asked. She reached toward Evie's forehead with the back of her hand, but Evie dodged it, turning and grabbing the otoscope again.

"I'm better," she said as she unnecessarily reexamined Cassiopeia's ear canal. Quickly changing the subject, she said, "The progress you all have made on this building is phenomenal. The remodel looks amazing."

"What do you think about *this* space?" Ashanti gestured to their surroundings. "It's nice having a dedicated exam room, right?"

"There are no words," Evie said. "Don't get me wrong, I still love Barkingham Palace's original location, but I am *so* glad Ridley convinced you to stop worrying about the cost and buy this building."

"Convinced me? She bullied me." Ashanti laughed. She scooted onto the exam table, picked up the Maltese, and sat it in her lap. "But I'm grateful for our bossy friend sticking her nose in my business too. I've always adored this building. I knew it would be perfect for a second location."

"When do you think you'll be ready to accept more pets?"

"Hopefully soon." She ticked items off on her fingers. "I'm interviewing two more people on Monday, including a new dog groomer. The last of the beds for the signature suites should be here in another couple of weeks. I'm going to do a few more test runs, but I'm hoping by the end of the month I will officially be the owner of a fully functioning doggy daycare chain!"

She kicked her legs out and wiggled her feet like a five-year-old on a park swing. Evie couldn't contain her smile. Her friend deserved this.

When the subject of that viral video came up yesterday, she hadn't been surprised that Bryson knew what Doc had been referring to. Six months later and the video of Ashanti's French bulldog and her boyfriend Thad's standard poodle sharing a doggy treat made its way into Evie's Instagram feed at least once a week.

Ashanti had started selling the homemade treats as a side hustle. After Duchess and Puddin' became internet sensations, a national pet food company bought the doggy treat portion of the business for millions, giving Ashanti the capital to expand the daycare by purchasing this second, much larger location.

"Hey, I wondered if you could do me a favor," Evie said as she moved the exam light back into place. "I know the waiting list for Barkingham Palace is out the door and down the street, but do you think you can find a spot for my new dog?"

Ashanti stopped in the middle of scratching Cassiopeia's backside. The dog responded with a displeased bark.

"Umm . . . did I hear that correctly, or do *I* need ear drops?" Ashanti asked. "Did you just say you have a dog?"

Evie nodded. "I visited The Sanctuary yesterday and fell in love with the sweetest pug and beagle mix. He is *so* adorable. I had to bring him home."

"Hold on." Ashanti made a time-out signal with her hands. Cassiopeia barked again. "Rewind this conversation back thirty seconds. How did you convince Cameron to finally get a dog? He's always been adamant that he didn't want one."

Evie had every intention of eventually coming clean to her friends about what had transpired over the past couple of days, but maybe she should have thought this through. Her bandwidth for dealing with this right now was at a negative seventy-five.

"Ev?" Ashanti prompted.

But she also knew her friend well enough to know that Ashanti wouldn't let this go. She could be as tenacious as any of the dogs in this daycare when it came to getting to the bottom of a story.

Conceding that her chances of leaving here today without telling Ashanti the truth were slim, Evie decided to rip off the proverbial Band-Aid.

She sucked in a deep breath, looked Ashanti straight in the eyes, and said, "I didn't convince him to do anything. We broke up, and I kicked him out of the house. Cameron and I are done."

CHAPTER FIVE

Evie would have laughed at the shocked look on Ashanti's face if her own mood hadn't just plummeted to the bottom of the sea with that pronouncement. Despite knowing she'd done the right thing by putting Cameron out, it still stung.

She loathed to admit that she was still hurting, but dammit she was! How could she not be after all she'd given to their relationship?

"Evie!" Ashanti screamed. "What in the heck are you talking about? You broke up?" She clutched her head. "You broke up with Cameron and you are just now telling me! You've been here all afternoon!"

"Actually, it's only been about two hours," Evie corrected. "I had a doctor's appointment this morning."

"Wait." Ashanti made the time-out signal again. "Wait. Wait. Wait. What happened? Start at the very beginning and don't you *dare* leave anything out."

There was another knock at the door. Jasmine Walters, the receptionist Ashanti had hired for Barkingham Palace's second location, poked her head into the exam room.

"Hey, do you need to sign for the shipment of prescription dog food, or can I do it?" the younger girl asked.

"You can sign for shipments," Ashanti said. She lifted the Maltese from her lap and held it out. "And will you ask Maxine to clip Cassiopeia's nails?" The moment the door closed, she turned back to Evie. "I need to know everything. When did you decide to break up with Cam?"

Evie blew out another sigh. She *so* was not up for rehashing this.

"When I went home Wednesday to get the earrings I'd borrowed from you and caught him screwing another woman in our bed." Evie snapped her fingers. "Shit, I still forgot to bring your earrings."

"What!" Ashanti slammed both hands on the exam table. "That rat bastard!"

"Won't argue with you there." Evie pulled out her phone and turned the screen to face Ashanti. It was riddled with red notification bubbles.

"He's left a dozen voicemails over the past two days, but I don't care what he has to say. He knows that cheating is the one thing I will never forgive him for. And for him to bring that woman into my house? Into my bed?" She returned the phone to her pocket. "Nope. It's over. I'm done."

Ashanti slipped off the exam table and perched her butt against it. She shoved her hands in her hair.

"Evie, I just don't understand. You and Cameron are... well, you and Cameron. Sure, the two of you have broken up a few times, but you're engaged now. I thought you were in it for the long haul."

"So did I," Evie said. That little zing of hurt pierced her chest again.

"What did he say when you caught him?" Ashanti asked.

"That I was blowing things out of proportion."

She gasped. "He did not!"

"And he called me ridiculous," Evie added. "Oh, and did I mention they were doing it on my satin sheets?"

"Not the green ones!"

"Yes, the green ones."

"He really is a rat bastard," Ashanti said.

Evie shook her head. "I'm done, Shanti. I've taken him back in the past, but this is different. I can't do it. I won't."

"What about the clinic? Do you think you can still work there?"

Evie hunched her shoulders and let them fall. "I've been going back and forth in my head, trying to picture what it would look like. The last time Cam and I broke up, we managed to continue working together, even though it was *the* most uncomfortable work situation you can imagine. The entire staff was walking on eggshells for a month."

"But you figured out a way to coexist through that rough patch."

"I know," Evie said. She stared at the portrait of Duchess dressed as Marie Antoinette that hung on the wall.

She wished it was as simple as just figuring out a way to coexist with Cam, but the situation wasn't as black and white this time around. She'd been mired in the awful swirl of grayness of this mess Cameron had made of their relationship for two days; she still couldn't decide what to do.

Wait a minute. What was she even thinking right now?

Of course she knew what to do: expunge Cameron Broussard from every facet of her life. It really *was* that simple.

"This is more than just a rough patch," Evie said. "I tried to come up with a solution last night, wondering if maybe we could work on different days of the week, but . . . " She shook her head. "I can't do it. It's his practice. I don't want to be beholden to Cameron for anything, especially my livelihood."

Ashanti frowned, then nodded. "I get it." She blew out a sigh. "Well, you know you always have a job here. It may not be a full-time job, but it's something."

"It's everything to me," Evie said. She leaned over and bumped Ashanti with her elbow. "I love you, chick. Thanks for always having my back."

"Always," Ashanti said. She folded her arms across her chest. "So, you want to go slash Cam's tires? Put sugar in his gas tank?"

Evie burst out laughing. "Now you sound like Ridley." She could only imagine what the most audacious member of their trio would have to say about this situation.

"It's too bad Rid isn't here," Evie said. "I could use her advice."

Ashanti pulled her phone from her back pocket. "We're not living in the Dark Ages. Just because an ocean is currently separating us doesn't mean we can't get her input. Although we both know what Rid's going to say about this."

Ridley would have definitely cut Cameron's dick off if she had been the one to walk in on him.

"You don't think she's still at the office, do you?" Evie asked. "I don't want to disturb her work."

"It's almost seven in London. Hopefully she's keeping

better work hours there than she does here," Ashanti said a second before Ridley answered the phone.

"Hey, girlies, what's up?" Ridley greeted. "Have you caught those two dogs hooking up on camera again?"

"No action on the webcam," Ashanti said. She looked at Evie with that raised brow again. "Or *was* there a camera?"

Evie shook her head, then asked Ridley, "You're not at work, are you?"

"Of course I am. If I don't do everything, nothing gets done. The people in this office are as incompetent as those in the New Orleans location." She lifted a clear mug filled with light brown liquid to her lips.

"Are you drinking tea?" Ashanti laughed. "They're turning you into a true Londoner."

"Nah, that would never happen," Ridley said. "True Londoners remember to first look right when crossing the street. I almost walked in front of a car again today."

"Please bring your butt back home before you end up splattered across Abbey Road," Evie told her.

"Graphic," Ridley said. "And if I get splattered, it would be on Brompton Road while on my way to Harrods. So, what are you two doing calling in the middle of the day? Don't you have jobs, or is everyone slacking off now that I'm not around?"

Evie paused for a beat before she said, "There have been some...interesting developments here at home." She gave Ashanti permission to get Ridley caught up on the drama that had become her life.

Five minutes later, Ridley's reading glasses were gone and the pen she'd shoved behind her ear had been flung clear across the room.

"I knew it!" Ridley said. "I knew that motherfucker would eventually do something like this. I knew he couldn't be trusted!"

"Really?" Evie asked. "Yet, you didn't say anything to me, your friend who has been engaged to the motherfucker for four years?"

"Girl, you know damn well I have never liked Cameron's crusty ass. But anytime somebody tried to tell you something, you'd say we just didn't understand him. I told you the last time you broke up that you needed to kick him to the curb for good."

"She did," Ashanti injected. "I was there when she said it."

"Well, you should have been more forceful," Evie said.

"And alienate one of my best friends?" Ridley asked. "After I realized you actually were in love with him, I stopped trying to make you see what I saw in Cameron. He wasn't worth losing my friend."

She knew Ridley didn't particularly like Cam—and she would never tell Rid, but Cameron felt the same way about her. She would brush off Ridley's snide remarks, figuring it was nothing more than a personality clash between two strong-willed individuals who would never see eye to eye.

"I've always thought you were too good for him," Ashanti said.

"You did? Why didn't you say anything?" Evie asked.

She shrugged. "You and Cameron come from the same social circles. I assumed that's just the way things worked in your world."

"The two of you have been my best friends for as long as I've been with Cameron, and neither of you thought to tell me how you truly felt about him?"

"I—" Ridley started, but Evie cut her off.

"Okay, Rid, yes, I know you don't like him, but you don't like anybody."

"That's fair." Ridley shrugged.

Evie's phone buzzed in her pocket yet again. She didn't have to look to know it was Cameron, although she took it out and glanced at it on the off chance that it wasn't.

"Is that him?" Ashanti nodded toward the phone.

"Yes," Evie said with a sigh.

"Tell him to shove his phone up his raggedy ass," Ridley said.

Evie read the text. "He says we need to talk."

"Is he honestly trying to get back together with you?" Ashanti asked.

"He knows that isn't a possibility," Evie said. "I think he's more concerned about the practice."

"Maybe you should talk to him, just to hear what excuse he tries to give you," Ashanti suggested.

"The fuck she should!" Ridley said. "Let his ass rot in the men's section at Nordstrom where he belongs."

Evie and Ashanti looked at each other and simultaneously rolled their eyes. They'd both known how Ridley would react, and she hadn't disappointed.

"No, I know what you should do," Ridley continued. "You should find the finest man in New Orleans and fuck him in front of Cameron."

"No!" Ashanti and Evie screamed at the same time.

"Why not?" Ridley asked.

"Jumping in bed with some random stranger is the last thing I need right now," Evie said.

Unbidden, Bryson's face popped into her mind, but she

quickly pushed the image away. He may not have been a random stranger, but he held the second to last spot on her list of potential candidates for a one-night stand, right above Cameron.

"I think it's best I take a break from dating for a bit," Evie said. "Jumping into another relationship so soon doesn't seem like a smart move."

"Who said anything about a relationship?" Ridley asked. "I said you should find someone to fuck, not marry."

Evie massaged her right temple. "It's late for you, Rid. We should let you go."

"Late? Girl, please. I'll be here until midnight," she answered. "Keep me up-to-date on that fool's shenanigans. Make him get on his knees and beg you to take him back, then kick him in the teeth."

"It's a wonder you've never been arrested," Evie said.

"She was that one time, remember?" Ashanti said.

"It was Mardi Gras!" Ridley defended. "Who hasn't been arrested during Mardi Gras?"

Ashanti and Evie both raised their hands and burst out laughing. This was why she loved these two. Even when her life was a shit show, she could always count on them to lift her spirits.

"I'll call tomorrow with an update," Evie said.

"I will be expecting one," Ridley told her.

"You're still coming back to the States next week, aren't you?" Ashanti asked. "I want to make sure you're back for the grand opening of The PX now that it's finally happening. Dom has been great with building buzz for it. Thad and Von are gearing up for a full house."

Ridley's entire demeanor changed, and Evie had no doubt it was because Ashanti had brought up Von Montgomery.

Von and Ashanti's new boyfriend, Thaddeus Sims, had served in the military together. Last year they retired and moved to New Orleans to open a sports bar geared toward active-duty military and veterans. They'd had a soft opening for their bar, The PX, late last year, but a bunch of setbacks had delayed the grand opening of the entire complex.

It was after that soft opening that Ridley had gotten weird whenever Von's name was mentioned. Ashanti was convinced the two had hooked up, even though neither Von nor Ridley had owned up to it. Soon after, out of the blue, Ridley took this assignment at her company's London office.

Evie never thought she'd see the day when a man sent Ridley King running clear across the ocean, but it was obvious that's what had happened.

"My flight is next Friday, but plans may change," Ridley said. She followed with a quick "I'll talk to y'all later" before disconnecting the call.

Ashanti and Evie looked at each other. "Something is up with her," they said at the same time.

Evie checked her Apple Watch, then began gathering her things. Waffles had spent his final night at The Sanctuary so that he could get his full set of vaccinations and microchipping, but Odessa said he would be ready by the end of today. Evie wanted to get all the supplies she needed before she brought him home.

Her heart did a little backflip. Her joy at becoming a pet owner again was one of the only things sustaining her at the moment.

"Hey, Ev, this isn't my business, but I'm making it my business," Ashanti said. "You really should think about getting tested."

"Already done," Evie answered. "That's why I was late getting here today. I explained to my doctor that it was an emergency. So far, I'm clean, but there are a few results that won't be in for a couple of days." She shook her head. "I swear, if Cameron gave me something, I will castrate him."

"Ouch." Ashanti grimaced. "Let's not go around castrating anyone. Although he kinda deserves it." She enveloped Evie in a hug. "I'm sorry this is happening."

"I guess I am too."

Ashanti jerked her head back. "You guess?"

"No, I am," Evie said. "I definitely am. I'm angry and I'm hurt, but I just...I'm not devastated, you know? I've cried on and off for the past two days, but I can't decide if I'm crying because I'm mad or because I'm heartbroken." She looked over at Ashanti. "What does it say about the state of my relationship with Cameron if I can't tell if I'm heartbroken now that it's over?"

"The same thing that a four-year engagement says about it," Ashanti said. "How many times have you told me that you just couldn't figure out why you weren't ready to take that next step? You may not have figured it out up here"—she tapped Evie's temple, then placed her palm on her stomach—"but there's something in here that must have known all along."

Was Ashanti right? Had there been something in her gut all this time telling her that marrying Cam was a mistake?

"And here I thought my cold feet were due to my parents' sham of a marriage," Evie said with a humorless laugh.

Ashanti's sad smile nearly did her in.

"You're going to be okay, Evie. You know that, don't you?"

"Will I?" Evie asked. "Are you going to pay my bills?"

"Besides the fact that you have Mama and Daddy Warbucks waiting in the wings, you don't have a mortgage and your car is paid off," Ashanti said. "But I do have a couple mil in the bank if you need a loan." She threw both hands up in the air and did a praise dance. "God, it feels good to say that!"

"Amen, amen," Evie said, pretending to wave a church fan.

"Seriously, though," Ashanti said. "If you need anything, it's yours. I know you don't like going to your parents if you can help it."

"And this is why I love you the best," Evie said. She scrunched up her nose. "Saying that doesn't have the same satisfaction when Ridley isn't around to hear it."

Ashanti shrugged. "Just call yourself a bunch of cuss words and it'll be like she's right here."

"True." Evie laughed.

She lifted her backpack over her shoulder and, after kissing Ashanti on the cheek, left Barkingham Palace. She got behind the wheel of her SUV but didn't start it. Instead, she just sat there, staring at her phone.

Cameron had texted again. It wasn't like him to be so... needy. So desperate. They'd had their share of fights over the years, and he usually went with the silent treatment. It was his way of teaching her a lesson.

Evie rolled her eyes.

It had taken her much longer than it should have to learn her lesson, though it wasn't the one he thought he'd been teaching her.

Ashanti was right, Cam really was a rat bastard.

She started the SUV and pulled away from the curb. There was a pet boutique in the French Quarter she'd been meaning to check out. Now she had a reason to go.

CHAPTER SIX

Bryson evened out his breathing, pulling in slow, deep breaths and letting them out just as slowly. He leaned forward, angling his body until he was in the perfect position.

"Seven ball. Right center pocket."

He pushed the cue stick forward with a smooth strike, sending the maroon ball spinning across the worn green felt. It clanked against the five ball he'd sunk a few plays ago.

"Impressive," Derrick Coleman said. His former classmate's brow dipped as he frowned. "I wouldn't have thought you'd have the time to perfect your technique, as busy as your schedule is."

"I don't. I haven't played since we graduated," Bryson said. He shrugged, trying to suppress his grin. "Maybe I'm just that good." He quickly knocked the eight ball into the top left pocket, ending the game.

"No, I'm just that bad," Derrick said, taking both his and

Bryson's cue sticks and setting them in the rack. "My pool debt was almost as bad as my student loan debt."

"So why did you choose to come here tonight?" Bryson asked. He clamped a hand on Derrick's shoulder as they headed back to their table.

"I wanted to see if I could continue my losing streak from eight years ago," Derrick answered. "Thanks for proving that I could. Success tastes sweet."

"Happy I could help," he said.

Derrick flipped him a middle finger and Bryson burst out laughing.

Short and boisterous, Derrick had always reminded him of Kevin Hart. The two of them had bonded over being the only two Black men in the program the year they started vet school at LSU. It would have been too much to ask that he and Derrick end up as lab partners. Instead, Bryson had been stuck with that asshole Cameron Broussard.

Derrick had surprised him tonight by driving in from Baton Rouge to hear him speak at the Louisiana Veterinary Medical Association's quarterly meeting. Seeing a friendly, familiar face in the crowd had lessened the nerves that had popped up as he'd stepped onto the dais, but despite both Derrick and Doc being there to cheer him on, those nerves had pestered him for far longer than Bryson was used to.

He'd spoken before audiences ten times the size of the one he'd addressed tonight, but there was something about being in front of the home crowd that made tonight even more nerve-wracking. There had been people there who knew him before he became *the* Bryson Mitchell, DVM.

At this point in his career, he enjoyed a level of prestige that few in his profession could ever hope to attain, but he also knew that, to some, he would always be nothing more than a basketball jock who'd managed to claw his way out of the bayou and into veterinary school. Instead of allowing that to intimidate him, Bryson had used it as fuel.

He'd opened with his usual story of how fate led him to transferring in his final year of vet school from LSU to Tuskegee University, the only historically Black university with a school of veterinary medicine. And how that eventually led to him joining a team of scientists studying 3D-printing technology only weeks after finishing the university's veterinary medical-surgical program.

Ten minutes into his presentation and he could tell by the crowd's rapt expression that he had them. He didn't let go of them until the very end. He still had a buzz flowing through his veins from the standing ovation he'd received at the conclusion of his talk.

Yet, there was one thing that continued to dampen his mood.

Bryson had spent his entire presentation searching for a specific face in the crowd, but it never materialized.

Was he surprised Evie never showed up? Not really.

But it still stung, particularly after so many at tonight's chapter meeting noted how odd it was not to see her in attendance. *He* was the reason she hadn't been there. He didn't believe that excuse she'd given Doc for a moment. Her entire demeanor had changed when she discovered that he was tonight's keynote speaker.

He massaged the corded muscles at the back of his head.

Their server was waiting for them when they returned to their table. Bryson added a water with lemon to Derrick's order of fries and a beer from a local brewery.

As he settled into his seat, he tried to hold on to the lightheartedness he'd experienced while playing pool, but Bryson could already feel that brief feeling of joy slipping away. He just wasn't up for it tonight, and not only because Evie had been a no-show at tonight's chapter meeting.

He glanced around the packed sports bar and resisted the urge to look down at his watch to see if enough time had passed to make excuses and head out. He had hoped being back at one of his favorite hangouts from that summer he'd worked at The Sanctuary would put him in a better headspace, but the only thing being surrounded by this loud chatter did was remind him that this had never really been his scene.

Back when he was at The Sanctuary, he'd joined Derrick, Evie, and the handful of other volunteers who'd been in the program because he'd finally found a group of people who made him feel as if he belonged, but even then he'd preferred an evening at home with a Walter E. Mosley detective novel or watching Animal Planet.

Tonight, he just wanted his bed.

His bed. The one he'd left in his condo back in Five Points, not the lumpy one at the short-term rental he had here in New Orleans until he could find a place of his own.

The server returned with their drinks and a basket of fries, and Bryson shook off the urge to check airfare to Raleigh-Durham. He couldn't let a horrible mattress and one bad night send him scrambling back to North Carolina so soon. He had yet to even see his parents who—surprise, surprise—were on yet another Caribbean cruise.

He was a Louisianian again. He had to accept everything that came with that.

"Hey, you okay?" Bryson looked up to find Derrick chomping on a French fry. "You can at least show some excitement over beating me at pool instead of making it look like another day at the office."

"My workdays are a helluva lot more exciting than whipping your ass at pool," Bryson said. He dodged the fry Derrick lobbed at him.

"I'm just messing with you," Bryson said. "And I'm good. Just tired. I always experience this adrenaline rush before I give one of these talks, but once it's done—"

"You're drained." Derrick nodded. "I get it. Not that I spend my time flying around the country—oh, wait, didn't you give a speech in Puerto Rico last year? Make that flying around the world—giving speeches."

"Technically, Puerto Rico is still the United States," Bryson pointed out.

"Whatever." Derrick gave him the finger again. "All I'm saying is that you've come a long way since those days of administering rabies vaccinations at The Sanctuary."

"I've done all right."

"Just all right? I do more clout chasing using your name than my own. I'm damn proud of you, man."

"I was lucky. I worked hard too," Bryson quickly added. He'd be damned if he downplayed the blood, sweat, and frustrating tears it had taken him to get to this point in his career. "But I also know luck played a role. If the student who had originally been chosen for that research team at Tuskegee had not transferred to UC Davis, I would be spending most of my days repairing perineal hernias."

"Instead, he's the one who probably spends his days with his hand up a Yorkie's ass," Derrick said.

"Boston terrier," Bryson said. "Or a corgi. Those are the breeds most prone to perineal hernias."

Derrick lobbed another fry at his head. "You're still such a fucking nerd." He wiped his fingers on a napkin, then said, "I hate to be the one to start the goodbyes, but I gotta bail. Nicole has already sent three 'Have you left New Orleans yet?' text messages."

Thank God. He hoped his relief didn't show on his face.

"You better get out of here before she sends another one," Bryson said. He stood and gestured to the table. "I got this." He slipped three twenties from his wallet and dropped them on the table to cover their drinks and Derrick's fries. "Thanks for making the drive from Baton Rouge. I appreciate it, man."

"You know I wouldn't miss the chance to see the great Bryson Mitchell in action."

"Your ass," Bryson said.

"I'm just messing with you." Derrick laughed. "Hey, we need to get together again before you leave town. How long will you be in New Orleans?"

Bryson paused for a beat. He hadn't shared this news with anyone outside of his immediate family, Doc Landry, and the upper management at the surgical hospital.

"Permanently."

Derrick stopped in the middle of putting on his jacket. "Come again?"

Bryson grinned. "I just accepted a position at the Animal Surgical Center of Southeast Louisiana in Metairie," he said, then shrugged. "I'm home."

"I can't believe you waited until now to lay that news on me," Derrick said. "What made you make that move?"

"I've been thinking about it for a while," Bryson said as

he followed Derrick out of the bar. "I want to be closer to my parents, for one thing. When the surgical center contacted me, I answered instead of letting the call go to voicemail. The rest is history."

They stopped at Derrick's black sedan, which was parked just outside the door.

"North Carolina's loss is Louisiana's gain," Derrick said. "I'll be back in New Orleans in a couple of weeks. I'll hit you up."

Bryson pulled him in for a one-arm hug and tapped him on the back. "Be safe on that drive back to Baton Rouge," he said.

He waited until Derrick was in his car before continuing on to his Jeep, pausing while a party of six filed out of the Mexican restaurant next to Cooter Brown's. He slipped behind the wheel of his granite-colored Wrangler Sahara and backed out of the parking space.

He drove up Carrollton Avenue toward the small place he'd rented on Bayou St. John. He had never seen more creative photography than the pictures that had been used in the ad for this short-term rental. It was half the size he'd anticipated and the floors creaked if he looked at them too hard.

The only upside was that it faced the water.

Bayou St. John was a far cry from Bayou Cane, Lake Boeuf, and the other spots he grew up swimming and fishing in, but he would take what he could get. The real estate agent he'd hired had several condos on Lake Pontchartrain for him to tour next week. If he was going to move back to Louisiana, he damn sure was going to have a view of the water.

As soon as he entered the house, Bryson dropped to his haunches and held his arms out for Bella, the sable and white papillon who had been abandoned at one of the clinics where he'd done his clinical rotation. She jumped into his arms, gave him the required lick on the chin, then started barking up a storm.

"I'm sorry, I'm sorry," Bryson said, smoothing down the hair on her butterfly-shaped ears. "I told you it was going to be a long night."

He plucked a treat from the jar he kept on the table next to the door. He had another in the kitchen and in his bedroom, because if there was one certainty in this house, it was that Bella would get her treats.

He carried her into the bedroom and sat her on her dog bed—there were also living room and kitchen dog beds—and changed out of his suit and tie. Bryson grabbed a pair of sweats and a T-shirt from one of two suitcases that lay open on the floor. He was determined not to be in this Airbnb long enough to unpack, but he also knew he could only live out of suitcases for a couple of weeks before he started to get antsy.

Bella barked.

"No more treats," Bryson said. "I wasn't *that* late."

He glanced over at the lumpy mattress, hating the thought of sleeping on it but knowing he should turn in for tonight. He'd made plans to have a walk-through at the surgical hospital tomorrow, which was open twenty-four hours, seven days a week. He didn't want to waste time learning the place when he started on Monday. He wanted to be able to jump right in.

But he also knew if he got in that bed right now, he would spend the next two hours staring up at the ceiling. He was still too wired from his LMVA presentation and hanging out at Cooter Brown's.

"Come on, girl," Bryson said, scooping up Bella. He

grabbed a can of blackberry sparkling water from the fridge and took Bella out to the small front porch.

As he settled into the worn wooden rocking chair, he could admit that the view of downtown earned the house another notch in the plus column. The crown of the old Hibernia Bank Building was lit up in purple, gold, and green to usher in the Mardi Gras season.

Bryson leaned over and whispered in the dog's ear. "We've gotta get out of this neighborhood before Mardi Gras, Bells."

He would rather run his nails down a chalkboard than deal with the crowds that would descend on this neighborhood and those that surrounded it in a few weeks. Maybe he would be able to convince his parents to stay home for five minutes so they could have a proper visit during that time.

He pushed off with his foot, sending the chair on a gentle rock.

Trailing his fingers through Bella's soft fur, Bryson leaned his head against the back of the rocking chair and finally allowed his mind to go to the place he'd been fighting to keep it from for the past two days. He closed his eyes and called forth the image of Evie in that simple sweater and jeans. It had been hanging out on the periphery of his consciousness, waiting for the chance to torture and entice him.

It shouldn't have come as a surprise that she was as beautiful as ever, yet the sight of her had nearly done him in. He should have been better prepared for the moment he first saw her; he'd known he would run into her eventually. He would probably run into her boyfriend soon too.

Boyfriend? It had been eight years. No doubt they were married by now. Probably even had a couple of kids.

His muscles flinched.

He had never allowed himself to go there, and he sure as hell didn't want to think about it tonight. Or ever. He didn't want to spend a single brain cell pondering what it was like for Evie to give birth to Cameron Broussard the Second.

He'd purposely avoided any information about them after he left LSU, knowing that news of their wedding would shred him. Even years later, the thought of that asshole having the heart of the amazing girl Bryson spent a summer falling in love with galled him.

And therein lay his problem.

He'd fallen in love with her, but she had been another guy's girl. The one guy who chapped his ass more than any other.

Of all the men for her to choose over him, his asshole of an ex-lab partner was, by far, the worst.

"You don't know if she chose Cameron over you," Bryson said.

He hadn't given her the chance to choose. Instead of talking to Evie like an adult after his confrontation with Cameron just before the start of the fall semester, he'd ghosted her like a coward, hauling ass to Tuskegee.

He drank down what remained of his drink and crushed the can with his fist.

Well, there was nowhere for him to run now. He was here, and so was Evie.

"Welcome home to me."

Bryson held Bella to his chest, pushed up from the rocking chair, and went inside.

CHAPTER SEVEN

Bryson studied the black-and-white screen as he glided the transducer along the German shepherd puppy's right side. Based on when the owner suspected the dog had ingested the foreign object, it would no longer be in the stomach.

"How long has he owned Rocket?" Bryson asked Chloe Oliver, the surgical tech who'd been assigned to him today.

"Christmas," she said. "Justin—that's the owner—said his girlfriend gave him Rocket as a Christmas present. It's his first time ever owning a dog."

"I guess he didn't realize puppies can be as inquisitive as babies when it comes to putting things in their mouths. He'll need to pay better attention to him. Hold on," Bryson said. He guided the wand back a few centimeters. "I think I found it. Let's turn Rocket onto his back."

He helped Chloe maneuver the puppy, who was much more manageable after the sedative Bryson had given him.

He usually tried to avoid even mild sedation during non-invasive procedures, but Rocket had lived up to his name. The moment they'd placed him on the table, the dog had shot up and dove off the side like . . . well . . . a rocket.

"Let's see if I'm right," Bryson said. He zoomed in on the cranial region of the abdomen. "Yep. Look here at the duodenum."

Chloe squinted from where she stood, gently rubbing Rocket's head. "I'll be damned."

"Does that look like a '68 Custom Camaro Hot Wheels to you? It looks like one to me," Bryson said.

"Sure does," she said. She shook her head. "Do you think it would have had a chance of making it through if it hadn't turned horizontal?"

He shook his head. "He's lucky it hasn't torn through the small intestine already."

Chloe leaned over and kissed the dog on his head. "Poor baby must be in so much pain. Let's hope his owner is willing to pay for surgery."

"He said that Hot Wheels is worth a thousand bucks. It's going to cost more than that to get it out, but I'd say you're worth it," he spoke directly to the puppy as he ran a hand along his flank. "I'll consult with Dr. Wu, then talk with the owner. Start prepping Rocket for surgery. Whether he's willing to pay for it or not, I'm not letting this dog suffer."

"Um, Dr. Mitchell. Do you—"

"I know the laws regarding informed consent," Bryson told her, chuckling at the alarmed look on her face. "Don't worry, I won't go against the owner's expressed wishes. I will just make sure Justin wishes to move forward with the surgery." He winked. "I have my ways."

Bryson peeled off the gloves and tossed them in the trash as he left the examination room. Adam Wu, who led the team of doctors who specialized in soft tissue surgeries, was walking toward him.

"How's the first official day on the job?" Adam asked.

"I have a six-month-old German shepherd who swallowed an extremely valuable Hot Wheels car. It's lodged right there in the duodenum."

He nodded. "Sounds about right. A simple splenectomy would have been too routine for a surgeon of your caliber."

"I'm sure that's coming through the doors next," Bryson said.

Rocket's owner had been joined by his girlfriend by the time Bryson met with them in one of the six patient consult rooms at the hospital. Three hours later, he was back in the consult room, handing the man his freshly washed die-cast Camaro.

To Bryson's relief and pleasure, Justin Lewis wasn't nearly as concerned about the collectible toy car as he was about the puppy he had not even known two months ago. It never ceased to amaze him how quickly a pet became the center of a family's life.

He went over the next steps in the recovery sequence, explaining that Rocket would remain at the hospital for at least one more day for post-surgery monitoring before being released.

"You'll be given care instructions when you come to pick him up tomorrow. You'll have to watch him because he's an active one."

Justin threw his arms around Bryson while his girlfriend continued to wipe tears of relief from her eyes. Bryson accepted a more restrained hug from the girlfriend before walking them to the lobby.

Rocket's owners had barely pulled out of the parking lot before a gorgeous American bobtail with a distended abdomen was brought in. Bryson had handled enough cholecystectomies on ruptured gallbladders to be able to successfully pull off the operation blindfolded, but he wasn't an arrogant asshole, so he performed the surgery with eyes wide open.

One of the techs came in to bring the cat to recovery and Bryson went out to talk to his owners. When he returned to the operating room, Chloe was setting up fresh surgical tools for the next emergency that entered the door.

"You're getting baptized by fire on your first day," she said as she covered the gleaming instruments with a clean cloth.

"I don't mind," Bryson said. "It feels good."

And it did. This is the type of day he had envisioned during those long hours in the library when he was an undergrad. It was hard to say no to those huge speaker fees, but if he had a choice between giving a presentation to a ballroom full of veterinary surgeons or escorting a ten-year-old to the recovery room so she could get a glimpse of the cat he'd just saved...

There was no choice.

"I'm heading out for the day, but I'm available if you need me," Bryson told Chloe.

"What about the onboarding period? You shouldn't be scheduled for on-call duties during your first two weeks."

"Nah." Bryson shook his head. "I don't need any kind of adjustment time. Call me if necessary."

"Hmm." Chloe's brows arched. "Dr. Wu said you would fit in well here. Now I understand what he meant."

Bryson smiled to himself as he walked down the powder-blue corridor toward the rear of the hospital. He stepped into his office first and changed into clean scrubs. Then he walked over to the last room on the right, which served as the in-house daycare for the staff's pets. He found Bella curled up against a three-foot-tall teddy bear in the corner of the room.

"What are you doing there?" Bryson said, scooping her into his arms. "That thing would smother you if it fell over."

"I had my eyes on her," called a teenager who was trying to wrangle a shih tzu with pink bows tied around its ears.

She came over and offered a hand to Bryson. "I'm Aurora, Dr. Guidry's daughter. I take over for Elizabeth in the afternoons. She said to tell you that Bella did great but will probably be exhausted tonight because she played with the other dogs all day."

"You made some new friends today, Belly Welly?"

Bella licked his cheek, then turned in toward his chest and went back to sleep.

"Thanks for looking after my girl," Bryson said to the teen. It was her mother, Dr. Jennifer Guidry, who had first sought him out. He'd met the ortho-surgeon at a symposium in Chicago last fall and later discovered that she had gone there with the sole purpose of luring Bryson back to Louisiana.

He secured Bella in her pet carrier and, after making one last sweep through the recovery wing, exited the back of the building and into the employee parking lot. His cell started ringing with a number he recognized but couldn't place. Bryson climbed into his Jeep and waited for the phone to connect to the vehicle's Bluetooth before answering.

"Hello, this is Bryson Mitchell," he said as he strapped in Bella's carrier.

"Hey there, Bryson. It's Odessa."

Ah, it was the number for The Sanctuary. *That's* why it seemed familiar. He'd removed it from his contacts years ago, after scrolling past it one too many times and experiencing that pain in his chest that struck whenever he encountered something that reminded him of Evie.

He cleared his throat.

"Hey, Odessa. What's going on?" Bryson asked as he backed out of his designated parking spot. When he'd pulled in this morning, the first thing he did was snap a pic of the metal sign with his name on it and send it to his brothers and nephews. He was back home to stay. The sign made it official.

"I'm calling on behalf of Dr. Landry. He needs to talk to you. Today," Odessa emphasized.

Bryson slammed on his brakes.

"What's wrong? Is Doc sick?"

"No, no. It's nothing like that. Just...can you come to The Sanctuary?"

Bryson pulled back into his parking spot and brought up the calendar on his phone. He had a call with an old colleague from the team at Tuskegee scheduled for six, but he could push that to Wednesday.

Still, why would Doc want to meet with him when they'd just gotten together for lunch a few days ago? And why did he want to meet in person? Couldn't he just call?

"Bryson, you still there?" Odessa asked.

"Yeah. Yeah, sorry about that," Bryson said. He put the car in reverse again and slowly backed out. "Tell Doc I'll be right over."

"He also asked if you could stop over at Maple Street Animal Clinic and see if Evie is available to join you. It's on your way."

He slammed on the brakes again.

"He's tried calling her cell phone, but it's going directly to voicemail," Odessa continued. "I tried calling the clinic, but they must be busy there today. I was put on hold twice. What Doc wants to discuss concerns you both, so it would be better if you're both here."

Doc wanted to see both him and Evie? Together?

What in the hell had he done to piss off the universe?

It's not that he wanted to avoid Evie forever, but he needed more time. He had to mentally prepare himself before sharing space again with the one person who had affected him more than any other woman. The one who'd gotten away.

The one you let *get away. The one you pushed away when you ran like a coward. The one you practically handed over to Cameron Broussard.*

Fuck his brain right now.

"Bryson?" Odessa said.

"I'm sorry. Yeah, I'm leaving the animal hospital right now," Bryson said. "I'll head straight to Evie's clinic."

He ended the call with Odessa and looked over at his dog. "This is going to suck so fucking bad, Bells."

Bella yipped.

Seeing Evie again was one thing. Being in the vicinity of his old lab partner would send him to a level of hell Bryson wasn't up for visiting.

"Only for Doc," Bryson said. "He's the only reason I would subject myself to this shit."

He tightened his grip on the steering wheel and, through gritted teeth, said, "Siri, get me the directions to Maple Street Animal Clinic."

Even saying the name of the practice Cameron had

inherited from his dad made Bryson's ass itch. He'd suffered through countless hours of that cocky nepo baby talking about all he would do to the clinic once it passed down to him.

"You're ten times more successful than that asshole," Bryson reminded himself. Bella barked her agreement.

The navigation system took him almost back to the bar where he and Derrick had hung out Saturday night. Bryson had forgotten just how close the Broussards' practice was to all the places he used to frequent that summer. Audubon Park, which included the Audubon Zoo, was less than a mile away. The Sanctuary was within walking distance of the zoo, and Doc's house was only a few blocks from the animal refuge, not far from the Mississippi River.

The sense of loathing that pooled in Bryson's gut as he maneuvered the Jeep into a spot across the street from the animal clinic was sizable, but he couldn't let it show on his face. He had to be cool and collected the first time he saw Cameron after all these years. He would embody the rockstar, in-demand surgeon the rest of the veterinary world saw him as.

Granted, most rockstar veterinary surgeons didn't go around carrying an eight-pound papillon with glittery painted nails, but it couldn't be helped. He wasn't leaving Bella alone. He unhooked her pet carrier and hoisted it out of the Jeep.

Maple Street Animal Clinic was housed in a camelback cottage in a neighborhood that boasted some of the most charming homes in New Orleans. Back when they were in vet school, the exterior of the building had been pink and looked like a cross between a preschool and a gingerbread house, with pastel-green shutters and a blue door. There had been a mural of animals frolicking in a meadow painted on the side.

Now the building was slate gray with white shutters and black trim. If not for the elegant wooden sign in the front yard indicating it was an animal clinic, the structure could be mistaken for the boutiques one would find lining Magazine Street and in the French Quarter. Cameron always talked about targeting a more sophisticated clientele than his dad had. He guessed this new look was part of that. Bryson was surprised he hadn't changed the name to match the outside. Something French, or some shit like that.

He walked up the steps but stopped when he reached the porch. He had to ready himself to face Cameron again after all these years. His old lab partner would either be condescending, or he would pretend they were friends and try to kiss up to him like several people had Saturday night at the LVMA meeting. Either would make Bryson want to hurl his fist at him.

"We're gonna just say no to violence, Bells," Bryson said.

He switched Bella's carrier to his right arm and opened the door.

The first thing he noticed was how the exterior renovations had not extended to the interior. Other than new paint on the walls, everything looked the same. From the yellow Formica countertop at the reception desk to the oak shelves that held a variety of prescription dog foods. Both had seen better days.

"Good evening," the receptionist greeted, then held up her hand while grabbing the phone's receiver. "One minute."

Bryson couldn't recall the name of the woman who'd worked for Charles Broussard, but he did remember how much Cameron bitched about her.

The receptionist ended the call and handed Bryson a

clipboard. "You can sign in here. We just need your name, your dog's name, and what brings you in."

"Oh, I'm not here to see the doctor," Bryson said. "Well, actually, I *am* here to see the doctor, but not for my dog."

The receptionist's forehead creased in confusion, and who the hell could blame her?

"I'm sorry," Bryson said. "I'm here to speak to Dr. Williams."

Or was it Williams-Broussard? He couldn't see Evie dropping her maiden name entirely. Her family was more prominent than Cameron's when it came to New Orleans high society.

"Oh, uh..." The receptionist hesitated. "Dr. Williams is—"

Before she could finish, Evie entered the lobby from the hallway that led to the back, carrying a cardboard banker box. Her steps faltered when she saw him.

"Bryson?" Her forehead crinkled. "What are you doing here?"

"He asked to see you," the receptionist said. She pointed to the phone. "And Dr. Broussard said to tell you that he's coming back to the office at five, so if you don't want to see him, you should leave."

"Oh, is that what Dr. Broussard said?" Evie huffed out a laugh and shook her head.

It was Bryson's turn to wear the crinkled forehead look.

Had he heard the receptionist correctly? If Evie didn't want to see Cameron, she should leave? What was going on here?

"This is the last of my stuff," Evie continued. "If there's anything I've missed, please just hold it here at reception and I'll come by and pick it up tomorrow."

The receptionist nodded, her expression solemn. "Good luck, Dr. Williams."

"Thanks," Evie said. Her smile was forced. He could tell by the tightness around her mouth.

He needed to get over to The Sanctuary, but that would have to take a back seat until he figured out just what in the hell was going on here on Maple Street.

"Evie—"

"Would you mind getting that?" she asked, gesturing to the door with her chin.

Remembering the manners his mama taught him, Bryson set Bella's carrier on the floor and lifted the box from Evie's arms. He nodded at the carrier. "Can you carry Bella for me?"

"I can carry the box," Evie said.

"I know you can, but I've got it," Bryson said. "Now, where am I bringing it?"

"You never answered my question. I asked what are you doing here?" Evie said. "And why are you wearing scrubs? I'm confused, Bryson."

That made two of them. Or three of them, counting the receptionist. Shit, Bella was probably confused too.

"First, tell me where to bring the box; then we can clear up all the confusion."

Evie picked up the carrier and led him out of the clinic. She pointed to the vehicles lining the curb.

"It's the gray SUV," she said.

She pressed a button on the key fob as she descended the steps. By the time they arrived at the SUV, the trunk door had lifted, but the cargo area was already filled with boxes.

"You can put it on top of that flat one," Evie said.

Bryson set the box where she instructed, then hooked his thumb at the trunk and asked, "What is all this, Evie? What's going on?"

She looked over at the clinic, then, after releasing a deep sigh, looked back at him and said, "I'm clearing out my things. This is my last day at Maple Street Animal Clinic."

CHAPTER EIGHT

A news chopper flying overhead drowned out Bryson's response, but Evie had always been good at reading lips. Especially his. She'd spent an entire summer suppressing the urge to burst out laughing at the silly comments he would mouth as Dr. Landry explained the procedures he was performing on rescues at The Sanctuary. Among other things.

Yeah, she had intimate knowledge of Bryson Mitchell's lips.

Once the chopper flew past them, Evie answered the question he'd choked out.

"Yes, I am serious," she said. "I no longer work at Maple Street Animal Clinic."

Based on the way his forehead creased, it looked as if he was having a hard time processing her statement. That made two of them. She still had not fully grasped that she would no longer work here either.

But Evie was having just as difficult a time processing the fact that Bryson was standing in front of her. He started to speak, but she held up a hand.

"Before you ask another question, I need *you* to provide some answers. What are you doing here? And by here I mean in New Orleans?" She gestured to his clothing. "And why are you wearing scrubs? I assumed you'd flown back to Raleigh after your presentation Saturday night."

His brow arched in surprise.

"What? You think I don't know that you live in Raleigh?" Evie said with a laugh. She may not have had contact with him for the past eight years, but she had googled him once or twice.

Okay, fine. She'd lost count of the number of times she'd looked him up over the years. Scores of veterinarians probably did the same. His research was some of the most exciting to happen in their industry in decades.

Yeah, you looked him up because of his research.

"I no longer live in Raleigh," Bryson said. He gestured to his clothes. "And I'm dressed this way because I came straight from my new job at the surgical hospital in Metairie."

Evie tried to close her mouth, but she would have had an easier time running a full marathon backward. She could not have heard what she thought she heard.

"Excuse me? Your new job where?"

His phone rang. He grabbed it from the back pocket of his scrubs.

"That's Odessa," Bryson said before swiping across the screen and answering. "Hey, Odessa, tell Doc I'm on my way. I'm with Evie now." He glanced at her. "Give us another fifteen minutes."

Evie shook her head, as if that would help to clear the jumbled mess crowding it.

"Bryson, what is this new job? And what's happening in fifteen minutes? What is going on?"

"I can take Bella," Bryson said, reaching for the dog carrier.

"I've got the dog," Evie said. She held up the carrier. The adorable papillon staring back at her was the exact opposite of the kind of dog she would expect him to own. "Hi, Bella, I'm Evie," she said. She returned her attention to Bryson. "Start explaining, please."

"Are you holding my dog hostage?" Bryson asked, a hint of amusement coloring his voice.

"Maybe," Evie said. "Now, answer my questions."

The left side of his mouth tilted up and Evie was immediately catapulted back to that summer she'd spent staring at that smile. She shut the door on the memories. She was *not* going there.

"Well?" she prompted.

"To give you the short-and-sweet version, I'm the new surgeon on staff at the Animal Surgical Center of Southeast Louisiana. And, if you have time, Doc needs us at The Sanctuary in fifteen minutes." He held up his hands. "Don't ask me what it's about because I don't know. Odessa called as I was leaving the hospital. She said Doc has been trying to get in touch with you, but his call keeps going to voicemail."

Evie frowned. "I have my phone on do not disturb," she said. Only the people in her favorites could get through to her. "And you don't know what Doc wants?"

Bryson shook his head.

"Did he—" she started, but the sight of a Mercedes-Benz

turning into the driveway that ran alongside the clinic put a halt to her words.

"Shit, that's Cameron," Evie said. "I wanted to be gone before he got back." She handed Bryson the dog carrier. "I need to get my dog from the daycare in another forty-five minutes. Hopefully whatever Doc needs won't take too long."

"I'll meet you there," Bryson said.

The Sanctuary was less than a ten-minute drive from the clinic. She caught sight of the gray Jeep Bryson had driven off in and parked her SUV at the curb in front of the nondescript building next to The Sanctuary.

Bryson was waiting at the entrance. With the dog carrier in his left hand, he used the other to open the door for her.

"Thank you," Evie said.

Odessa stood from behind her desk when they entered. She didn't look in distress, which Evie took as a good sign.

"Is everything okay with Doc?" Evie asked.

"I already told this one here that Doc is fine," Odessa said, hooking a thumb toward Bryson. "There's been a few... developments," she said. "He just wants to discuss them with the two of you. He's in his office."

Evie led the way to Doc's office, which was at the very end of the hallway, at the back of the building. Bryson remained a couple of feet behind her, but it didn't stop her from feeling his nearness on her skin.

She rapped on the closed office door.

"Doc?" Evie called.

The door instantly swung open, as if Doc had been standing there waiting for them.

"Hey, hey! Come in!" he said, waving Evie and Bryson inside. He gestured at the dog carrier. "Who's this?"

"This is Bella, the most spoiled papillon you'll ever meet," Bryson said.

"Well, let her out of that cage," Doc said. "She needs to run around."

"She's fine," Bryson said. "She's had a full day today. She'll be snoring in about three minutes." He set Bella's carrier on the floor and perched against the edge of Doc's crowded desk. "What's going on, Doc? Why did you call us here?"

Evie tried valiantly not to stare at the way the corded muscles in Bryson's arms flexed as he folded them across his chest. It didn't work.

She turned her focus to Doc, whose expression had darkened considerably since his jovial greeting. Something was definitely off here.

"What's wrong?" Evie asked. "Are you sick?"

"I'm fine," Doc said. He let out a sigh. "It's the rescue that's in trouble."

"The Sanctuary?" Evie and Bryson asked simultaneously.

"You asked about the mentorship program the other day, Evie," Doc said. "The truth is, the program hasn't been in operation for more than a year."

Evie's hand flew to her chest. "Doc! Have you been handling the workload here by yourself?"

He nodded.

"Why didn't you say anything before now?" Bryson asked.

"Stubbornness, if you ask Odessa," Doc said. "Honestly, I thought I could turn things around on my own. I've been applying for grants, and I dipped into my retirement."

"Doc!" Evie said again.

"You've been funding this place on your own?" Bryson asked.

Doc responded to their concern with a dismissive wave. "I'm fine. What am I going to do with the money? It's not as if I have family to pass it on to," he said. "These pets *are* my family. But it's not enough, and as much as I don't like to think about it, I'm getting old. I can't do this on my own."

"You shouldn't have to," Evie said.

Guilt engulfed her. She'd neglected The Sanctuary over the past year. She'd assumed all was going just fine but hadn't bothered to check in on Doc or the rescue.

"I'm sorry for not being here for you," Evie said.

"It's not your—" Bryson said.

"There's no need for—" Doc said.

Evie stopped them both, holding up a hand. "I should have been here," she reiterated. "I'm sorry I haven't been, but I am now. What do you need from me, Doc? I happen to be between jobs right now, so if you need to restart the mentorship program, I'm willing to lend a hand."

Doc shook his head. "Eventually. Maybe. But that would come later. With the increasing cost of food and medicine, I'm more concerned with keeping the doors open," Doc said. He looked to Evie, then to Bryson. "I asked the two of you to come in today because I'm hoping you can help come up with a way to save The Sanctuary. Based on where things stand right now, we have enough to operate for another two months, maybe three if Odessa figures out a way to stretch the budget. Do you think you can do that?"

The two of them? As in her and Bryson? As in her working *with* Bryson?

"I know you're still settling in, Bryson, but—" Doc started.

"I'm good," Bryson cut him off. "I can handle it. What about you, Ev? Are you in?"

"I—" She looked to Bryson, then quickly averted her eyes, focusing on Doc. "I have to think about it," Evie said. She immediately felt like a filthy rock at the bottom of a scum-filled pond. But how else was she expected to react to the thought of working alongside Bryson?

"I understand," Doc said. "It's a big commitment. And you all lead busy lives."

She wasn't imagining the disappointment she heard in Doc's voice. She felt even worse.

"I'm sorry, but I need to pick up Waffles," Evie said. "He's been at doggy daycare all day."

She stood and chanced a glance at Bryson. There was disappointment on his face, too, but it was accompanied by something else. Something closer to annoyance.

The fucking nerve of him. He steps back into her life after eight years and has the audacity to be annoyed that she wants to take a minute to process all of this? The fucking nerve!

"I'll be in touch, Doc," Evie said before leaving the office.

She didn't know what she was going to do, but one thing she would *not* do was allow herself to be rushed into this. She had been through too much in only one week's time. She would not commit to working alongside Bryson Mitchell unless she was sure she could handle it.

If she would ever be able to handle it.

CHAPTER NINE

Evie sat behind the wheel of her idling SUV, observing the landscapers as they clipped away at the ten-foot-tall Italian cypresses that bracketed either side of the two-story arch leading to her parents' doorway. The men were meticulous in their technique, snipping with precision until the tops were perfectly aligned. It was a perfection her father demanded of everyone who worked for him. Evie was surprised he wasn't out here supervising.

The sprawling mansion was her father's pride and joy. Located in one of New Orleans's most exclusive neighborhoods, with a view of the manicured golf course at English Turn Golf & Country Club visible from the backyard, he saw it as the ultimate symbol of how far he'd come from his upbringing in public housing.

She couldn't complain. It had been a nice house to grow up in, if one didn't mind living in a museum that was constantly used to host dinner parties and soirees.

She glanced in her rearview mirror at Waffles, who was nestled in his brand-new doggy car seat. For someone without a job—her part-time gig at Barkingham Palace was *not* sufficient employment—she was having way too much fun spending money at the pet boutique. She'd told herself only necessities, but that was two sweaters and three bow ties ago.

It wasn't as if she would go hungry. She had money in the bank. And as much as she silently judged her parents' extravagant lifestyle, Evie knew they were her safety net. They would give her whatever she asked for if the need ever arose.

It won't get to that point.

"Okay, Waffles," Evie said. "I will need you to be on your absolute best behavior. No loud barking. No scratching any furniture. And, by all means, do not have an accident on the floor. You will not be allowed back in the house."

Her mother would likely have a conniption the moment Evie walked through the door with her dog, but she would have to get over it. Evie and Waffles were a package deal.

"You ready?" she asked.

Waffles remained silent.

"Yeah, me neither," Evie said.

She could think of a million other places she'd rather be right now instead of in her parents' driveway. For the briefest moment, Evie had considered letting her mother's call go to voicemail, but trying to avoid her was the *most* impractical exercise in futility. Dr. Constance Williams always got her way in the end.

Her phone rang. She answered through the SUV's Bluetooth.

"Are you going to spend the evening staring at the house

from your car, Evelina?" her mother asked before Evie had the chance to even say hello.

"I— A song I hadn't heard in a while was playing on the radio," Evie said. She rolled her eyes. Five seconds into a conversation with Constance and she was already coming up with unnecessary lies. "I'll be there in a minute."

"I'm in my office. The temporary code for the front door is four-eight-two-five," her mother said before disconnecting the call.

Evie cut off the engine.

"Okay, Waffles, no more hiding in the car." She got out and went to the back seat, unclipping her dog's harness from the car seat and hooking it onto the leash before lifting him out and setting him on the ground. "You'll probably have to spend the visit in the sunroom, but it's enclosed and air-conditioned."

Waffles barked.

"You'll like it. I promise."

Evie looked from her dog, who stared at her with the goofiest expression—my goodness, but she loved him so much already—to the house.

"Okay, I'll make you a deal. Give me ten minutes with Constance, and I'll take you to get a pup cup on the way home."

Another bark.

"Deal," Evie said, then started up the walkway toward the front door. The landscapers paused and nodded as she approached.

"Good evening," Evie said. "It looks great out here."

Both men beamed in a way that told Evie it was the first time they'd received praise for their work in a long time. That tracked. Her father felt that a paycheck was the only praise a person deserved.

She punched the temporary code into the keypad. Her parents were not the type to give unfettered access to their home, even to their grown children. Although Evie wouldn't be surprised if her brother, Marshall, had weaseled the permanent code out of their father.

She entered the house and was instantly hit with the scent of lemon verbena. It had been her mother's favorite for as long as Evie could remember. Based on the sheen that covered the marble floors and the fresh flowers in the vase that sat in the center of the entryway table, the cleaners had come through earlier today.

Evie grabbed a bottle of water from the kitchen, noting there was only one place setting at the smaller table in the informal dining room where her parents normally took their meals. Guess Dad had to fend for himself tonight. Not that it surprised her.

She walked back across the foyer and formal dining room to her mother's office.

Constance Williams, MD, sat behind her desk wearing the reading glasses she hated to admit she needed. At sixty-five, she was still incredibly active, working full-time as the head of cardiology for the largest hospital system in South Louisiana. She served on the board of directors of several local nonprofits, and as Evie learned just last month, spent what little downtime she had kicking ass and taking names as the top pickleball player at the country club she and her father belonged to—which, ironically, wasn't the one in their backyard.

Evie wasn't surprised that her mother excelled at her

newest hobby. As the first Black woman to run a cardiology department in the region, Dr. Williams had a long-standing reputation for kicking ass and taking names. As much as they butted heads, Evie had always been intensely proud of her mother's accomplishments. Now, if only her mother could reciprocate that pride when it came to Evie's career accomplishments, maybe then their relationship could resemble that of a normal mother and daughter.

Stop asking for the impossible.

Constance tolerated her daughter's career choice, but she would never forgive Evie for not following in her footsteps.

Her mother had two laptops open, her head volleying back and forth between the screens as if she were watching a tennis match.

"You know, if you get one with a bigger screen, you can have two windows open on the same computer," Evie offered.

"I don't want a bigger computer," her mother answered.

She took the glasses off and placed them on the desk. Once she finally focused on Evie, the tiny lines in her forehead deepened with her frown.

"You're not in scrubs. I thought your practice didn't close until six. How did you have time to change clothes?"

Seriously? That's the first thing she noticed?

"It's good to see you too, Mother," Evie said.

"It's good to— Evelina, what is that?" Constance pointed at Waffles.

"Took you long enough to notice your new grandpup," Evie said. "Constance, meet Waffles. Waffles, say hello to your grandmother, Dr. Williams, but you can call her Grandma Connie."

"Really, Evelina? A dog?"

"I'm a veterinarian. Why are you surprised that I have a dog?"

"Because you've been a veterinarian for years and this is the first dog you've had since that scraggly little thing you left here when you went to college."

"I'm sure Sparks would be touched that you remember her as that scraggly little thing," Evie said.

Constance pointed. "You know how I feel about dogs in the house. Take him to the sunporch."

"Told you your grandma would send you to the porch," Evie said as she tugged Waffles's leash.

"And stop referring to me as that dog's grandma," her mother called.

It was probably best that she comply. The last thing she wanted to do was trigger the "All our friends are becoming grandparents, when will we get our turn?" discussion again. Funny how Marshall was the oldest, but he was never accosted with that question.

Of course, if her mother did bring up the idea of grandchildren, it would be the perfect way to break the news of her split with Cameron.

Evie batted the thought away. She wouldn't be able to keep the news from her family forever, but the idea of telling her mother about the breakup, quitting the practice, and all the other drama of the past few days made her head hurt.

"Okay, Waffles, give me ten minutes," Evie said after getting him settled on the sunporch. "And don't pee on the rug."

She returned to her mother's office to find her back at the computer.

"One minute," Constance said before Evie could speak. She spent another five seconds typing into the computer, then swiveled in the chair and folded her hands atop the desk. "I would like you to come over to the house this coming weekend. The event planner, Tami, will be here to present her vision for the anniversary party, and I would like your input."

This again.

Her parents could barely stomach eating nightly meals together, yet her mother insisted on throwing this elaborate party to celebrate their fortieth wedding anniversary.

"I'll have to look at my schedule," Evie said. Her mother's right brow arched. Evie suppressed the urge to roll her eyes. "But I'm sure I can be here," she said.

Make no mistake about it, Constance Williams *always* got her way in the end.

"I am not asking you to visit a torture chamber, Evelina."

"You sure about that?" Evie said.

Her mother gave her that same look she had been giving her since she turned thirteen. She should have learned by now to whisper the backhanded comments under her breath, but no.

"You did not make me suffer through bridge traffic just to tell me that you want me to be here when the decorator comes over, did you?" Evie asked.

"I guess visiting your mother isn't enough of a reason," Constance said as she stood from behind the desk. She walked over to the built-in shelves on either side of the picture window that looked out onto the front lawn and pulled something from behind the display copy of the book on women's heart health she'd co-authored years ago.

Evie frowned when her mother placed a small velvet drawstring bag in her palm.

"What's this?" she asked.

"I found it while going through some things in my closet yesterday."

Evie pulled the bag open and gasped. She shook out the piece of costume jewelry she had not seen in years.

"Grandma's brooch! Where did you find it?"

She'd coveted the frog with blue stones for eyes when she was a little girl.

"It was in a small box of her things. I debated whether I should even give it to you. You're already too much like your grandmother."

A firecracker. That's what her grandmother used to call Evie when she was younger. She, too, used to say that Evie was just like her.

Evie wrapped her arms around her mother.

"Thank you, Mommy."

Constance's brow arched. "Oh, now it's Mommy?"

"When you give me an amazing surprise like this? Yes! Here." Evie jutted out the left side of her chest. "Pin it on me."

Constance's lips twisted with irritated amusement as she opened the clasp on the brooch. "Don't forget to remind Cameron that the theme for the anniversary party is red. I want to make sure everyone is coordinated."

Great. Way to kill her happy mood.

She would probably regret this, but Evie decided to rip off the Band-Aid.

"Cam won't be able to make it to your party," she said.

Her mother's forehead creased in affront. "He's known about the party for months. Why would he make other plans?"

"No." Evie shook her head. "He won't be there because we broke up."

The silence that stretched around the room was so

profound—so intense—Evie could practically feel it on her skin.

"What did you say?" her mother asked.

Evie pushed out a deep breath. "Cameron and I broke up," she repeated. "He moved out of the house, and I left Maple Street Animal Clinic. So, if you hear of any veterinary practices hiring, point them my way."

To her surprise—*not*—her joke fell flat.

"Evelina!" Her mother raised her voice, something she rarely did. "What are you saying? How could you do this?"

"*I* didn't do this. Cameron did—"

"Four years," her mother said, cutting her off. "You were engaged for four years, after being together for ten. Is that why he left you? Because you wouldn't set a date for a wedding? I warned you that Cameron would not wait forever for you, didn't I?"

"First of all, we haven't been together for ten years," Evie corrected her. "You're forgetting about the three separations. And our long engagement had nothing to do with the breakup."

"Well, then, what did? Why did you break up?"

"The *why* doesn't matter," Evie said. "What matters is that Cameron and I are no longer together. It was my decision to make, and you need to respect that."

"I will *not* respect this decision, because it is a horrible one," her mother said. "Being in a relationship with Cameron Broussard is the one good thing you had going for you."

Evie's head jerked back. A slap across the face would not have stung as much as the words her mother had just hurled at her.

"Did you really just say that to me?" Evie asked.

"I apologize." Constance had the graciousness to look contrite. "That was unfair and untrue. But, really, Evelina. You could have discussed this with your family before doing something so rash."

"So my relationship choices are done by committee now?"

"You know what I mean," her mother said.

Yes, she did. And therein lay the problem.

The last time she and Cameron broke up, Evie had decided she was finally done. It wasn't until her mother got into her head, bombarding her with all the ways she and Cam were a perfect match, that Evie had caved and taken him back.

She and Cameron were a perfect match in the ways that were important to her parents. They looked good on society blog posts and write-ups in the local paper following a charity gala. He was the consummate son-in-law for her parents, but they would have to accept that Cameron would not be her husband.

"I'm sorry if you don't agree with my choice, but I've made it," Evie said. "I am capable of deciding what is best for my own life."

"And just what do you plan to *do* with your life, Evelina? You left your fiancé and his vet practice. What will you do now? Go back to rescuing every stray you find on the street?"

"You say that like it's a bad thing," Evie said. "I may not be a heart surgeon, but my work still matters."

Constance threw her hands up. "I'm not having this conversation with you again." She went back to her desk and sat. Not two seconds later, she popped back up. "You wanted to be a vet and we let you become a vet—"

"You did not *let* me become a vet. I chose to become one," Evie said.

Yes, they'd paid for her education, and saved her from a mountain of school debt, but it didn't give them the right to control her life.

"You're making a mistake," her mother said. "Cameron is a good man. He comes from a good family."

He was not a good man, and he came from a rich, well-connected family. But Evie knew if she said those words to her mother, it would only extend this argument. She was over it.

"I'm sorry you don't approve," Evie said. "But the decision to leave Cameron is mine, and mine alone. And I've made it."

She stopped herself before she could tack on *Deal with it*. She was only willing to go so far with the disrespect, and telling her own mother to deal with it crossed the line.

Instead, she left the office without another word and went to the sunroom to retrieve her dog. She had to fight the urge to head straight to the doggy boutique—not because she didn't have the money to spend on him, but because retail therapy wouldn't make her feel any better. She had enough shoes in her closet to attest to that.

"We don't need to buy stuff to prove our worth," Evie told Waffles, strapping him into his car seat.

"And I sure as hell don't need Cameron to prove it," she muttered as she rounded the circular driveway.

She pulled up to the first stop sign and spotted her dad's bright yellow Lamborghini coming toward her in the opposite lane. Evie waved at him as she drove past and thanked the Lord for perfect timing.

She loved her father. She loved her mother. She did not love her mother and father together.

Even before she understood how to properly categorize what her parents shared, they had shown her what a loveless marriage looked like. It looked like two people who actively hated each other but stayed together for appearance's sake. The sole purpose of the anniversary party Constance was planning was to continue shoring up the lie.

Despite the fact that her father's philandering was the worst-kept secret in New Orleans, her mother was prepared to smile and pretend the last forty years had been wedded bliss, because as two of the city's most prominent Black doctors, their partnership mattered more than their vows. Or their happiness.

Evie refused to settle for that type of relationship. She'd made that promise to herself as a fifteen-year-old, when she first learned of her father's infidelity.

She could still remember the hot, embarrassed flush that rushed over her when he walked through the doors of the French Quarter restaurant where she had been invited to celebrate a friend's sixteenth birthday. Even worse than seeing her father out with that other woman was her mother's lack of a response when Evie told her about it two days later. She had prepared to see her entire life change. Divorce, separate homes, having to choose who to spend holidays with.

Instead, her mother had brushed it off and told her to get ready for violin lessons.

Evie had quit the violin a few months later, just about the same time she'd quit trying to understand her parents' relationship. She would rather be alone than endure such a pitiable excuse of a marriage.

Despite what her mother believed, she did not need Cameron or his practice to give her life meaning.

"And just what do you plan to do with your life, Evelina? Go back to rescuing every stray you find on the street?"

"Why the hell not?" Evie said. She looked at Waffles in the rearview mirror. "I rescued you, and look how much it's changed my life already."

She couldn't take in every stray in New Orleans, but she knew how she could help save them.

CHAPTER TEN

Bryson bobbed his head to Nas's collaboration with Lauryn Hill, "If I Ruled the World," as he secured the final suture in place. He secured the knot, then snipped the pink nylon.

"And that's that," he said. He smiled at the surgical tech. "Thanks for your help with the surgery. I appreciate it."

"Are you kidding? I had to win a game of Rock, Paper, Scissors to make it into this operating room," Eli Parker said as he lowered the volume on the sound system. "Competition to work with you is fierce."

Bryson laughed. "Is that what's going down in the employee break room?"

He did his best not to let that tidbit go to his head, but hearing shit like that was like a steroid shot to his ego.

"I'm sure there will be the opportunity for every surgical tech to join me in the operating room," he said. "I just started here and don't plan on going anywhere anytime soon."

Eli shook his head. "Doesn't matter. All the techs will want to say that they've performed the most surgeries with you. Next time, I'm challenging them to a dance-off." He did a hand and shoulder move circa a 1980s hip-hop video.

"Doesn't seem like a fair fight," Bryson said as he inspected the site where he'd made the small incision to remove the Egyptian mau's bladder stones. The feline was one of the most expensive domesticated cats in the world, but it was just as susceptible to common ailments as the strays living on the streets. Bladder stones showed no mercy.

"If not for the pink stitches, I wouldn't know where to find the incision," Eli said from just over his shoulder.

That's the point, young grasshopper.

His unwillingness to come off like an arrogant dick prevented Bryson from speaking the words out loud.

"I just do the best I can to reduce the recovery time as much as possible," he said instead. "Bianca's owner asked us to call once the surgery is done, but I want to hold off until she comes out of anesthesia. I'll be in my office. Just give me a ring once she's awake and produced her first post-surgery urine."

After cleaning up, Bryson checked in on Bella, who was frolicking around the playroom with her new best friend, a cockapoo named Ginger, before going into his office. He pulled his cell phone out of the desk drawer where he'd stashed it and grimaced at the forty-plus text messages waiting for him.

He read the two from his mother first, telling him that she'd cooked his favorite—beef stew with potatoes and carrots—and was putting some in the freezer for him. She'd followed it with another text that their neighbor Ms. Lucille Green had brought over a container of shrimp étouffée that would be placed in the freezer alongside the stew. Bryson hadn't factored in the added bonus of having both his mother and her friends filling his freezer with food when he'd made the decision to move back home. It more than made up for the few nights he'd had to sleep on the lumpy mattress in the short-term rental.

Hopefully that would soon be a thing of the past. Another text was from his Realtor. A two-bedroom condo with a view of the water had just come on the market in the building near Lake Pontchartrain that Bryson had set his sights on.

He shot her a quick text back.

Interested. Set up a tour asap.

He was tempted to tell her to put in an offer, but if he planned to make this his permanent home, he couldn't be hasty about it. Regardless of the current, highly competitive real estate market his Realtor continually reminded him that they were in.

The rest of the texts were from the group chat with the vets at his old practice in Raleigh. There was no reason for him to still be in a chat that discussed the day-to-day workings of a place where he was no longer employed, yet every time he made an attempt to leave it, he held back.

Bryson stared at the phone. He'd just told his Realtor he wanted to tour a condo but couldn't let go of a group chat? Either he accepted that he lived here now, or he didn't.

He started typing. Stopped. Then started again.

Sorry to be that guy, but I'm going to remove myself from the group text.

A flurry of "sorry to see you go" and "miss you" and "trying to lure you back" texts came through.

He smiled, but finally went through with removing himself from the text.

"That wasn't so hard," he said.

Now, if only he could figure out how to deal with the other issue he was having, all would be right in his world.

"Yeah, that's not happening," he muttered.

He set his elbows on his desk and rubbed the bridge of his nose.

With the exception of when he was performing a surgery, his mind couldn't seem to focus on anything but Evie. Ever since she walked back into his life wearing those jeans that hugged her curves to perfection, he had to make a concerted effort to direct his attention elsewhere, and it was already starting to wear on him.

For a while Monday afternoon, Bryson had felt a glimmer of hope that he could exist in this city with Evie as his friend and colleague. He'd accepted within moments of her leaving The Sanctuary that such an existence would not be feasible. He could not simply be friends with her. He had never wanted to be only a friend to her. From the first moment he saw her, he'd wanted more.

As if that ever would have happened back then.

He and Evie came from two entirely different universes. His success of the last few years had evened the playing field, but only slightly. Her upbringing, her family's money and standing within New Orleans's social circles, was something that would always be out of his reach, no matter how much success he achieved.

He no longer aspired to be part of that lifestyle. He was

satisfied with what he'd accomplished. But back then? Back then, he would have done anything to be part of Evie's world.

For a moment, he *had* been part of it.

When Evie showed up at The Sanctuary the summer he volunteered, Bryson viewed it as a test to his character. He'd known that if he could spend the summer working alongside her without crossing that line he had been desperately wanting to cross, then he could achieve anything. But then she'd started to respond to his corny jokes, and their innocuous exchanges had become decidedly more flirtatious.

It was all the incentive he'd needed. Once it became obvious that she was feeling him just as much as he was feeling her, he gave a middle finger to the part of his brain that told him a girl like her could never be serious about a guy from the wrong side of the swamp.

Bryson rested his lips against his folded hands.

He'd spent an entire year after he left Louisiana dissecting just what had made him take such a drastically wrong turn when it came to Evie. Why had he run instead of fighting for her? Was it because of Cameron? Was it because her rich, successful parents would never have approved of him back then?

None of that *should* have mattered. He'd allowed it to. He'd allowed Cameron to get into his head, along with his own hang-ups. And in doing so, he had lost—he didn't want to think about what he'd lost, what he and Evie could have shared.

He dropped his head back into the headrest of his desk chair.

"Fuck," he whispered.

He'd known returning to this city would be like a plunger, bringing up all this old shit he'd put off dealing with for years. What surprised him was how thoroughly thoughts of Evie had taken over his life.

He had to quash this, and quickly. Even if Evie was remotely interested in being anything more than a friend, the timing was off. He needed his focus to remain squarely on his job and on readjusting to life back in Louisiana.

His cell phone rang. Bryson slipped it from his desk and sat up straight when he saw the name on the screen.

EVIE WILLIAMS

Unlike with The Sanctuary's number, he'd never been able to bring himself to delete her contact from his phone. Apparently, she hadn't gotten rid of his either.

Don't read too much into it.

He still had the number of a man who'd once tried to sell him solar panels for his car saved in his phone. Evie still having his number wasn't as consequential as he wanted it to be.

Not that he wanted it to be of any consequence.

"Evie. Hey," Bryson said.

"Hey," she replied. "I hope you don't mind me calling out of the blue like this."

"Not at all," Bryson said. "A little surprised, but I don't mind. Was there something you needed?"

There was a brief pause, then, "I've been thinking about our meeting with Doc."

His pulse quickened.

"What about it?" he prompted when she didn't continue.

"Knowing The Sanctuary is in trouble and that the mentorship program isn't even operating doesn't sit right with me."

"Yeah, I've been thinking a lot about it too," Bryson said. Not nearly as much as he had been thinking about her, but

The Sanctuary had been on his mind. "That mentorship program was a vital part of my training. I hate the thought of the community losing both the program and The Sanctuary."

"Yes, well, that's why I called," Evie said.

A knock on his office door interrupted them.

"Dr. Mitchell." It was the surgical tech he'd worked with on that Hot Wheels car extraction. "Captain Jack is prepped for his sialoadenectomy," she said.

Shit.

"I'll be there in a minute," Bryson said. "Hey, Evie, I have to deal with a salivary mucocele in a fourteen-year-old Chihuahua. It shouldn't take more than an hour."

"Go," she said. "Call me when you're done."

The surgery took a little longer than Bryson had anticipated because, as he'd feared, the gland was infected. He had been forced to go into the procedure without all of the information he should have had because the owner had declined to do a pre-op CT scan. He got it. The CT scan would have added another thousand dollars to the already expensive surgery, but it only made his job more difficult.

It was yet another reason why operations like The Sanctuary were vital to the community. The world needed more places that offered pro bono veterinary care. If they somehow managed to save the rescue, he would suggest to Doc that he implement a program that helped to defray the cost of surgeries for low-income pet owners.

Suggest it to Doc? Who was on the verge of retiring?

"You cannot run The Sanctuary," Bryson murmured under his breath as he shucked off his gloves. He was certain that's why Doc had taken him to the rescue following their lunch last week. Wanting to give him that lapel pin had only been an excuse to get him into the building, but Evie being there had thrown everything off. Bryson was just waiting for Doc to bring up the subject.

He could *not* run The Sanctuary. He had enough on his plate with this new job, new move, the speaking engagements still on his calendar. Doc would have to find someone else.

He made his way to the waiting room to talk to Captain Jack's owner. His steps faltered when he caught sight of Evie standing next to the wall covered with photos of past patients.

"Uh, Mrs. Stewart, I just wanted you to know that everything went well with Captain Jack's surgery," Bryson said, watching Evie out of the corner of his eye. "We found a slight infection, which will require an extra night of IV antibiotics, but he should make a complete recovery."

Evie had turned at his voice and was watching him with open curiosity.

"Does he have to stay here to get those antibiotics?" the woman, who looked to be in her seventies, asked.

"Yes. He needs to be monitored."

She frowned. "How much more will that cost on top of the surgery?"

Did it matter? She had just spent nearly four thousand dollars getting that salivary gland surgically removed. Was she going to allow her dog to die of an infection because it would cost an extra two hundred?

Bryson took a mental step back. Who in the hell was he to pass judgment? Maybe she didn't have an extra two hundred dollars. Maybe she had scraped together every cent she had for the surgery. He knew better than most what it was like to have to make tough financial choices. He'd spent the better part of his life doing it.

He took Mrs. Stewart's hand in his. "I know it's hard not to stress about the cost, but please don't. The receptionist can tell you about programs that will allow you to pay in installments so that you don't have to cover everything all at once."

The worry marring her features lessened. "Thank you again for all you did for my little Jack." She gave his hand a gentle squeeze before slipping past him and walking over to the reception area.

Bryson turned to Evie, who had crept a few feet closer to him.

"What are you doing here?" he asked.

She disregarded his question and nodded toward Mrs. Stewart. "That couldn't have been easy. I've seen too many people have to make the hard choice of providing care or saying goodbye to their pet because they can't afford the expense. I'm glad you encouraged her to save her dog."

"I didn't really give her any other option," Bryson said. "It's a habit I'm trying to break, if I'm being honest. The choice isn't mine. Sometimes, saving the animal isn't what's best for it or for the owner. But Captain Jack still has a few years left in him, and I have a feeling he's her only companion. She needs that dog as much as the dog needs her."

The corner of Evie's mouth curved up in a crooked half-smile and his skin grew hot. Shit.

"Why am I not surprised that you turned out to be this kind of vet," she said.

Bryson cleared his throat. "What kind of vet is that?"

"The kind who approaches patient care with both the owner and the pet's well-being in mind."

He shrugged. "It's part of the job."

"Not every doctor sees it that way," she said. "But of course you do. Like I said, I'm not surprised at all."

Bryson tried to dismiss the way his pulse amped up as they stood in the reception area. He should at least try to get a handle on his body's reaction to her.

"Um, what are you doing here, Ev? I thought I was supposed to call you back?"

"I just dropped Waffles off at doggy daycare—I want him to socialize for at least a few hours each day—so I decided to drive over. It would be better to discuss this face-to-face." She glanced around the reception area and pulled her bottom lip between her teeth. "Is there somewhere we can go to talk? Someplace a bit more private?"

His mouth suddenly felt as dry as the Mojave.

He was a grown man. He could handle this.

"Sure," Bryson said. "Follow me."

CHAPTER ELEVEN

Even though Evie walked at least three feet behind him, Bryson could feel her nearness on his skin. It pressed against him like a physical weight—a reminder that she was within touching distance. It had been well over a week since he'd returned to Louisiana and he still had not fully grasped the fact that he was close enough to Evie Williams to touch her.

It defied comprehension that she could still have this kind of effect on him after all this time. It wasn't as if he'd spent the past eight years pining for her. Maybe that first year—he could admit to obsessing over what he'd walked away from and the relationship they could have had if he'd stayed and fought for her. But he had gotten over Evie. He had made sure of it.

He'd dated more than his share of women, both casual and serious relationships. He had come close to getting engaged. Hell, he had nearly become a father. If not for an early pregnancy miscarriage, there would be a little Bryson Junior running around.

Yet, of all the women he'd dated since the last time he saw Evie, none had made his heart bounce against his rib cage the way it did at this moment.

Maybe when he had more time he could find a quiet place to sit and contemplate just what in the hell it was about Evie that had caught hold of him and would not let him go, even after all these years.

They reached his office and Bryson motioned for her to go in ahead of him. She entered and began a slow perusal, examining the Andy Warhol–inspired portraits of Bella he'd hung on the walls, along with his framed degrees. They were copies. The originals hung in their place of honor at his parents' house in Houma, ninety minutes southwest of New Orleans.

Evie slowly turned, her attention traveling from the ultramodern adjustable standing desk to the equally modern light fixtures above.

"So, this is how the specialties live," she said, a trace of envy coloring her voice. "Must be nice."

Was she actually going there?

"Really, Evie?" Bryson asked. "You sure you want to talk about how the other half lives?"

She spun around and stared at him with raised brows. "What?"

"Do you remember back when we were at The Sanctuary and your car wouldn't start? I brought you to that behemoth of a house you lived in."

Pulling his fifteen-year-old Nissan Altima into that circular driveway had been the beginning of the end of whatever he'd hoped to have with Evie. Bryson had known from that very moment that he would never fit into her world.

"That's my parents' home, not mine," Evie said. "I live in a humble little house once owned by my grandmother." She walked over to the lone chair across from his desk and sat. "It's a cute house, but not a mansion by any stretch of the imagination."

"Well, I'm in a short-term rental with the most uncomfortable bed known to man, if you want to know how the specialties *really* live."

She tilted her head to the side, her brow lifting again in inquiry.

"How short-term is that rental?" she asked.

"What do you mean?"

"I mean, are you planning to rent something more permanent, or are you still trying to decide if you're going to stay?"

Well, damn. He was quite the open book, wasn't he? But he was no longer vacillating between staying in New Orleans or returning to Raleigh.

"I'm home," Bryson said. "At least for the foreseeable future. In fact, my Realtor may have found me a condo. She sent a virtual tour, but I plan to visit before I make an offer."

"You're buying?" Her voice rose in surprise.

"Specialties," he said; then he winked. "It's how we roll."

Evie burst out laughing and every muscle in his body grew tight. It was that lyrical laugh he remembered. The laugh he'd become instantly addicted to the first time he'd heard it. He'd spent an entire summer chasing after that laugh, behaving like a lab rat repeatedly pulling a lever for another hit of dopamine. He'd been willing to go to whatever lengths necessary to hear that sound again and again and again.

Don't turn into a lab rat.

Bryson leaned forward in his chair and set both elbows on the desk.

"Just so we're clear, I'm joking. There's nothing inherently special about the 'specialties.'"

"No, no, no," Evie said. She held her hands up. "Don't downplay your success on my account. You worked for it."

"You helped. I honed a lot of those skills trying to show off for you that summer."

"Show off for me, or for Doc?"

"Definitely for you," Bryson said.

She looked away but couldn't hide the twin, dusty rose spots that blossomed on her light brown cheeks. His chest tightened at the sight. Exquisite. She had always been the most beautiful, most alluring being he'd ever encountered. It was nice to know some things never changed.

"That was a long time ago," Evie said. She shifted in her chair. Crossed her legs, then recrossed them.

Shit. He'd made her uncomfortable.

Maybe if he could find a way to not fucking flirt with her within ten minutes of having her in his office, she wouldn't be sitting there looking like she wanted to bail.

"Of course, the competition between me and Derrick played just as big of a part," Bryson said. "Like a couple of know-it-all assholes, we were always trying to show each other up."

She laughed, and some of the tension in the room began to dissipate. "Neither of you were know-it-alls," she said. "And, in the end, the animals at The Sanctuary benefited, so no harm done."

She sat back in her chair, appearing more at ease. A small

smile tilted up the corners of her gorgeous lips as she rested her folded hands in her lap.

"All joking aside, I'm proud of everything you've accomplished, Bryson," she said. It was the sincerity in her voice that caused his breath to hitch.

He had to clear his throat before he could speak. "Thank you," he answered. "That means a lot coming from you."

"You're welcome." She glanced down at her folded hands, then back at him. "I'm not surprised at what you've accomplished," she added. "And it's nice to see that you not only lived up to those ridiculously high expectations you set for yourself, but also surpassed them."

"You're the one who thought my expectations were high," he said. "I don't think they were high enough."

"Are you kidding me?" Her hands shot in the air before falling back into her lap. "You are one of the most highly regarded veterinary surgeons in your field. What more can you want?"

Bryson made a show of looking around the office. "Do you see a Leo K. Bustad Veterinarian of the Year Award anywhere?"

Evie rolled her eyes. "You really are ridiculous."

"Not ridiculous. Just a high achiever," Bryson said with a grin. "It's a carryover from my days on the basketball team. Coach used to tell us after every win that winning wasn't enough. We should strive for annihilation." He cocked his head to the side. "Now that I think about it, some of the shit Coach said to motivate us was messed up."

"Uh, yeah. I'd say so." Evie laughed again.

It was like another dopamine shot, straight to his fucking brain. He craved that laugh the way he craved air.

As much as he tried to stave it off, it was impossible not to get drawn in by her, or the ease in which they'd fallen back into the banter they once shared. She had always been so damn easy to talk to. And to look at. And to kiss.

She stared at him from the other side of the desk, a subtle hint of amusement still lifting the corner of her mouth and shimmering in her eyes. The four feet separating them was both too much space and not enough. He had to fight the sudden, overwhelming urge to rise from his chair, lean over the desk, and close the distance separating them.

And you thought your flirting made her uncomfortable?

Just because she looked at him with something other than derision—just because she and Cameron were no longer together—didn't mean she would welcome any kind of advances from him. They were different people from who they had been eight years ago, when they were still a couple of veterinary students who couldn't keep their hands off each other.

If he was lucky, he would get the chance to know the person Evie had become over the past decade.

She was the first to break eye contact. She sat up straight and tucked a lock of her curly, natural hair behind her ear.

"Back to the reason I came to see you," Evie said.

"Uh, yeah. Of course," Bryson replied, clearing his throat again.

"I've been thinking about what Doc told us the other day regarding the rescue. I—we—can't allow The Sanctuary to go down without a fight."

"We?"

"Yes, we," Evie said. "I mean, if you're up for it."

"What exactly are you thinking we should do?"

"Well, that's what we need to figure out. Something in

my gut is telling me that Doc isn't giving us the full story, but I'm not sure that matters. Nothing will change the fact that The Sanctuary is worth saving."

"I agree," Bryson said.

She let out a relieved breath, her smile returning. "Good," she said. "I didn't think I would have to twist your arm, but I was prepared to do so if necessary."

Bryson clamped down on the quip he nearly made about her getting physical with him, because what the fuck? He could *not* say shit like that to her.

It was the lighthearted back-and-forth; it made it feel like old times.

It is not old times, he reminded himself. He would repeat those words until they took hold.

"I was hoping that we could maybe brainstorm some ideas on how to save the rescue," Evie was saying. "I've already jotted down potential fundraisers. Did you know The Sanctuary still has that old WordPress blog as its official website?"

"The one you set up during your downtime that summer?"

She nodded. "It is so inadequate. There's nothing about how to adopt an animal, or a place for people to donate. It's one of a number of things that needs to be addressed." She held up her hands. "I'm not saying a new website will automatically save the rescue, but we have to start somewhere. That is, if you plan to join me."

"I'm in," Bryson said. "Of course I am."

Sure, he had a thousand things on his plate, but in what world could he say no to Evie? He'd made that mistake once. And paid for it.

"Doc is going to be so relieved," he said. He picked up his cell phone. "I'll call him and let him know what's going on?"

"Not yet." Evie reached across the desk and covered his hand.

Bryson stilled. The impulse to lift her hand to his mouth and press a kiss to it nearly overwhelmed him. No, the inside of her wrist. He wanted to brush a kiss over the delicate skin there, to feel the pulse point beating against his lips.

Stop it!

Evie pulled her hand away and sat back in her chair, oblivious to the chaos she'd wreaked within him. He was in fucking shambles from a simple touch.

"There's something we need to discuss first," she said.

"Okay," Bryson said, his blood chilling at the seriousness in her tone. The tension in the room had increased tenfold in a matter of seconds.

"If we're going to work together on this effort to save The Sanctuary, I can't spend the entire time feeling as if I'm going to jump out of my skin whenever we're in the same room."

His brows spiked. "Is that how you've been feeling around me?"

"You know things have been awkward, Bryson," she said.

"It's been years since we've seen each other, Ev. Things are bound to be awkward."

Especially after the way things ended between them.

"Time has nothing to do with it," she said. She pulled her bottom lip between her teeth. "I think the easiest way to go about this is to leave the past in the past."

Bryson jerked his head back. That wasn't what he was expecting to hear.

He'd spent so many hours contemplating just how to explain his actions from eight years ago to Evie, if ever given the chance. The one thing he had never contemplated was for her to not want to hear an explanation.

"This doesn't have to be weird or uncomfortable if we make a decision right now that it won't be," Evie continued. "Our focus should be on saving The Sanctuary, not on our feelings."

Bryson rested his fingers against his lips.

Could they simply close the door on that part of their past and just move on? Pretend none of it happened?

Did he *want* that?

If they ignored the bad way it ended, that meant they had to ignore the good parts too. He wasn't sure he was onboard with that.

Evie glanced down at her phone.

"I need to get going. Waffles isn't officially on the roster at Barkingham Palace yet, and I need pick him up before the afternoon clients get there." She looked at him. "Are we good here?"

Bryson nodded. "Go pick up your dog."

He started to stand when she did, but she held up her hand. "Don't. I'm fine. I can see myself out. Why don't you call Doc and let him know what we discussed."

"I can do that," he said.

She graced him with one of those smiles he could easily lose himself in before she said, "Thanks for not making this too difficult. I'll be in touch."

Bryson waited until she closed the door before settling back against the headrest and closing his eyes tight.

Had he just agreed to ignore that, at one point, he had been completely in love with Evie?

Leave the past in the past.

Bryson blew out an agonized breath.

"Good fucking luck with that."

How was one to prepare themselves for weeks of the sweetest torture imaginable? He had a feeling he was about to find out.

CHAPTER TWELVE

Ridley, girl, what is this?"

Evie burst out laughing at the tall, furry hat Ashanti placed atop her head.

"It's not for you; it's for the dog," Ridley said. "It's a hat like the guardsmen at Buckingham Palace wear. I figured Barkingham Palace's mascot should have one." She looked over at Evie. "Sorry, I didn't bring one for your mutt. Granted, I didn't know you *had* a mutt."

"No worries." Evie waved her off. "It's sweet that you would have bought Waffles a gift if you had known he existed."

"That's a silly name, by the way," Ridley told her. She glanced over to where Evie sat with her legs tucked underneath her on the sofa, Waffles snuggled in her lap. "But he does look like he has a blob of syrup on his head."

"Thus the name," Evie said, running her fingers along Waffles's fur.

She had been fully prepared to keep her dog secured in his travel crate while she and Ashanti helped Ridley settle in from her two-month stint across the pond, but Ridley told her not to bother locking him up. Six months ago, she balked at the idea of a dog in her downtown high-rise condo; now she was bringing home doggy souvenirs. As far as Evie could tell, London had been good for her friend.

"Thank you for thinking of Duchess," Ashanti said. "I'm sure she'll love it."

"I'm surprised she isn't here. You and that damn dog are usually joined at the hip."

"She's at The PX with Thad and Puddin'. They're putting the finishing touches on the Cigar Room. It looks amazing. They went with the deep raspberry-colored accents." She kissed the tips of her fingers. "Perfection."

"When is the grand opening?" Evie asked. "Well, the re–grand opening?"

"Thad is shooting for the end of next month, but Von thinks they'll be ready within the next four weeks."

"Have you started searching for a new job, Ev?" Ridley asked as she lifted a designer blazer from a designer garment bag.

Evie sent Ashanti a look. That obvious subject change had not gone unnoticed, but she and Ashanti had decided before coming to Ridley's that they wouldn't push her to talk about Von. Although Evie really, *really* wanted to push. She wanted the whole story when it came to what went down between her and Thad's best friend.

The fact that Von refused to talk was also telling, at least according to Thad, via Ashanti.

Evie would get a full account out of Ridley eventually.

Right now, there were other things she needed to discuss with her friends, and Rid had given her the segue she needed.

"I've put off the job search for the moment," Evie said. "I have another project I want to handle first, and I'm hoping you and Shanti can help brainstorm a few ideas. You remember The Sanctuary near Audubon Zoo, Rid?"

"The pet rescue where you interned that one summer?" Ridley asked.

She nodded. "I used to help out often before things got so busy with working at the clinic and at Barkingham Palace, but I hadn't been there in well over a year."

"Sorry," Ashanti said.

"No need to apologize," Evie said. "It's not as if you forced me to work for you. I do feel bad about abandoning the rescue, though. And I discovered a few days ago that things have gotten really bad there. As in, it may shut down. The mentorship program has already been disbanded."

"No way," Ashanti said. "I always regretted that I never got the chance to take part in that program."

"Well, no one will if The Sanctuary closes," Evie said. She lifted Waffles from her lap and moved her feet from underneath her, setting them flat on the floor, along with her dog. "I've decided to put off the job search for now so that I can focus on trying to save The Sanctuary."

"Exactly how much will it take to save it?" Ridley asked.

Good question.

"One of the issues we're facing is the fact that we don't think Doc Landry has given us the full picture of how bad things are."

"Oh, how is Dr. Landry?" Ashanti asked. "I loved him as a professor."

"Doc is Doc," Evie said with a shrug. Ashanti's nod signified that her answer was sufficient. "But we didn't really need Doc to tell us that things aren't going well. It was obvious to us by the state of the facility."

"Who is this *us* you keep mentioning?" Ridley said.

Shit. She hadn't caught what she was saying, but of course Ridley did. With a healthy intake of breath, Evie prepared herself for the fallout from her next words.

"Um, Bryson Mitchell is also going to help with the effort to save The Sanctuary. I'm meeting him for dinner this evening so that we can come up with an initial plan."

"Wait a fucking minute!" Ridley said, tossing the cashmere sweater she was folding onto the floor as if it were a dirty rag. "Bryson Mitchell? That fine-ass basketball player you dated back in school?"

"I never dated him," Evie said.

"Bullshit," Ridley said.

"We volunteered at The Sanctuary together that summer. We did not date."

"Come on now, Ev. Don't try to rewrite history," Ashanti said.

"What?" Evie said, going for the most innocent look she could manage.

"Girl, do you not remember that weekend Shanti and I spent with you at your parents' house that summer? We could play connect the dots with the hickeys that man put on your neck."

Evie felt her entire body flush with the most intense heat ever. She absolutely remembered that weekend. She'd met Bryson at The Sanctuary for what was supposed to be a quick check-in on a Doberman that had been rescued from a storm drain. The check-in turned out to be not so quick.

"Fine, I can admit that things got a bit... overly friendly that summer," Evie said. "But we were not a couple. We were just having a little fun."

"You should have fucked him," Ridley said. "I told you that back then. Instead, you returned to LSU that fall and went back to Cameron's crusty ass."

Because Bryson left Louisiana without so much as a goodbye.

Evie pushed down the rush of indignation and hurt that bubbled to the surface.

"That all happened a long time ago," she said. "It has nothing to do with what's happening with The Sanctuary today."

"The hell it doesn't," Ridley said. "Is he married? Because if he isn't, you better fuck that man now. Make up for time lost." She pointed a stiletto heel at her. "Better yet, fuck him in front of Cameron!"

"What is with you and this new fascination with voyeurism?" Ashanti asked.

"I'm not sure, but it's become my preferred porn genre." Ridley shrugged. "But I don't want Ev to fuck the basketball star in front of Cameron for my benefit. Although I would love to see him lose his shit over you getting your back blown out by someone better than him. This is for you, Ev. You deserve it."

Evie pushed up from the sofa and walked over to the glass-topped dining room table where Ridley was sorting her unpacked clothes. She picked up the cashmere sweater from the floor and added it to a pile on the table.

"No one will be getting their back blown out anytime soon," Evie said.

"Ahem." Ashanti cleared her throat.

"A-fucking-hem," Ridley followed.

Evie held up both her middle fingers. "You can both go to hell," she said.

The three of them burst out laughing.

"All jokes aside," she continued. "I just broke up with Cameron. What would it look like to have me dating this soon?"

"Like you have common sense and good taste," Ridley said.

Evie shook her head. "I think it's better I just chill for a while when it comes to men. I'd rather focus on The Sanctuary. It's filled with sweet dogs that are probably more loyal than any man I know."

"True dat," Ridley said.

"What do you need from us regarding The Sanctuary?" Ashanti asked.

Evie pressed her palm to her forehead and slid into a cream-colored leather seat at the table.

"Honestly, there's so much that I'm not sure where to even start." She held her hands up. "No. That's a lie. I do know the first place to start. The website is an atrocious, obsolete mess. Oooh!" She reached across the table and picked up a blue and white package. "Can I have a cookie?"

"It's called a biscuit," Ridley said in a horrible British accent. Then, in her normal voice, said, "Take the entire pack. I brought a bunch of them home with me."

Evie pulled out a thin cookie—biscuit—and bit into it.

"There's nowhere for people to donate online to The Sanctuary," she continued. "There's not even a Facebook page."

"That's a minimum," Ashanti said.

"Even I know they should have a Facebook page, and I hate that hellscape," Ridley said.

"Do you think Kara can build us a website?" Evie asked. Ashanti's seventeen-year-old sister was a genius at that kind of stuff. She had been in charge of Barkingham Palace's social media when everything went viral last year. "I'll pay her out of my own pocket."

"It's a nonprofit, so it would count toward her community service hours."

"Perfect," Evie said, her shoulders drooping with the relief that washed over her.

She'd anticipated Ashanti and Ridley coming through for her, and they did not disappoint. Not that she ever expected them to. She had been able to count on Ashanti since the day she met her back as an undergrad at LSU. The same went for Ridley, though her help tended to come with a side of salty commentary Evie could often do without.

"Is that all you need from Kara? A website?" Ashanti asked.

"The website is just the start. The Sanctuary doesn't have a social media presence at all." Evie grabbed the package of cookies—these were coming with her—and went to collect her bag and her dog. "I'll let you know what comes out of my dinner tonight with Bryson."

"I know one thing that should come—" Ridley started, but Evie stopped her, pointing two fingers in her direction.

"Don't finish that statement."

Ridley held her hands high. "I'm just saying."

"Let's go, Waffles," Evie said. "We have fifteen minutes to get to the restaurant."

"You're bringing the dog on your date?" Ridley asked.

"Yes, and it's not a date," Evie said.

She put her hands in the air again. "If you say so."

"Have fun on your non-date," Ashanti added with a laugh.

Goodness, what was she going to do with those two? Well, besides keep them. Evie knew she would never find better friends.

CHAPTER THIRTEEN

Evie noticed Bryson's Jeep pull into the paid parking lot across the street from the restaurant, and her already accelerated heart rate sped up even more.

"Okay, Waffles, they're here," she murmured to her dog.

It had been a long time since she'd been out on a first date—this was not a date! Damn Ridley and Ashanti for putting that in her head. Although the semantics of whether it was a date didn't matter. What mattered were the butterflies flittering around her stomach as if she were a two-year-old on a sugar high. If she didn't get control over her nerves soon, she wouldn't be able to eat a thing.

Her eyes tracked Bryson's movements as he waited at the crosswalk at the corner of Magazine and St. Joseph's Streets.

"Over here," Evie called from underneath the pink awning that covered the restaurant's entrance.

"This is . . . uh . . . colorful," Bryson said as he approached her. He gestured to the mural featuring three fluorescent flamingos painted on the building's outside wall.

"Flamingo A-Go-Go is one of the most pet-friendly restaurants in the city," Evie said. "They even have dog entrées on the menu. I thought it was the perfect spot for these two to meet."

Bella and Waffles had already begun the ceremonial first-meet butt sniff. Waffles moved from Bella's rear to her left ear, then to her front paws. Evie held her breath as Bella repeated the paw sniff, then a quick sizing up of Waffles's junk, before she went to sit at Bryson's feet.

No growls. No yapping. No teeth baring.

Evie released her breath. "Thank God."

"Glad that's done," Bryson said at the same time, letting out a huge sigh.

"Were you nervous they wouldn't get along too?"

"Bella can be temperamental," Bryson said, wrapping the end of her leash more securely around his hand. "But it looks as if your dog passed the sniff test, pun very much intended."

Evie rolled her eyes. "Still with the stale jokes."

"I am nothing if not consistent." His grin lit up his entire face.

Two women, each carrying the newest Telfar bag, strolled past them, their gazes locked on Bryson.

Evie wanted to tell them to back the hell off, then remembered this was not a date and Bryson was not her man. She could not blame *any*one for looking. He was gorgeous. Always had been.

"What is he, by the way?" Bryson asked, seemingly oblivious to the fact that he was the subject of several fantasies right now. "He looks like a pug and beagle, with a bit of something else."

He held the door open so she and Waffles could walk in ahead of him.

"I've decided he has a little rat terrier in him but won't be sure until his DNA test comes back," Evie said.

"Interesting combo."

"It gives him personality," she said. "And before you ask, yes, he runs the house, even though I've only had him for a week."

The restaurant's interior was as cheerfully flamboyant as the exterior. Because the dreaded humidity New Orleans was known for hadn't made an appearance yet, Evie requested patio seating. The hostess guided them outside to a table next to a fountain with pink flamingo metal sculptures.

Almost immediately, another woman stepped up to the table with two waters, announcing herself as their server. Evie ordered chicken, rice, and black bean dinners for the dogs and loaded French fries for her and Bryson to share.

"We must get the shrimp," she said. "They're fried and then drenched in this amazing sauce that has macadamia nuts. It's ridiculously good."

Evie looked over to find Bryson grinning at her after the server walked away with their orders.

"What?" she said.

He shook his head. "Nothing."

"No, not nothing," she said. "What is it?"

"It's just that when I think of home, I don't think French fries and macadamia shrimp."

"Hey, you can get red beans and rice and shrimp étouffée whenever your little heart desires it, but you won't get that when you're out with me. I've eaten those dishes my entire life. I'm good."

His forehead creased in confusion. "So what do you eat?"

"Everything else," Evie said. "There's a new restaurant representing another culture opening every week. We'll have to go to my favorite Thai place soon. It's even better than the one everyone used to rave about near LSU. Oh, and there's this Haitian restaurant in Tremé that is unbelievable."

"It sounds like I have some good meals to look forward to," Bryson said. "Thanks for the invite."

"Wait, I didn't—" Evie shook her head. Thinking back to what she'd just said, she realized she *had* invited him. Still, she didn't want him getting the wrong idea.

Ashanti and Ridley had joked about her dating, but she wasn't ready to date anyone yet, even someone she'd admittedly had feelings for years ago.

Especially someone who'd had her crying and confused in her childhood bed because he wouldn't answer her calls or texts and then left the entire state without a word to her. No thank you, sir.

"Um, just so we're clear, these are strategy sessions," Evie said. "Nothing more."

There was a hint of disappointment in the rueful tilt of his lips.

He nodded. "I understand, Ev."

Did he?

She didn't owe Bryson a single thing after the way he'd ghosted her. In fact, she had every right to shut him out completely.

Except she couldn't.

In the few days since he'd barreled back into her life, she'd been mired in this jumbled cloud of resentment, confusion, and nostalgia over how things ended that summer. She had no doubt her anger at Cameron played a part in just how intensely she was leaning into that nostalgia, but this wasn't about Cam. This was about Bryson, and how despite being engaged to another man for the past four years, there had always been a tiny piece of her that thought, *What if?*

She pressed a hand to her stomach.

Acknowledging that she'd felt something for him—even a tiny bit—while she was with Cameron triggered an uneasy feeling in her gut.

"Stop overthinking," Bryson said.

She jerked back. "What? I'm not," Evie said.

"Yes, you are," he said. "I told you, I understand. I keep thinking of you in terms of the Evie from that summer, but that isn't who you are. I'm not the same person I was back then either, thank God. I'm trying to remember and respect that things are different. Forgive me if I slip up."

Evie's eyes softened as a gentle warmth spread throughout her.

This. This is what was so unique about him. Other men, including the one she'd been engaged to, would try to gaslight her into thinking she was being ridiculous. This is why it had been so easy to fall for him that summer. It's why she had to be careful right now.

The server arrived with the dogs' meals first, each delivered in pink dog dishes with water on one side and the chicken, rice, and veggies on the other. She also set two plates on the table and let them know their meal would be out soon.

The growls Evie had expected when Bella and Waffles first met emerged.

"Aht, aht!" she reprimanded. "You each have your own. No need to get territorial."

Waffles and Bella both quieted and started in on their respective bowls.

"So, what magic potion did you slip the dogs?" Bryson asked. "It took months before I could get Bella to obey."

"No magic," Evie replied with a laugh. "Waffles and I quickly came to an understanding regarding temper tantrums. We both agreed not to have any." She scrunched up her mouth. "I kinda had a screaming fit the other day and it scared him. He ran behind the couch and I had to coax him out with rotisserie chicken.

"I felt horrible, of course. I promised him that I would not rant at the air again. When I took him to the park and he started barking at a group of kids playing Frisbee, I made him promise the same."

Bryson grinned. "And did he?"

"In my mind he did," Evie said.

The deep timbre of his laugh reverberated along her skin. It caused those earlier butterflies to take flight again in the pit of her stomach.

The server arrived then with their food, setting the oval plate in the center of the table. Evie started dishing the loaded fries and shrimp onto the smaller plates, grateful for something to do with her hands.

"So, how recently did you lose your last dog?" Bryson asked as he stabbed his fries with a fork.

Evie tipped her head to the side. "What do you mean?"

"You adopted Waffles from The Sanctuary the day I was there with Doc, right?"

"Oh, yes. Um, my last dog died about twelve years ago, back when I was an undergrad."

He stopped with the fork halfway to his mouth. "You're kidding, right?"

"Cameron never wanted a dog," Evie explained with a shrug. "He didn't want pets of any kind. Not even a goldfish. He said we saw enough animals at work; we shouldn't need them in our home."

"Talk about a fucking red flag," Bryson muttered.

"I said the same thing after I kicked him out," she exclaimed. "I'm not sure how I didn't see it."

"Does Cameron even like being a veterinarian?" Bryson asked. "Back when we were lab partners, I always got the sense that he was there because it's what was expected of him. You know, because it was the family business. I'm not sure he ever really wanted to be there."

Evie took a sip of her water. "It's what I've suspected for a long time. But then, I went through something similar with my family, so I didn't want to examine Cameron's motivations too closely. He's a good vet—I'm not defending him or anything, just stating a fact. He is good at his job—but he's not a loving vet. Everything is always straightforward and no-nonsense for him."

"I have different pet voices for different breeds, even though the pets are under anesthesia for ninety percent of the time we're together," Bryson said.

Why did that not surprise her?

"Because there is no question that you love your job," Evie said. "I hope that surgical hospital knows how lucky they are to have you."

He smiled that smile again, the one she wished she could see on a continual loop.

"Based on the way they've rolled out the red carpet, I would say they do. But if you ever feel the need to remind them, by all means, you're welcome to come over and do just that."

Heat spread through her as she connected with his quiet, amused gaze. How many times had their eyes met in this same way across the exam table at The Sanctuary, or while sharing lunch underneath the branches of one of the massive oak trees in Armstrong Park?

It was that soothing sense of familiarity that jarred her out of her daze. She could not allow herself to get sucked in by the hypnotic pull of old memories.

"I want to be up front with you," Evie said. "I am not in a place where I can be anything more than a friend. But you were my friend, Bryson. Before you became anything else, you were a *really* good friend."

His Adam's apple undulated as he swallowed and nodded.

"You were a good friend too, Ev." He shook his head. "I'm sorry—"

She put up both hands.

"No. Nope. We already agreed that the past is in the past." Evie sucked in a deep breath, giving herself the chance to rethink this. But she didn't need to rethink it. She knew what she wanted to do.

"Let me propose something," she continued. "New Orleans has undergone a lot of changes since that summer you spent here." Another deep breath. "What do you say to me helping you get reacquainted with the city? No pressure. No expectations."

Bryson blinked. "Uh . . . okay. I, uh, I would like that."

"I mean, we're already on this mission together to save The Sanctuary. It just makes sense. Unless you don't—"

He cut her off. "I already said yes. You don't have to convince me, Ev."

She nodded, pulling her bottom lip between her teeth.

"Okay, then," Evie said. "Well, why don't we start talking strategy? That's why we're here, right?"

"Yes," Bryson said. "So, the no-brainer is to start a crowdfunding campaign. It takes the least amount of work, and you can grab all of those people who just want to throw twenty bucks to a good cause in order to feel good about themselves."

"I agree," Evie said. "Also, I'll admit to being one of those people when life gets hectic. Often, it's just easier to donate cash. As for The Sanctuary, I've already talked to a good friend about revamping the website. As soon as that's up and running, we should start a GoFundMe. But that won't be enough. We will need actual fundraisers."

"No doubt," Bryson said.

"What do you think about a 5K charity run?"

"Won't work," he said, swirling a fried shrimp in the sauce that had trickled to the bottom of the bowl.

"Why not? I've taken part in those before."

"The permits you'll have to get from the city will be a pain in the ass. Then you have to pay the police department for securing the route. And don't forget the people you will piss off for closing down streets. It's just not worth it."

He had a point.

"Okay, that's fair," Evie said. "Now, I think *this* idea would be a ton of fun. We host a scavenger hunt! We charge a registration fee and hide items for the participants to collect all around the French Quarter."

"I guess that's a little better," he said with a shrug. "But it seems like a lot of work on the front end."

Evie threw her hands up in exasperation. "It will all be work! You have to put in some effort if you want to achieve your goal."

"Why are you getting testy with me?"

"I am not getting testy." She pointed to his phone. "Look up the word *testy* and tell me if that describes me right now."

His eyes glittering with amusement, he slid his phone from the table and swiped across the screen. Evie's eyes narrowed as she watched him type with his thumbs. He turned it to face her.

"Irritated, impatient, and somewhat bad-tempered. If I snapped a picture of your face right now and submitted it to Merriam-Webster, they would use it as an example of *testy*."

Evie rolled her eyes. "Whatever," she said, trying not to laugh.

"You always made it way too easy to get under your skin."

The grin playing at the edges of his lips made her want to choke him. Or kiss him.

"And you were always quick to do it," she said, pitching her napkin at his head. There would be no kissing.

Bryson caught the napkin in one hand, then made a production of folding it neatly and handing it back to her. She snatched it from his fingers.

"I'm not apologizing for throwing this at you," Evie said, setting the napkin on the table.

"I'm sure you've convinced yourself that I deserved it," Bryson said.

She gave him the same treatment she'd given Ashanti and Ridley earlier, pointing both of her middle fingers at him.

Bryson's head snapped back with his shocked, sharp laugh. Evie tried to hold it in, but her own laugh bubbled up so quickly that it escaped before she could stop it.

"You can be so annoying," she said.

He repeated his assertion from earlier when they'd first arrived, his brown eyes alight with amusement.

"I am nothing if not consistent, Ev."

He broke your heart once. Never forget that.

She would have to hammer that reminder into her brain. She feared if she didn't, she would fall for Bryson even quicker than she had the first time.

CHAPTER FOURTEEN

Bryson tracked the slow, methodic up-and-down motion of the stark white sail bobbing along Lake Pontchartrain. The movement had lulled him into this peaceful, relaxed state that he couldn't seem to shake himself out of.

To be fair, he hadn't tried to shake himself out of it. Staring out the floor-to-ceiling windows in his newly purchased condo, it was the first time he truly felt at peace with his decision to move back to Louisiana. He could stand here doing this exact thing for hours.

He glanced at his watch.

Shit. It had been nearly a half hour since he'd stopped to take in the view. The can of sparkling water he'd been drinking had long since lost its fizz, and Bella had since awoken from her nap, but every time he thought of stepping away, something on the water caught his attention.

"I'm not going to get any work done when I'm at home, will I, Bells?"

His dog peered up at him, then went back to gnawing on her chew toy.

As much as he wanted to, spending the day staring out at the calm lake waters was not on the agenda. The packet of new-hire paperwork he'd been putting off couldn't be ignored any longer, not if he wanted health insurance. The forms he'd been asked to complete in the condo association's management portal weren't as urgent, but it made sense to knock those out while he was at it.

Bryson tore himself away from his outstanding view—the number one reason he'd offered over asking price for this condo to ensure he got it—and went into the kitchen for another drink.

His phone rang, a picture of his mom at his graduation from Tuskegee filling the screen.

"Hey, Ma," Bryson answered. He put her on speaker and set the phone on the counter. "How was the recital last night?"

She and his dad had traveled to Baton Rouge to his nephew's choir recital. Bryson would have made the seventy-mile trip if anyone had bothered to tell him about it. He'd called and gotten her voicemail. When he called again a few minutes later, she'd sent a text telling him to stop calling because the recital had just begun.

His "What recital?" text went unanswered until after the concert concluded.

He owed his brother a call so he could chew him out for not telling him about last night's performance. The whole point of moving back home was to do things like attend choir recitals and baseball games and whatever else his nephews had going on in their lives.

Bryson knew it was probably just an oversight. They were still getting used to him being back home. But he'd still felt like shit for the rest of the night.

"The recital was fine," his mother answered. "Marcus's voice cracked during his solo, so of course he now thinks the world is over."

"Eighth grade," Bryson said. "Tough age. Are you ready for dinner next Saturday night?" he asked, grabbing another can of water from the refrigerator. "I still think you should let me hire a car to pick you two up and drive you here. You and Dad can spend the night and I'll drive you back on Sunday. I'll even go to church."

"Uh-huh," his mother grunted. "Did you go today?"

"I plead the Fifth."

"You need to find a church family out there," she said. "You're not going to drive an hour and a half to Houma for church every Sunday."

"Maybe I *will* make the trip every weekend. At least that way I'll get to see you and Pop on a regular basis."

"Don't make promises you're not going to keep to me or to the Lord," she said. "Anyway, I called to tell you that your father and I can't make the dinner next Saturday."

"What? Why not?" He popped the top on his water.

"What was that noise? Is someone shooting?"

Bryson rolled his eyes. "Nobody is shooting. I told you my condo is in a safe neighborhood. Now, why can't you two come over for dinner?"

"Because our favorite cruise line emailed a last-minute

deal that we can't pass up. Fifty dollars a night for a balcony room."

"Another cruise?" Bryson took the phone off speaker and cradled it between his shoulder and ear. "You literally just got back home from a cruise."

"Fifty dollars per night, Bryson! Do you know how big of a savings that is?"

"It's not really saving anything. They only sent the deal because they know you're going to spend twice the cost of a regular cruise in the casino."

"We've already paid for it," she said. "We'll do dinner when we get back. I'll even cook for you."

"What if *I* wanted to cook for *you*?" He didn't want to cook. He never wanted to cook. But he was in full-on ornery teenager mode now.

Bryson pulled a red Solo cup from the pack he'd bought yesterday—he had a date with the homeware department at Macy's tomorrow—and emptied the can of sparkling water into it.

"What was the point of me moving back home if you and Pop are never here?"

"You expected us to change our lifestyle just because you decided to move back? And you're not home; you're in New Orleans."

"Closer to home," he amended, modulating his tone because, first of all, he was too old to keep up the ornery teenager crap and, second, his mother was at least partially right. He hadn't expected his parents to drop everything and race over whenever he called, but he thought they would carve out at least *some* time for him.

The irony that he was the one complaining about not seeing them when it had been the other way around for so many years was not lost on him.

"How long is this upcoming cruise?" Bryson asked.

"Only seven days," she said. "Look at it this way. It will give you more time to make your new place presentable."

"What makes you think my new place isn't already presentable?"

He gave the open-concept kitchen and living room a quick glance. Save for his sofa and a coffee table his neighbor two doors down had offered after their college-aged son returned home with excess furniture, the space was bare. His own furniture was scheduled to be delivered from Raleigh on Thursday, but maybe he could pick up some decor when he shopped for plates and glasses. He could use a vase, maybe a few paintings. And a rug. A rug would be good.

"Fine," Bryson said. "But please let this be the last time you cancel, Mama. Being able to see you and Pop on a regular basis was the biggest factor in my moving here."

"We're not canceling, just postponing," she said. "Now, tell me, how are you liking your new apartment?"

He looked out the window again and grinned.

"I'm loving it," he said. "And it's a condo, not an apartment. It's my home."

"Homes have yards."

"Why are you so bullheaded?"

"Because I've earned the right to be," his mother said. "I need to go. I refuse to have my picture taken on formal night in that same green dress. I told your father since we're getting the cruise for such a cheap price, he can afford to buy me a new gown. I'll talk to you later, honey."

"Talk to you later," Bryson said. "I love you, Ma. Tell Pop he owes me a phone call."

"You know that man hates talking on the phone."

"Too bad. I can't manage to see you two in person, so a phone call will have to do."

Just as he ended the call with his mother, a text from Evie popped up. The enormity of the smile that stretched across his face at the sight of her name on his phone was embarrassing as hell. It's a good thing Bella was the only one here to witness it.

"Don't tell anyone how infatuated I am, Bells. Keep this between you and me."

Bella didn't bother to respond.

Bryson tapped on Evie's message. It was a link to a website.

"Whoa," Bryson said when he clicked on it. He sent her a text.

Nice work!

A few moments crept by before she responded.

Right? But I can't take credit. The three dots appeared, then, Can you talk?

Bryson immediately called, because apparently, displaying even a drop of chill when it came to her was beyond his capabilities.

"So, who deserves the credit for the website?" Bryson asked when the call connected. "It's awesome."

"That would be Ashanti's younger sister, Kara. She put that together in a single afternoon."

"Damn. Even more impressive."

"I know! Hello, by the way," Evie said. "Sorry for disturbing you with what's essentially work on a Sunday afternoon. I promise not to blow up your phone with texts the entire time we're working on this project."

"For future reference, you can text me at any time, Evie. And for any reason. It doesn't have to be about The Sanctuary."

He considered buffering his statement with a platonic qualifier, like *That's what friends do*, but decided to let it stand. She could interpret his words however she wished.

There was a prolonged pause on the other end of the line before she answered with a simple "Thank you."

Well, shit. How was *he* supposed to interpret *her* answer? Was that the thank-you of someone who wanted to remain friends or had she read something more into his offer?

And why in the fuck was he even going there?

Evie had made it crystal clear where things stood between them. They were old friends working to save a rescue that was dear to both of them. The last thing he wanted to do was push her away by coming on too strong.

"So, now that the website is done, does this mean we're moving to the crowdfunding campaign?" Bryson asked, bringing the conversation back to The Sanctuary.

"Kara is working on graphics as we speak," Evie said. "But I wanted to talk through a few more fundraising ideas we came up with while I was at Ashanti's."

There was a static sound, then rustling.

"Ev?"

"Sorry," Evie said, once back on the line. "Hey, I'm on my way to the City Bark with Waffles," she said. "Do you and Bella want to join us?"

"What is City Bark?"

"It's a dog park in City Park. Just google NOLA City Bark and it'll give you directions. It's one of the nicer dog parks around—worth me driving across town for Waffles to visit it. There's lots of equipment and space for them to run around."

Bryson thought about the mountain of work he *should* do this Sunday and knew within seconds that none of it was getting done.

He looked over at Bella, who was back to napping. He'd taken her for a walk a couple of hours ago, so she was probably good for the rest of the day.

"Sure," Bryson said to Evie. "I'll meet you there in thirty."

He disconnected the call.

"Okay, Bells, it's time for you to take one for the team," Bryson said. "We're going to the dog park."

CHAPTER FIFTEEN

Evie sidestepped a gnarled tree root that had penetrated the concrete sidewalk. Anytime she walked along St. Charles Avenue, it was an exercise in dodging tripping hazards, but the added distraction of Bryson's bare arm brushing against hers played such havoc with her concentration that she was bound to face-plant sooner or later.

"I'm sorry again about City Bark," Evie said. She jerked forward as her dog went in chase of a blowing leaf. "Stop it, Waffles."

"Why are you apologizing?" Bryson asked. "Did you give those teens the paint and glitter they used to pollute the doggie pools?"

"No. And if I ever see them in person, I'm going to jail."

"It's not worth jail time," Bryson said.

"That's not the point. I hate when a handful of little assholes ruin things for everyone else."

"The park said they'll have the pools cleaned out within a day or two. Besides, the dogs seem to be having just as much fun here."

They'd come back to the area of the city they were both familiar with. Miracle of miracles, they'd both found parking spots on St. Charles Avenue near Audubon Park within a few yards of each other.

"Yeah, but there isn't a designated dog park here," Evie said. "I've learned that this one likes the freedom to run unleashed."

As if he'd heard her, Waffles tried to take off again.

"Stop it," Evie said, tugging his leash. He wiggled his body the way she did when she thought a bug was on her. "Waffles, calm down."

"Okay, I know you haven't had a dog in a long time, but you're still a veterinarian, Ev. You know commands don't work that way. *Stop it* and *calm down*, especially in that wishy-washy tone you're using, won't cut it. You were more assertive at the restaurant the other day."

"Believe it or not, I have never been good at controlling my own dogs," she said with a laugh. "It used to drive my mother out of her mind. The worst was when she would come home from the hospital and find the dogs in my bedroom instead of the pool house or sunporch."

Bryson stepped aside so that two younger girls wearing pink and white sorority sweaters could pass them.

"I'm still not sure how you ended up in this profession," he told Evie. "You come from a family that doesn't like dogs and were engaged to a man who also doesn't like them."

"I never said Cameron didn't like dogs; he just didn't want one of his own."

He slid her a sideways glance.

"Fine," Evie said. "And, honestly, if it wasn't for Ashanti, I'm not sure I would have become a vet. I told you this story back when we volunteered at The Sanctuary, didn't I?"

He shook his head. "Nope."

They were probably too busy getting into the kind of mischief she didn't want to think about right now.

"Well, it's true," Evie said. She told him how she was all set to apply to medical school so that she could follow in her mother's footsteps as a cardiologist.

"Ashanti pointed out that I always seemed more fascinated in her coursework than my own. I knew I wouldn't be happy as a cardiologist, but never even considered doing anything else until Ashanti said two simple words to me: *Why not?*"

"And that's all it took?"

"That's it." She nodded. "I've never regretted it, despite the backlash I still occasionally get from my family. I honestly cannot imagine doing anything else."

"That must make this time right now difficult," he said. "Not having a practice to go to. Have you started putting out feelers?"

"Not yet. I'll get a new position eventually," she said. "I want to focus on The Sanctuary right now. I'm lucky that I *can* take some time off to focus on something else. At least this time when I start the job hunt, I know I'm getting the position based on merit."

"Wait, do you think you didn't deserve to work at the clinic on Maple?"

"Whether or not I deserved to work there is moot. It was a foregone conclusion that I would." She hunched her shoulder.

"That's the problem. I have never been in a position of having to rely on myself—I've always had this safety net."

"You mean your superrich parents?"

"Stop it." She bumped him with her shoulder. "They are not *super*rich."

"Remember, I've seen their house, Ev. Compared to most people, they're superrich."

She rolled her eyes. "They make a good living," she said. "And, yes, it's nice knowing I can go to my parents if I need anything, even though I'm a perpetual disappointment to them both."

She raised her hand when he started to speak.

"That's a joke. Well, kinda," she said. "But it's not just my parents; Cameron has also been a safety net. I knew before I graduated that I would work at his practice. I never imagined myself anywhere else."

"There's nothing wrong with having a safety net. A lot of people would kill for that."

"I know how lucky I am."

"Do you?" Bryson asked.

"Of course I do," she said. "Why would you ask me that?"

"Because, in my experience, I've found that people tend to look at what they *don't* have and what *isn't* going right in their lives instead of focusing on the good stuff. It seems to have gotten worse since the pandemic."

"That isn't me," Evie said. "And what we all went through with the pandemic only served to show me just how blessed I am."

One of St. Charles Avenue's signature green streetcars rolled past them. The sound of its steel rails rattling always put Evie in a New Orleans state of mind.

"If I share something with you, do you promise not to get upset or hold it against me?" Bryson asked once the noise from the streetcar abated.

"I can't make that promise because I have a feeling it's going to piss me off," Evie said.

"Probably." He stuffed his free hand in his pocket and stared straight ahead. "Once I saw your parents' home, it changed the way I thought about you. You started to be one of them to me."

Evie stopped walking. "Excuse me? One of *them*?"

"A rich kid," he clarified. "I know, I know. It was unfair. You never acted like you were better than anyone else, and you never tried to make me feel as if I was less than simply because I didn't come from the right area code. But I was pretty messed up back then."

"Bryson, you were a basketball star on campus. Everyone else worshiped the ground you walked on."

"I wouldn't go that far," Bryson said. "And that's part of the issue. Everyone knew me because I could dribble a ball. Ninety percent of the people on campus had no idea what my major was, or my GPA, even though it was mentioned at least three times per game. They didn't care about that. I helped the team win basketball games. That's what mattered. And I had to prove myself as an academic over and over again."

"What does that have to do with the area code you came from?"

"Because I had been relying on my athleticism to get me *out* of that area code for years before I ever started at LSU. Since junior high school, actually. It's a weird dynamic, but I came to both depend on my ability to play basketball and resent it."

He tapped the side of his head.

"I've always had this brain. I've always done well in school. But even from an early age, what was in here didn't matter. I was tall, Black, and had an athlete's build. *That's* what people saw. That's what people's assumptions were based on. It's a lot easier to show people that you can make a three-point shot than do a math problem, so that's what I became known for."

Evie could see how much it still affected him, and she understood why he'd come to resent it. But she would be lying if she didn't admit that his words stung.

"I didn't know what area code you'd come from when we first met," Evie said. "And, if you want to know the truth, I didn't know you were a basketball player either."

His head swung around. "You didn't?"

"Nope." Evie shook her head. "Ashanti was the one who first pointed it out. I called her after the first day we met. The day I started volunteering at The Sanctuary."

"That wasn't the first time we met," Bryson said.

"Yes, it was."

He was shaking his head. "It was the first time you talked to me, but it wasn't the first time we met."

"I would have remembered—"

He cut her off. "I met you once before, just outside of the vet med building on campus," Bryson said. "I'd noticed you standing on the steps outside the entrance and asked if you needed something, but then Cameron came out of the building before you had the chance to respond. I found out later that he'd kept you waiting for a half hour while he hung out in the lab with a couple of guys from his frat."

Evie stopped walking. "Oh my goodness," she said. "That was *you*!"

"That was me," he said. His voice had taken on a hoarseness that she felt on her skin. "You may not have noticed *me* before then, but I'd noticed you, Ev. Well before we volunteered at The Sanctuary."

Evie's chest expanded with an oddly warm feeling. To know she had been on his radar, even back then, sent her mind into dangerous places. Places that made her wonder if things would have ended up differently if Cameron hadn't chosen that moment to come out of the vet med building. One small change, a few minutes, could have altered everything about the past decade.

"I guess we've come full circle, haven't we?" she asked.

"Not yet." Bryson shook his head. "Full circle would mean... well, it would mean something else. At least to me. But we're leaving the past in the past, right?"

She glanced at him, then quickly averted her eyes.

"Uh, yeah," she said.

The confusion she'd experienced way too much lately reared its head again. Her chest tightened with the uncomfortable feeling of not knowing what she really wanted.

She'd told herself it was best to keep things strictly platonic and professional when it came to Bryson. They were no longer a couple of young college kids still trying to figure out where they belonged in the world. They were adults. They'd seen more, experienced more. They'd lived.

It didn't change what happened eight years ago, but it added context she hadn't considered before tonight. Before this very moment.

What exactly was she afraid of when it came to moving beyond friendship with Bryson? She knew herself well enough to recognize if she was moving too fast and too soon, didn't she? Then again, she thought she knew herself well enough to recognize if she was being cheated on.

"Stop overthinking things, Ev."

She startled just as Bella moved in front of her. Evie nearly tripped over her leash.

"Whoa." Bryson wrapped his arm around her middle to steady her. "You okay?"

She nodded. "I'm good." She stepped out of his embrace, but the sensation of his palm against her waist lingered.

They approached the entrance to Audubon Park, across from Tulane University.

"Can we grab a seat for a bit?" Bryson asked. "Bella's walking slow, which means she needs to rest."

Evie glanced down at his dog. "How old is she?"

"My best guess is between ten and twelve, but I can't be sure. She was brought in for a surgery and her owner never came back to pick her up." They walked over to Gumbel Fountain and took a seat on one of the benches that circled the bronze sculpture and its surrounding pool of water. "It wasn't the first time it had happened, but there was something about Bells that just wouldn't allow me to leave the hospital without her."

"Does she realize how lucky she is to have the world-renowned veterinary surgeon Bryson Mitchell as her rescuer?"

"She couldn't give two shits," Bryson said with a laugh. "As long as I keep her supplied in T-R-E-A-T-S, she's good."

Evie laughed. "I'm pretty sure Waffles would join Pennywise in the sewer if he was holding a bacon-flavored Milk-Bone instead of a balloon."

"You mind if Bells sits up here with us?" Bryson asked,

lifting the papillon from the ground and placing her on the bench between them. Bella immediately curled up and closed her eyes.

"Let's see if this one will sit still for a few minutes," Evie said.

Just as she reached down for Waffles, a squirrel ran down the trunk of one of the huge oak trees surrounding the fountain area and darted in front of them.

Waffles bolted, yanking his leash from her grip.

"Waffles!" Evie yelled. "Get back here."

"Shit. I'll get him," Bryson said.

Evie watched in fascinated horror as Bryson chased after Waffles and the squirrel. Her dog tore through the flower beds, kicking up dirt in his wake. She looked around to make sure there were no police or park employees. This dog was going to get her banned from one of her favorite spots in the city.

"Stop!" Bryson called.

He tried to catch the leash that still trailed behind the dog, but Waffles was too fast. Bryson nearly slipped and Evie was appalled by the giggle that escaped.

This was *not* funny. Except that it was. At least a little.

The squirrel zipped out of the flower bed and headed for the fountain.

Oh shit! No!

"Waffles don't!" she called.

But he did.

With a leap, Waffles dove into the shallow pool, splashing water everywhere. He ran to the center of the fountain where the squirrel had climbed onto the bronze sculpture.

Waffles's barking had attracted the attention of several park-goers. Evie could feel her face heating with embarrassment.

Bryson clapped his hands and, in a stern voice, said, "Waffles. Come."

Waffles ignored him.

"I can't believe this," Evie said underneath her breath. She started for the fountain, then stopped when Bryson climbed into the water and snatched up her dog, who continued to bark at the poor squirrel. He held the sopping-wet Waffles at arm's length as he walked back to the bench.

"Might I suggest dog training. Maybe then he will listen to commands," Bryson said.

"I am *so* sorry." Evie took Waffles from him and pushed the handle of his leash onto her wrist.

Bryson looked down at Bella. "Did she really sleep through all of that?"

"Like a baby," Evie said. Bella looked angelic; her body still curled on the park bench.

He shook his head. "Um, I hate to cut the evening short, but . . ." He motioned to his pants, which were soaking wet from just under his calves and down.

"I understand," Evie said. She pulled her lower lip between her teeth.

Bryson's eyes narrowed. "Are you laughing?

She shook her head, then nodded. "I'm sorry," Evie said, breaking out in a full-on belly laugh. "I'm so sorry. This is horrible." She wiped at the tears trailing down her face. "I can't believe you climbed into the fountain."

"How else was I going to get him?" he asked with a laugh.

"Thank you," Evie said. "I really appreciate it, Bryson."

"Anytime," he returned. His warm brown eyes were alight with amusement.

She thought about how Cameron would have reacted in this same situation and nearly laughed out loud at the contrast.

It was just as she'd feared. Bryson was making it very hard not to fall for him again.

CHAPTER SIXTEEN

The harsh fluorescent light beaming down from the metal arm that extended six feet above the exam table was giving him a headache, but Bryson did his best to ignore it and concentrate on the task at hand. He carefully snipped at the necrotic tissue covering a hind leg wound on a mutt that had been brought to The Sanctuary by a Good Samaritan just after he and Evie arrived. The woman said she'd found him rummaging through the garbage behind a nearby restaurant.

The light slid down the metal arm, clunking Bryson on the top of his head.

"Shit." His hand went to his head, but he stopped just before touching it. There was only one box of gloves in the entire rescue. He didn't want to contaminate the pair he had on. "Odessa? Can you come in here?"

The receptionist was there in a matter of seconds.

"How's he doing?" Odessa asked, her attention on the dog.

"He'll be just fine if I can get this light to stay in place long enough to get through the procedure," he said. "It keeps slipping."

"That happens. Give me a sec." She left the room and, moments later, returned with a roll of gray duct tape.

"Seriously?" Bryson asked.

"We have to do what we have to do." Odessa shrugged. She came around the back of the table and started sliding the light up the metal arm. "Tell me where to place it?"

Bryson shook his head. This was ridiculous. And tragic. How much could it cost to replace this thing? And get more gloves?

"Go up a few inches," he said. "Down. Right there."

She peeled off a long swatch of tape and wrapped it around the light and arm.

"There you go. That should last for a while."

"How long has it been like this, Odessa?"

"You don't want to know," she said. She held her hands up. "We've had to make do since the grant money dried up. Doc has been doing what he can, but it's been a one-man show since the mentorship program ended."

"Why didn't he say anything before it got to this point?" Bryson asked.

"Because he's a stubborn old man."

"Why didn't *you*? I mean, are you even taking a salary?"

"I don't need a salary," she said. "Joe's pension takes care of my bills."

"So you're an unpaid volunteer at this point," Bryson stated.

"I work here because I *want* to work here." She wrapped her arms around her chest. "It keeps me out of that quiet house."

Her softly spoken words doused what was left of his fight. What good was it to complain to Odessa? She and Doc were both doing the best they could. If he wanted to point a finger at someone, he should look in the damn mirror.

Odessa patted him on the shoulder. "I'm glad you're back home, Bryson. This place needs you. I'm not sure if it will be enough, but it does my heart good to see you and Evie trying to save it. The same goes for Doc. He has more hope in his eyes than I've seen in a long time."

Bryson swallowed and nodded. "I'm not sure if we can save it either," he said. "But we're going to do what we can."

He felt like the biggest lump of shit as he watched Odessa exit the room.

What did it say about him that he'd used The Sanctuary's mentorship program to bolster his credentials, then left without a backward glance? Doc shouldn't have had to reach out. Bryson knew damn well he should have been here well before things got to this point.

Unfortunately, it all felt a bit "too little too late."

Though, not if Evie had anything to say about it.

He still thought she was just on the other side of delusional for thinking they could save this place, but the determination he'd sensed in her told him that she would do it with or without his help. Maybe he was just as delusional to think he could work alongside Evie and not lose his mind.

"You're definitely delusional," Bryson muttered as he used gauze to dab at the healthy tissue he'd unearthed.

He'd had the hardest time going to sleep last night after their evening in Audubon Park. He'd felt like a fool climbing into that water to go after her dog, but he would do it again without hesitation if it meant he would see that smile brightening Evie's face or hear her lyrical laugh.

There was a knock on the open door to the surgical room.

"Hey!"

A shot of adrenaline rushed into his veins at the sound of Evie's voice. It was a reaction that he'd come to anticipate. The key was to hide his body's reaction so that he didn't scare her off.

"Hey, what's up?" Bryson asked. At least his voice didn't give him away.

"Just dropping by to see if you need help with the debridement. Those can be a little tricky."

He caught the grin tipping up the corner of her mouth.

"I think I've got it," Bryson said.

"You sure? When you spend your time performing high-risk surgeries, the simple things become complicated. I wouldn't want you to miss a step."

Bryson tried to hide his smile; the mirth in her voice made it impossible.

"Have you finished cleaning that Pomeranian's teeth?" he asked, not bothering to hide his own amusement.

"What was left of them," Evie said. She came into the room and perched against the prep table. "I ended up having to extract four. She hasn't woken from the anesthesia yet."

Folding her arms over her chest, Evie blew out a tired breath and said, "If I wasn't already preparing to do whatever I could to save this place, I would be after today. The guilt over not helping out sooner is going to eat at me for a long time to come."

"Join the club," Bryson said.

"At least you have the excuse of not being in the state. Maple Street Animal Clinic is less than five miles away. Even if I'd taken the time to swing by once a week, I would have noticed The Sanctuary was in trouble."

"What good does the guilt trip do for you or The Sanctuary?" Bryson asked. "You're committed to helping fix it. Focus on that." He nipped the last bit of dead tissue from the wound and bonded it with gauze and tape. "This should heal in a few weeks," he said.

Evie rubbed her hands over her crossed arms, despite it being a comfortable temperature in the surgical room. "Being here in this room brings back a lot of memories."

Bryson cocked one brow. "You sure you want to go there?"

She glanced away, then back to him. "We made more memories in this room than . . . you know what."

"Funny. I can barely remember anything but *'you know what'* while in this room," he said.

When they'd volunteered here, he'd taken advantage of every chance he could get to taste Evie's mouth. But it was that one time in this very room, toward the end of the summer, when things had gone further than they'd ever taken them. Those memories had lingered at the periphery of his brain for months after he left. His mouth on her neck. One hand on her breast, the other inside the waistband of her scrubs. Then moving lower.

If he closed his eyes, he could still feel her hot, slick flesh constricting around his fingers. That sensation had obliterated all other memories from this place.

Bryson cleared his throat. "But I guess you're right. There

were also the endless hours of cleaning up dog poop. Who could forget about that?"

She laughed, just as he knew she would. Meanwhile, he was fighting like hell to rein in the need those erotic memories had evoked. He still wasn't sure how this should all play out. He could continue to go along with pretending that all they'd shared eight years ago was a casual flirtation between friends that had gotten out of hand, but it didn't sit right with him. It belittled what they'd truly shared.

He'd fallen in love with her that summer, and Bryson was certain she'd felt something for him.

Even more unnerving, the pretending left little space for something more to develop between them. And the more time he spent with Evie, the more he was determined to make her see that the spark was still there.

Whether or not she'd only used him as a summer fling to get over Cameron back when they'd volunteered at The Sanctuary, which is what Cameron claimed, no longer mattered. Bryson was certain his ex-lab partner was out of the picture for good this time.

He just had to remember not to push. He needed to go slow.

But that was getting harder to do by the second.

"I need to get back to the first steps in my Operation Rescue the Rescue plan," Evie said. She held up her cell phone. "I took a few pictures and videos of the animals and the current state of the building. I'm hoping we can harness the power of Instagram and TikTok to bring attention to it in the same way Ashanti did with Barkingham Palace. It's amazing what one viral video can do."

"Yeah, that video of those two dogs was everywhere."

"And Ashanti used it to grow her business in ways you wouldn't believe. I'm heading to the daycare after I leave here," Evie said. "She's been planning a canine carnival as one of the lead-up events to the grand opening of Barkingham Palace's newest location, but now she wants to turn it into a fundraiser for The Sanctuary."

"No shit? That's so cool, Ev."

"That's Shanti," she said. "We're going to brainstorm carnival ideas this afternoon."

"You didn't tell me you were talking strategy today," Bryson said. "I thought we were doing this together?"

Her mouth dropped opened. "I—"

"I'm not just a pretty face." He tapped the side of his head. "I've got ideas up here."

She burst out laughing again. "I'm sorry I left you out. Would you like to join me at Barkingham Palace?"

Her smile was genuine and sweet and made him question just what in the hell he was thinking when he told this woman that he was okay with keeping their relationship friends-only. There was no way he could keep this pretend thing going.

"I just need to check in with the hospital," Bryson said. "I'm on call today, but it shouldn't be a problem."

"Perfect," Evie answered. She hooked her thumb at the door. "I'll take a few more pictures, then meet you in the reception area."

He finished clearing the wound and carried the sedated dog to his crate.

Bryson walked out toward Odessa's desk. "Hey, Odessa, are there cones that will fit the stray I just worked on?" He stopped short at the sight of his mentor standing near the reception desk. "Doc, I thought you said you wouldn't be able to make it in today?"

Doc looked up at him and the hair on the back of Bryson's neck immediately stood on end.

"What's wrong?" Bryson asked.

"Someone has finally decided it's time to tell the truth, the *whole* truth, and nothing but the truth," Odessa said. "Where's Evie? She needs to hear this."

Bryson's stomach bottomed out. He'd known there was something Doc wasn't telling. He'd felt it in his gut.

"I'm right here." Evie walked over to Odessa's desk. "Hey, Doc! I didn't expect to see you today."

"Mm-hmm," Odessa murmured. "You ready to tell them?"

"Tell us what?" It had taken Evie a few moments longer to recognize the situation, but Bryson could tell she saw it now.

"What's going on, Doc?" Bryson asked.

"Odessa's right. It's time I give you the whole story." His mentor settled his backside against Odessa's desk and folded his hands in front of him. "You both know the mentorship program was partially funded by the endowment left by Marsha Lawrence, right?"

"I still have the stethoscope with her name etched into it that we received that summer we volunteered," Evie said.

"Well, before Mrs. Lawrence became a benefactor, Dr. Stanley Shepard had already made a huge contribution. In fact, The Sanctuary would not have a home if not for him."

"You need to give them the abridged version," Odessa said.

"I'm getting there," Doc said. "Stanley owned this building. He's rented it to The Sanctuary for a dollar per year."

"I didn't know that," Bryson said.

Evie shook her head. "Neither did I."

"It's how we've been able to operate even in lean years, when there were hardly any donations. He kept it in his company's name for tax purposes but always meant to gift it to the rescue." Doc blew out a deep breath. "Stanley suffered a stroke last year and passed away just before Thanksgiving."

"Oh, I'm so sorry," Evie said. "Were you two close friends?"

"Not really. Stanley was a hard-ass. We were more competitors than friends." He hunched his shoulders. "Anyway, I discovered about a month ago that Stanley never got around to changing his will. Everything is still tangled up in the succession and probate process, but as soon as his estate is done making its way through the courts, his grandson plans to sell the building."

Evie gasped.

"Sell it?" Bryson asked. "Even though he knows his grandfather wanted to gift it to The Sanctuary?"

"Stanley's grandson doesn't care about The Sanctuary, or his grandfather's wishes. Stanley cut him out of nearly everything he owned, but he forgot about this building."

"Shit," Bryson cursed under his breath. This was even worse than he'd imagined.

"What about the rest of his family?"

"There is no one else. The grandson is an only child. Stanley's daughter, the boy's mother, was killed in an automobile accident years ago."

"Is there a way to fight him in court?" Evie asked.

"As far as I know, there isn't anything stating that Stanley planned to leave the building to The Sanctuary. It's just something we talked about while trying to best each other on the golf course. Based on Louisiana's estate laws, any assets that were not assigned in the will are automatically inherited by the legal heirs. That's Stanley's grandson. Besides," Doc said, "the money that would be spent on lawyer fees trying to fight it in court would be better put to use on the animals."

"Or buying the building," Bryson said.

"Or that," Doc said.

"Do you know his selling price?" Evie asked.

"The market value is just over one-point-eight million," Doc said. He let out a gruff laugh. "Stanley bought this place for a hundred thousand dollars back in the eighties."

"Times change," Odessa remarked.

"I guess they do," Doc said. "I considered buying it—even putting up my house as collateral—but the purchase price is more than I can afford."

"Well, this definitely changes the ball game," Evie said.

As far as Bryson was concerned, this ended the ball game.

It pained him to come to that conclusion, but it was the truth. He went into this thinking they would have to raise maybe thirty or forty thousand in order to keep up with The Sanctuary's operating expenses and bring back the mentorship program.

The fundraising ideas he and Evie had begun tossing around—the carnival at Ashanti's place, soliciting raffle donations from local businesses, setting up a crowdfunding campaign—were good, but they were not raising nearly two million dollars on GoFundMe. He didn't care how viral the campaign went online.

Maybe *he* could buy the building. It would be the kind of flex he had only dreamed of being able to pull off. He couldn't afford to purchase it outright—he'd just bought a million-dollar condo—but he could take out a business loan. He knew how to talk a good game. He would be able to convince a bank this was a solid investment.

And how in the hell are you going to pay it back?

Even with a loan, and maybe taking on more speaking gigs to cover the payments, the ongoing operating expenses would continue to climb. There would be maintenance on the building, staff salaries, and he hadn't factored in the cost of bringing back the mentorship program yet.

"So, what does this mean?" Evie asked. "Do we try to find another place to house the animals?"

"That isn't a viable solution," Bryson said. "The cost of outfitting another location with the equipment that would be needed would be just as cost prohibitive. And as someone who just dealt with the residential real estate market, I can only imagine how outrageous the commercial market is these days."

A somber pall fell over the room. It was so oppressive Bryson could practically feel it on his skin. They all knew what this meant, but no one wanted to say the words out loud.

"I should have told you both sooner," Doc said. "I just... I got so caught up in your plans to save The Sanctuary that I thought maybe it would all work out. What better duo to pull off the impossible than my two best veterinary students?" He sighed. "But I don't think it's meant to be."

Bryson hated to hear that defeated tone in his mentor's voice, but at this point they were all feeling defeated. This rescue had played a pivotal role in his life. Accepting that this was the end hurt like hell.

"It was still nice to see the two of you working together

again," Odessa said. She lifted her sweater from where it was draped on the back of her chair and threaded her arms through it. "Remember that I'll be an hour late tomorrow, Doc," she said.

"Is there an extra key?" Bryson asked. "I want to come in early to check on the stray whose wound I cleared today."

"I can do it," Doc said. "I want to spend as much time here as I can, now that I know it won't be operating much longer." He pushed up from his perch on the desk. "Let me go check on the animals now."

Bryson stuffed his hands in his pockets. "I guess there's no need to go to Ashanti's," he said.

"Actually, she texted me about ten minutes ago, postponing our brainstorming session. Her little sister Kendra has some after school awards banquet she didn't bother to tell Ashanti about."

"It's just as well," Bryson said.

"Yeah." Evie's brows pulled together, the corners of her mouth dipping in a pensive frown. After a few moments, she asked, "What are your plans for dinner?"

"Um, leftovers," Bryson said, taken aback by the unexpected question.

"Let me take you to dinner. We have some things to discuss. I'll text you the address. It's another dog-friendly spot, so you can bring Bella."

"I would have to go get her from home," he said.

"You leave her home alone all day?" She asked it in the same tone one would ask whether someone tortured live goldfish.

"Not all the time," Bryson said. "She comes with me to

the hospital when I'm working, but she also is just fine at home."

"Go and get that dog," Evie said. She lifted her phone from her pocket and typed something into it. "Meet me at the address I just texted you in an hour."

CHAPTER SEVENTEEN

Evie sat across the table from Bryson at Cafe Abyssinia, one of her favorite restaurants in the city. She'd asked for the outdoor picnic table underneath the huge, arcing oak tree branch. She sometimes treated herself to dinner and a good book, and this was one of her favorite spots to enjoy both.

"I feel very uncultured right now," Bryson said as he looked over the menu. He tipped it down and peered at her over the top. "I've never had Ethiopian food before."

"Really? Well, you're in for a treat," Evie said. "Do you mind if I do the ordering?"

He set the menu on the table. "Go right ahead."

The waiter returned to their table with a piece of chicken breast and a bowl of water for Bella and Waffles, then asked if they were ready to place their order. Evie requested the dish she always chose when she ate here, along with sparkling water and two glasses of tej, the traditional Ethiopian honey wine.

Once the waiter walked away with their selections, Bryson folded his hands on the table and said, "So, Doc Landry really laid one on us, huh? I knew there had to be more to the issues with The Sanctuary than he was letting on, but this goes beyond anything I'd expected."

"Same," Evie said.

He hunched his shoulders, then let them fall in defeat. "It was going to be an uphill battle to save it anyway, but there's no hope now."

Evie paused for a beat, then said, "I disagree. I'm not ready to accept defeat."

Bryson's forehead wrinkled with his incredulous frown. "Are you serious?"

The waiter interrupted them before Evie had the chance to respond.

"Here's your tej," the young man said. "And I told the chef this was the gentleman's first time eating Ethiopian cuisine, so he provided a small beyainatu. It's a sampling of the traditional vegetables, curries, and lentil stews served here."

"That's so sweet," Evie said. "Please pass along our thanks to the chef."

"Will do. I'll be back with your entrée."

The minute the waiter walked away, Bryson said, "Evie, you can't be serious about The Sanctuary."

"We'll get back to that. Let's eat first," Evie said. She was grateful for the pause in their discussion. She needed a moment to consider how to best approach Bryson with her idea now that she knew he thought saving the rescue was hopeless.

"Ev."

"I'll explain everything," she said. "The food won't be good if we let it get cold."

"Fine." Bryson shook his head, his skepticism unmistakable.

"Good. Now, since this is your first experience with the cuisine, we need a quick lesson in how to eat beyainatu." She broke off a piece of the spongy bread that covered the surface of the platter. "This is injera. It's a flat bread that also serves as your utensil. You use the bread to scoop up your food. Like this."

She demonstrated, picking up a helping of yellow lentils.

Bryson parroted her movements, choosing the gomen, a spicy, minced spinach.

"Oh my damn," he said around a mouthful of food. He looked down at the platter, then up at her, his eyes wide with excited wonder. "Why have I never eaten Ethiopian food before?"

"I can't answer that," Evie said. "I eat here at least once a month. Cameron isn't a fan, but I never let that stop me."

"He doesn't deserve food this good," Bryson said around a mouthful of the intensely seasoned potatoes.

"You're right," she said. "I hope he never has a satisfying meal again."

"Damn, you'll have to tell me what that asshole did to make you feel that way about him. I always did, but it took you a while to see the light."

She shook her head. "Not tonight. I don't want to ruin our meal with talk about Cam."

"Agreed," Bryson said. "This food is too good to let him spoil it."

"And you're just getting started. Wait until the doro wat gets here."

As if she'd heralded it, the waiter arrived with a clay pot

brimming with aromatic stewed chicken and vegetables. They gorged themselves on the flavorful dish and sweet, mead-like wine.

By Bryson's third pleasurable moan, Evie was ready to either jump out of her skin or jump *him*. She hadn't considered the unintended consequences of inviting him to a meal where he would be required to suck his fingers every two minutes.

"And here I thought I was moving back home to eat my fill of gumbo and jambalaya," Bryson said. "Looks as if I'll be adding Ethiopian to the list."

Lord help the women of this city who had to sit and watch this man lick curry from his fingers.

Evie had to clear her throat. "I'm happy you're enjoying it," she said.

The waiter returned. "Will you be ordering dessert this evening?" he asked.

Evie looked to Bryson with a raised brow. "Can you handle dessert?"

"I'm from the South. I will never say no to dessert," he said.

She ordered baklava and two Ethiopian coffees.

"Okay," Bryson said once they were alone again. "Can we finally get to the reason why I was treated to this amazing meal?"

Yes, she did have a reason for bringing him here that didn't revolve around staring at him slip his fingers in and out of his mouth. She had no idea such a thing should have been on her list of "must-sees" but she was profoundly happy to have discovered it.

She cleared her throat again. "Yes, we can. I want to discuss The Sanctuary."

"I figured as much."

"I think we should still try to save it."

Bryson stared at her over the rim of his wineglass. He drained the last sip of tej from it and then set the glass on the table.

"Have I had too much of this wine, or have you?" he asked.

Evie rolled her eyes. "I'm not even tipsy, and neither are you. I'm serious, Bryson. I don't want to give up on The Sanctuary."

"I know you heard exactly what I heard Doc say because you were standing right next to me when he said it."

"Yes, I heard what he said."

"And you still think there's a chance of us saving the rescue? The building alone will cost nearly two million dollars."

"I understand it's a lot of money. But—"

"Two million, Ev. And we don't know when the succession and probate will go through, which means we don't know how much time we have to raise that kind of money. But even if we *did* have an idea of the timeline, there's no way it will happen."

"Way to be positive," she said with a snort.

"Way to be realistic," he countered.

"The Bryson Mitchell I remember would not quit so easily," she said.

"The Bryson Mitchell you remember would not pretend he could snap his fingers and produce two million dollars out of thin air. Be for real, Ev."

"Can you please not shoot this down before I even have the chance to make my case?"

Bryson held his hands up. "Go ahead. By all means, make your case."

The waiter returned with their baklava. Bryson immediately broke off a piece and slipped it to Bella, who had been quietly resting at their feet.

"Don't give her that," Evie said.

"Why not? She likes sweets."

"You're a veterinarian. You know better."

"Life is short, especially for a dog. A little sugar won't hurt her." He broke off another piece. "I guess this means none for Waffles?"

"Nope." Evie shook her head and gave Waffles a piece of bread so he wouldn't feel left out. "I'm not going to sit here and debate what's best for your dog, but when she gets a tummy ache, call me."

"Will do." He winked. "So, now that we've established that I'm a bad dog owner and that it would take a miracle to save The Sanctuary, what's next?"

"We have established no such thing," Evie said.

"Ev—"

"Bryson, I'm serious."

"I can tell. And it's kinda scaring me, if I'm being honest. Face it, Evie, The Sanctuary is a lost cause."

"You don't know that," Evie said. "I still think we should look into buying another place. Or—and just hear me out—we could talk to this grandson of Doc's old friend. Maybe he has a generous bone hidden somewhere in his body and would be willing to donate the building. We should at least inquire about it."

"This is not going to work." Bryson set his elbows on the table and rubbed both temples. "Look, I have no idea what this grandson is like, but based on what Doc shared with us tonight, there's a zero percent chance of that happening, Ev.

The guy sounds like a selfish asshole. Even his own grandfather cut him out of his will."

He had a point. But Evie wasn't ready to concede hers.

"We'll never know unless we ask," she said.

He tilted his head to the side, a curious glint coming from his narrowed eyes.

"What's with this one-eighty, Evie?" Bryson asked.

"What do you mean?"

"You went from needing time to think things over when Doc first asked us to work together to save The Sanctuary, to now looking to create some miracle by convincing a selfish brat to donate two million dollars' worth of property? Where is this coming from?"

She reached for her coffee. Evie sipped slowly, her mind racing to come up with an answer that wouldn't make her look like she was selfishly using The Sanctuary's bad fortune as a way to make herself feel better about the state of her life. Because that's essentially what she was doing.

"Let's just say I had a change of heart," she finally answered.

"Nope." Bryson shook his head. "You don't get to take a page from Doc's playbook and come at me with this vague shit. It's more than just a change of heart." He picked up the baklava and took a bite. With his other hand he made a motion for her to continue.

"Remember when I told you I'm a bit of a black sheep when it comes to my family because I didn't go into medicine?"

"Yeah, I remember," he said.

He sucked the syrup the baklava had been soaked in from his fingers and Evie nearly lost it. She made a mental note to never invite Bryson Mitchell anywhere that required him to eat with his fingers ever again. She was not adult enough to handle it.

"Do you realize how accomplished a family has to be when you're a doctor and still get labeled the black sheep?" Bryson continued. He shook his head. "Those Williamses are something else."

"I know, right?" Evie said with exaggerated glee. "Lucky me!"

"I'm joking, Ev," he said. "You know you're a standout in everything you do. But what does any of this have to do with The Sanctuary?"

"Well, lately I've been feeling like there's something to what my family thinks of my lack of accomplishments."

He stopped chewing. "Now *you're* the one who's joking."

"Think about it, Bryson. What have I really accomplished on my own? I went from relying on my parents to fund my education—"

"Which is their responsibility," he said.

"Well, it wasn't Cameron's responsibility to give me a job, but I never even tried to look anywhere else because I knew I would work with him."

"As much as I hated it back then—and still to this day, if we're being honest—why would you look elsewhere, Ev? You and Cameron were together. You were engaged, weren't you?"

She nodded. "For the past four years."

He held his hands out as if he'd just spelled it out for her.

"It doesn't matter what's true or what makes sense," Evie said. She pressed her hand to the center of her chest. "What matters is what I feel in here, and I still feel as if I haven't accomplished anything meaningful on my own. Saving the rescue has meaning. It's something I can be proud of. Now do you get it?"

"Hmm." He nodded.

"Is that it? Hmm? That's all you have to say?"

"I'm not really sure what to say. I disagree that you need to save The Sanctuary in order to prove that you've accomplished something, but I can't change the way you feel about yourself. If this is what you want, go for it." He took a sip of his coffee. "I still think it's a lost cause."

"Bry—"

"But." He held up his free hand. "If you want to give it a try, I'm here to support you."

Gratitude expanded in her chest until it felt as if she would burst with it. She reached across the table and covered his hand.

"Thank you," Evie said.

He looked down at her hand, then focused his eyes on hers. Evie knew she should release him, but she didn't want to. Instead, she brushed her thumb back and forth over his hand as they continued to stare at each other across the table.

Finally, she pulled away.

"So, you'll help me?" she asked unnecessarily. He'd just said he would.

"Yes," he answered, just as unnecessarily.

She used her napkin to dab at the corners of her mouth, even though she hadn't taken a bite of their dessert yet. This pent-up adrenaline needed an outlet.

"I should warn you that I'm about to go all-in on this. Now that Doc has laid out just how serious the situation is, I plan to eat, sleep, and breathe Operation Rescue the Rescue."

"I wouldn't expect anything less," Bryson said, the corner of his mouth hitching up in a smile.

"I appreciate any time you can lend to the effort, but I

know that you're in a different situation than I am with the move and the new job. So, you know, no pressure."

He stared at her from across the table, his fingers toying with the rim of his mug. After several lengthy moments passed, he finally spoke.

"What if I want pressure?"

CHAPTER EIGHTEEN

Awareness and heat hovered in the air around them. It pressed against Evie's skin like the humidity that usually blanketed this city.

Bryson's words caused a cluster of sensations to stir deep within her belly, but it was the tone in which he'd spoken them that truly got to her. His deep, resonant voice set off sensations in a lower, more sensitive region.

"I—" Evie started, but words escaped her.

Bryson settled his elbows on the table again and clasped his hands together, agitatedly tapping his folded hands against his lips.

"I told myself I wasn't going to do this, that I needed to give you space. But fuck it. I can't pretend I don't want more from you, Ev. I can't keep pretending that I only want to be friends. I'm not that good of an actor."

"Bryson, please don't do this. I can't..." Evie massaged

the left side of her forehead, where an ache had immediately settled. "I can't do this right now," she finished.

"Just hear me out. When you came to my office and proposed working together for the sake of The Sanctuary, you said you wanted to leave the past in the past. You were talking about the way things ended that summer, right?"

She nodded.

"What about the rest of it, Ev? What about what happened *before* things ended? We spent an entire summer falling in—"

She cut him off. "It was just a little lighthearted flirting."

"Bullshit," Bryson said. "You were falling for me back then. I don't care how much you try to deny it, Evie. I know you were."

Should she continue to deny it?

Maybe while she was at it she could try to convince him that the sky was red and the ocean was orange. She had as much of a chance of doing the former as she did the latter.

"Okay, yes," she said. She noticed her hands were trembling and tucked them in her lap, underneath the table. "Yes, it was more than just flirting." Her voice trembled as badly as her hands. Evie took a breath and tried to inject humor. "When was the last time you looked at pics from back then?" she said with a laugh. "Who could blame me?"

"Don't do that," Bryson said. "Don't cheapen what happened between us. There was physical attraction on both our parts, but you know damn well it was more than just physical. I want you to admit it."

"What's the point in doing that now?"

"What's the point in not?" he countered. "Why can't you admit that you felt something for me back then?"

She glanced at him, then quickly looked away, afraid he would see the truth if he looked into her eyes.

"Ev?" he prompted.

"Bryson, don't—"

"Why can't you just admit it?"

"Fine!" She hadn't mean to scream, but then again, she wanted to scream at him and never stop. It's what he deserved for stirring up all these emotions she'd worked so hard to suppress over the years.

"Fine, you want me to admit that I had feelings for you?" she continued. "I had feelings for you. *Real* feelings. I tried not to act on them, but I guess I failed."

It felt as if her entire body were on the verge of bursting. Evie counted her heartbeat at least a dozen times before Bryson finally spoke.

"Was that so hard?" he asked. There wasn't a trace of smugness in his voice for getting her to admit how she'd felt. Instead, she heard sincere curiosity coming from him.

"Honestly, it was," Evie said with a laugh that sounded hysterical even to her own ears. "Back then, those feelings scared me. I'd just broken up with Cameron. It felt as if things were moving too quickly."

Which, ironically, was exactly how she felt right now.

But *was* it the same?

She was so different from the girl she'd been back then. Wouldn't it stand to reason that Bryson wasn't the same guy who'd walked away from her without a word?

"It's not moving quickly enough for me," he said. "I tried to pretend that I could just be your friend, but I can't. I want more, Ev."

Evie pressed her fingertips into her left temple and began

massaging it again. This was the last conversation she'd expected to have when they'd sat down for dinner. But now that they were having it, maybe she could finally get answers to the question that had plagued her for the last eight years.

"And I can't give you anything more without knowing why you left in the first place."

There. She'd said it.

For so long she'd told herself it didn't matter, but deep down she'd known that was a lie. Not knowing why Bryson left so abruptly had affected her life in ways she refused to acknowledge for the longest time.

Whenever Cameron brought up setting a date for the wedding, a nagging feeling would creep into her head, impeding her from taking that next step. This was the reason. Wondering why Bryson left. Wondering what she could have possibly done to send him running.

Wondering what could have been if he had stayed.

She was too much of a coward to ever put voice to that thought, but Evie knew in her heart it was true. Wondering what could have been with Bryson had made it impossible to marry Cameron.

She'd suppressed that question for so long, but now that he'd insisted they address it, she wanted answers.

"You want to clear the air, Bryson? Let's do it. Tell me why you left without so much as a goodbye. Actually, no." Evie held up her hands before he could speak. She was suddenly overcome by the fear of hearing an answer that she wasn't sure she could handle. "Forget I said that. It doesn't matter."

"Yes, it does," Bryson said.

"It doesn't—"

"It's what's standing between us, Ev. I've owed you an explanation for years. Let me . . . let me finally give you one."

There was a plea in both his eyes and voice that she couldn't ignore, and she wondered if he had been seeking to unburden himself for as long as she had been seeking answers.

She sucked in a breath. The significance of this moment was not lost on her. She reached down and lifted Waffles onto the bench beside her. He immediately rested his head in her lap.

"Okay," Evie said. "Why did you leave?"

He tapped his fingers against his lips.

"There were several reasons," he started. "I was approached by the surgical program at Tuskegee just as the summer was ending. I found out later that it was Doc who first contacted them. One of his college roommates was running the program at that time. Once they extended the offer, I couldn't turn it down."

"That explains why you left LSU," she said. "It doesn't explain why you left *me*."

"I know." He ran both hands down his face.

The server chose that moment to return to their table.

"Can I clear any of this for you?" he asked.

"Yes, thank you," Evie said. "Can I get another coffee?"

"Of course. You too, sir?"

Bryson shook his head. "No thanks. I'm good." He waited until the server had walked away before continuing. "I already alluded to why I thought things would never work between us," he said. "It started that afternoon when I brought you home and saw the house you lived in."

"That doesn't make any sense, Bryson."

"To you," he said. "But it made everything crystal clear to me. All I could see was this house that was so big everyone in my small hometown could probably fit inside of it. I sat in the driveway for several minutes after you went inside. I couldn't stop staring at that house. And the longer I stared, the more I came to realize that I would never fit into your world, Ev."

"So you decided to end things without asking me how *I* felt about how and where you fit into my world?"

"I already knew what you would say," Bryson said. "You would have said that you didn't see a problem with it."

"Because there was no problem."

He shook his head. "You don't understand. How you saw things back then is not how the rest of the people in your life would have seen them. Your parents would have never stood for you being with a guy like me."

"A standout student at one of the top veterinary schools in the South?"

"Who got there on a basketball scholarship," he said. "And you were already dating a standout student enrolled in that same veterinary program. The difference was that Cameron came from a wealthy family, while I came from a poor town on the bayou with parents who had to scrape together every penny just to provide what people in your world took for granted."

"For your information, my father would have loved you," she said. "He came from beginnings that were even more humble than yours. The fact that you'd come so far—he would have eaten that shit up."

"It's how I felt," he said. "I didn't say it was fair, but it is what it is."

"I hate when people say 'It is what it is,' as if there's no other way for things to be. It's a lazy excuse."

"I won't argue with you, Ev. I told you before, I was messed up back then," he said. He paused for a moment, then said, "I almost reached out to you after I left. About a month after I got to Tuskegee." He blew out a tired breath. "But then I found out that you and Cameron were back together. It just confirmed what I'd already known."

"And what's that, Bryson?"

"That you were meant to be in a relationship with someone like him. Someone with a background similar to yours, who could have brunch at the country club without eating his salad with the wrong fork—I know a salad fork these days, by the way. I learned a lot over these past eight years."

Evie closed her eyes tight. An ache had formed in her throat; it made it difficult to swallow.

"I spent years wondering why you left the way you did, and now that I know, I honestly wish I didn't," Evie said. "It's such a waste, Bryson. You made a decision for both of us. Did it ever occur to you that I should be the one to decide the kind of guy I want to be in a relationship with?"

"I don't know what else to tell you, Ev."

"Well, I asked," Evie said. She'd been afraid she wouldn't like the answer but never expected it would piss her off to the degree it had. It would have taken a simple conversation to put his worries to rest; all he'd had to do was come to her. Instead, he'd ghosted her.

The server returned with her coffee and the check.

"Take your time," he said. "It's slow tonight, and we don't close for another hour."

"Thanks," Bryson and Evie said at the same time.

She took a sip of her coffee, then set the mug on the table.

"So," Bryson said. "Now that you know why I left, how does it affect us going forward? Does it put us even remaining friends in jeopardy?"

"No." She didn't even have to think on it. "It was a long time ago. You said you were messed up then, but you're not the same person you were eight years ago."

"I'm not." He shook his head. "The man I am today would never have left you that way."

"The woman I am today wouldn't allow it," Evie said. "I would find you and demand answers instead of wondering for nearly a decade."

"Damn, Ev." He ran a hand down his face again. When he looked at her, the contrition in his expression washed away some of her hard feelings.

"The thing is, I don't know if I'm ready for a relationship so soon after ending things with Cameron," Evie said. "I know I am not getting back together with him, so don't even go there. But that doesn't change the fact that I just ended a ten-year relationship with a man I thought I would spend the rest of my life with. Yes, it was on again/off again, but this just feels too soon. You understand that, right?"

He sucked in a long, audible breath.

"I don't like it, but I understand it," Bryson said. He spread his hands flat on the table, then balled them into fists. "This feels like Cameron's winning. I really hate that son of a bitch."

"Stop looking at it that way," Evie said. "It was never a competition."

"No, but if I thought that I had a real chance with you back then, I would have made it one. You have no idea how hard it was to accept that the girl I'd fallen for was the girlfriend of the lab partner I hated to the very core," he said. "Life can be funny. Brutal, but funny."

"It's the weirdest coincidence that the two of you were lab partners. Cam had never mentioned you to me before," Evie said. "He'd talked about his lab partner, but he never called you by your actual name. It was always some kind of insult."

Bryson snorted. "I did the same."

"There was no love lost between the two of you. That was obvious." Evie paused, unsure if she should continue. But they were airing things out, so she did. "I've asked myself so many times what I would have done if you hadn't left," Evie said. "If I'd returned to campus to find you still there, as Cameron's lab partner.

"I got back together with him because there was pressure from my family to do so, and you were gone, so I just . . . " She hunched her shoulders. "I did what everyone thought I should do and forgave Cameron."

"Do you want to know just how pathetic I was eight years ago?" Bryson asked.

"You were not pathetic."

"Yes, Ev, I was. Because if I'd known I had even the *slightest* chance, I would have happily taken any crumbs you threw my way. If you had been willing, I would have snuck around with you behind Cameron's back. Hell, I would have poisoned that motherfucker if you'd asked me to."

Evie let out a surprised laugh. "Is that still an option?" She put her hands up. "Just kidding."

"I've got a little more to lose these days," he said with a wry grin. Bryson shook his head. "If I'd thought I had a chance to win you away from Cameron back then, I would have tried."

"Stop saying that. I was not then, nor am I now, a prize to be won," she said.

"You're right. I'm sorry," he said. "I blame your ex. He's the one who always made things into a competition when we were in class."

Evie rolled her eyes. "I'm not surprised."

A weighty silence fell over them as they stared at each other across the table.

"Why can't we start over, Ev?" he asked.

"Bryson . . . " She shook her head.

"Why not?" He slid from the bench on his side of the table and walked over to where she sat, sliding in next to her. He took her hands in both of his and gave them a gentle but firm squeeze. "Why not? You said you wanted to leave the past behind and start fresh. We can still do that."

Evie pulled her bottom lip between her teeth. "I just don't know, Bryson."

"Tell me friendship is all you ever want from me." His eyes bored into hers. "If you can say that with all honesty, then I'll let it go and never speak on it again."

Evie let her eyes fall shut. She wanted to pull her hand away but couldn't.

"It took me a long time to get over the way you left," Evie whispered. "Who knows if it would have been any better if you'd stuck around long enough to explain why you were leaving. I just know that the way it went down really hurt." She looked down at their clasped hands and then back up at him. "I don't want to ever hurt that way again, Bryson."

"I promise not to hurt you," he said.

Her heart constricted in her chest.

Could she believe him? How difficult would it be to pick up the pieces of her heart if he reneged on his promise?

Bryson cupped her chin in his palm. "We can start over." The words were soft and filled with a tenderness she didn't have the fortitude to fight.

She wanted to back away as he leaned forward, but she didn't. She couldn't. She'd dreamed of their mouths coming together more times than she would ever admit to over the years. She was powerless against the memories of his kiss. She needed to experience it again.

At the first brush of his lips, Evie's insides turned to mush. He was slow and gentle, not rushing the way they did when they were kids, afraid they would get caught.

This kiss was so much better. This kiss was between two adults who now understood just how meaningful it was to connect with a person in this simple, yet powerful way.

He applied the slightest bit of pressure, and she instantly caved, opening her mouth and letting him inside. His tongue swept across hers as his lips crashed into her. Desire burst to life within her, evolving from a slow burn deep in her belly into an inferno that engulfed every nerve ending.

It was her own desperate moan that knocked her out of the spell she'd fallen under. She pulled away and regretted it immediately.

But it was the right thing. This was moving too fast.

"Shit," Bryson whispered through a shaky breath. He rested his forehead on hers. "That went further than I intended. I told myself I wasn't going to push you."

"This is going to make working together very difficult," she said.

"It doesn't have to, Ev. I will respect whatever choice you make. This time, the decision is solely up to you."

"I just . . . I don't know, Bryson."

The disappointment that flashed across his face matched what she was feeling inside, but she had to be honest with him, and with herself.

"I need time to think about this," Evie said.

The mouth that had sent her to heaven a few minutes ago quirked up in a wry smile. "Take the time you need. Like I said, the decision is yours. And I'm not going anywhere."

CHAPTER NINETEEN

The breeze blowing in from the lake managed to cut through the thick humidity that had settled over the city today. The meteorologists on every news station had spent their afternoon forecast discussing how the unseasonably warm air was something they should start to expect as climate change continued to wreak havoc on the area. It was a good thing he liked the heat over the cold.

Bryson followed Bella's lead, running at a slightly less than easy pace as they made their way along the jogging trail that looped around West End Park. The fourteen-acre strip of green space that sat between the marina and Lake Pontchartrain had been an unexpected but welcome find as he began touring his new neighborhood this week. He'd been prepared to drive out to City Park for his afternoon runs. Instead, within five minutes of hooking Bella to the hands-free jogging leash that wrapped around his waist, they were at the park.

Today's run was about more than the physical exertion his body had demanded since his days as a student athlete. He was in desperate need of the mental clarity that always came with a good jog. Based on the thoughts that continued to permeate his brain, he would probably bring Bella back to the house after a half hour and then return to the park so he could go hard on the pavement. Maybe if he depleted himself physically, he could do the same for his mind.

That way he would be too mentally exhausted to do something stupid, like tell Evie that he would take her any way he could get her.

He could not stop reliving that coffee-flavored kiss they shared last night. It played over and over again, up until the moment Evie pulled away.

In twenty years, when he looked back on this era of his life, there were only two things he expected to find. Either this was the period in which he found lifelong happiness, or the one in which he began his downward spiral into becoming a lonely curmudgeon who scared kids who passed him in the park. He had a great-uncle who'd been that way. He wondered if unrequited love was the source of Uncle Butch's crabbiness.

Bryson tugged on Bella's leash as they neared the stone bridge that spanned the small lagoon on the eastern edge of the park. On a previous jog, they'd nearly had a head-on collision with a double stroller. He didn't want that kind of near miss ever again.

"Come here, girl," Bryson said, scooping Bella up and

holding her against his chest. He slowed to a walk and unsnapped the phone band from around his arm. He glanced over the few texts that had come through, but it was the voicemail from a number he didn't recognize with a 985 area code that snagged his attention.

The only 985 numbers he recognized were his own and his family's. No one else from that area code ever called his phone.

Anxiety squeezed Bryson's chest like a vise.

It had to be the hospital. Or the sheriff's office. Would the fire department call?

He clicked into his voicemail and readied himself for whatever news was about to turn his world upside down.

"Hi, Bryson. This is Althea Gordon, assistant principal at Southwest Terrebonne High School. Your mother gave me your number."

Bryson paused the voicemail and, still holding on to Bella, bent over and braced his left hand against his knee. He sucked in several deep breaths. He had to stop jumping to the worst-case scenario when it came to his parents. He was going to give himself a fucking heart attack.

He went back to the voicemail.

"I know this is very short notice, but one of our featured speakers for the school's Career Day had to pull out at the last minute. I mentioned it to your mother before she left on her cruise, and she said I should give you a call. Even though you didn't graduate from Southwest Terrebonne, we still consider you an honorary member of the Wolf Pack. I apologize for not calling sooner, but we would love to have you join us tomorrow."

Seriously, Ma?

She couldn't bother to make time for him, yet she had

no qualms about distributing his time out to others. It's a good thing he wasn't on call tomorrow and the one surgery he'd had scheduled was pushed back due to an infection that would need to be cleared first.

He called the assistant principal back and was relieved to get her voicemail. He wasn't up for holding a conversation right now.

"Hi, Ms. Gordon, this is Bryson Mitchell. I'm happy to join you all for Career Day. If you can send a text to this number with the start time, that would help a lot. See you tomorrow."

Still holding Bella against his chest, Bryson set off in an easy jog along the remaining bit of the running trail. He crossed Lake Marina Drive and, within minutes, was back in his condo. He considered returning to the park for a more rigorous run, but it didn't take much to talk himself out of it.

After topping off Bella's water bowl, he made his way to the kitchen for his own bottle of water. His phone chimed with an incoming text.

> Hey Bryson, this is Sierra Jackson. Your mom gave me your number.

"What the hell?" Why was his mother giving his number out like Halloween candy? And to his junior prom date, no less.

But he couldn't ignore Sierra's text. She had been sweet back in the day. She'd also refrained from remarking on the less-than-stellar two minutes it had taken from start to finish when they both lost their virginity on prom night.

He perched against the kitchen counter and banged out a quick text.

> Hey Sierra. Good to hear from you.

He uncapped a bottle of water and gulped down half of it without coming up for air. Sierra texted back within seconds.

> Your mom told me you moved to New Orleans. I'm in River Ridge now. Maybe we can get together?

Bryson set the water bottle on the counter and stared at the phone.

There were several ways to interpret Sierra's invitation. She was an old friend who possibly just wanted to catch up. They hadn't been super close as kids. They'd attended the same church but not the same high school. He'd only asked her to prom because not a single girl at the bougie-ass high school he went to appealed to him back then.

The three dots popped up on his phone, indicating another incoming text.

> To be clear, when I say get together, I mean in an adult way.

Well, damn. Guess there was no reason for him to interpret her meaning on his own.

Bryson ran a hand over his mouth as he continued to process the text and suss out its implications.

Maybe this is what he needed. After the way his kiss with Evie had ended, with her still not sure if she wanted to go beyond that kiss, why not see what else was out there? God knows this drought he'd been in had lasted longer than he'd planned. It had been nearly a year since he'd hooked up with anyone. His last time had been with a research vet he'd met at a conference in Seattle. They hadn't even exchanged numbers after.

Would it hurt to spend a night out with an old friend? A night that would end in guaranteed sex and would force him to finally put Evie in that friends-only category she obviously wanted to reside in?

He texted Sierra back.

> I appreciate the invitation, but this just isn't a good time.

"Fuck," Bryson whispered. Could he be a bigger glutton for punishment?

The ellipses popped up on the screen again. A few seconds later came her reply.

> Let me know when that better time rolls around so I can shoot my shot again. Take care.

"Fuuuck," Bryson said again. He threw his head back and stared up at the pristine white ceiling. What in the hell was he doing? There was absolutely no reason for him to turn down Sierra's invitation. Not a solitary one.

"You know why you turned her down," Bryson muttered.

He would be too disgusted with himself to look in the mirror after sleeping with Sierra, knowing that he would be thinking about Evie the entire time. He hated this. He hated the thought of turning away someone who actually wanted him because he couldn't shake the thoughts of someone who refused to commit to being more than a friend.

But that's the situation he found himself in, no matter how shitty.

He picked up his phone again and texted Sierra.

> If things change, you'll be the first one I call.

Then he flipped over to the texts he'd been exchanging with Evie, because yes, apparently he *could* be a bigger glutton for punishment.

> Are you up for a trip to the bayou tomorrow? The high school in my hometown wants me to speak at their Career Day. You've showed me around NOLA, thought I could return the favor. We can talk strategy on the drive.

He stared at the phone while he finished his bottle of water. No reply. No ellipses. Nothing.

"Not everyone is staring at their phone, waiting for random text messages to come through," Bryson said.

He carried the phone into his bedroom, keeping it in his left hand while he used his right one to pull a pair of lounging pants and a T-shirt from his drawer, along with a pair of boxer briefs.

Still nothing.

Bryson huffed out a derisive laugh, but he was more frustrated with himself than Evie's lack of a reply. What part of asking her to join him on a road trip to Houma even remotely resembled the "friendly acquaintance" she'd asked for? Tacking on that they could talk strategy was as transparent as plastic wrap.

"When did you turn into a joke?" Bryson muttered.

He got in the shower and made quick work of washing because he fucking refused to engage in his normal ritual of jerking off, not when he'd just passed on the opportunity to have an orgasm initiated by something other than his hand.

He slung the drying towel from the rack and angrily attacked his limbs, because that made total sense. Like it was his arm's fault that he was showering alone.

When he returned to his bedroom, he noticed his phone screen had just lit up. The swiftness in which he ran to it told Bryson all he needed to know about how far gone he was. She had him sprinting.

And yet, he couldn't stop the big, stupid-ass grin that broke out across his face when he read Evie's text.

> Sounds like fun. Let me know what time and where you want me to meet you.

Bryson quickly replied with a time and told her that he would drive over to her house to pick her up. She responded almost immediately, asking if he'd meet her at Barkingham Palace instead. She would be leaving Waffles at the daycare.

> I'm sure Ashanti can find a spot for Bella if I ask her nicely.

Bryson replied, Please do. Let me know what she says.

Evie answered with a thumbs-up emoji. He couldn't explain why that caused his grin to broaden, but it did.

He should stop pretending that there was even the slightest possibility that he would settle for anything less than Evie Williams's whole heart. He couldn't do it. When he finally got her to love him, he wanted it all.

CHAPTER TWENTY

It doesn't feel awkward. How are things not awkward?

Thirty minutes into their drive, and Evie still could not get over how comfortable the mood felt between herself and Bryson. She'd awakened with a weird feeling in her gut that had her picking up her phone to call and back out of today's trip. She had been so sure she wasn't ready to face him after their kiss a couple of nights ago.

Instead, she'd placed the phone on the charger and showered, determined to move beyond whatever discomfort they would face for the sake of The Sanctuary. Other than a tricky moment when he first arrived to pick her up—he'd hesitated before greeting her with a soft peck on the cheek—all had gone just fine.

Could it really be this easy? Could they fall back in love without having to go through the cringeworthy, uneasy phase of sussing out what worked and what didn't?

God, I hope so.

It would make this transition from friends to something else... something more... a lot easier.

Evie peered out the window as they reached the crest of the bridge over Bayou Des Allemands. One could argue that the whole of South Louisiana was one big bayou, but the difference in the landscape of this marsh compared to what she was used to in New Orleans made it seem as if she'd crossed over into another world. Tall cattails—Evie always thought they resembled a corn dog—waved back and forth, the stems bending toward the water.

"It's beautiful out here," Evie said. "You know, I don't think I've ever taken this drive before."

"Have you ever had a reason to?" Bryson asked.

She frowned. "I'm not sure what you mean. Why would I?"

"Exactly," he said. "Unless a person has something specific happening in Bayou Country, it's hard to get any of you city folk out here to visit us." He gave her an up-and-down glance from the driver's side. "You don't look like the type who would spend a day catching catfish on the lake, so I'm guessing that's a no."

"Excuse you," she said, giving him a playful slap on the arm. "Judgmental much?"

"Just pointing out the obvious."

"Should I also point out the obvious?" Evie asked.

"And that is?"

"That you're also 'city folk'?" She made air quotes.

"No." He shook his head. "I *live* in the city, but I will always be a country boy. Make no mistake about that."

She would love to point out how his tailored slacks and

that camel-colored cashmere pullover that fit him to perfection was the opposite of what you'd see on a country boy, but he would come back with some excuse to fit his narrative. He was maddening. And irritably handsome as he steered the car with one hand, which was even more maddening.

"Now," Bryson continued, "if you want the experience of a lifetime, you will let me bring you back here one weekend and go out with my dad's old pirogue to Dulac or Chauvin."

"I appreciate the offer, but I'll pass," Evie said. "I don't do bugs, and I know enough about the bayou to know there are bugs. Big ones."

"Coward."

"Unapologetically."

Their eyes met for a second and they both laughed.

"You're so ridiculous," Evie said.

"And yet you agreed to take this ride out to the bayou with me anyway," Bryson said. "What does that say about you?"

"That I'm a glutton for punishment," she returned.

"Ouch." He slapped his left hand to his chest. "Speaking of you being a glutton for punishment, there's something I've been wanting to ask, and now that I have your undivided attention, I can."

"Uh-oh," Evie said. "This sounds too serious for my liking."

"I want to know what my asshole of an ex-lab partner did to finally make you see that he is and has always been an asshole."

"Ah." She nodded. "Just to be clear, who's the glutton for punishment here? Me for having to tell the story, or you for having to sit here and listen?"

"Definitely you, but for staying with him for so many years. I don't know what you did in a former life to saddle yourself with that kind of a penance."

"It wasn't all bad," Evie said. "And I am not defending Cameron in any way. Just pointing out that there were *some* good years sprinkled between the bullshit."

He grunted.

Evie knew he didn't want to hear about the good parts, but she also wanted to be truthful.

"Cameron and I had a perfectly fine relationship," she said with a shrug.

He made a *Get on with it* gesture. "We only have about twenty minutes until we arrive at the school. Get to the part where Cameron is the asshole."

She burst out laughing again.

"Fine, I'll fast-forward through the not exactly exciting, but still pleasant years of the relationship. I thought things were just fine, but that all changed the day before I ran into you at The Sanctuary."

"What happened?"

Evie adjusted the seat belt at her shoulder and settled back into the seat. It occurred to her that Ashanti and Ridley were the only people who had been given the whole story.

"I dropped by the house unexpectedly and caught him in bed with another woman," Evie said. Remembering that afternoon still caused a slight ache in her chest, but it had already begun to lessen. Interesting.

"That figures." Bryson grunted again. "Asshole. How can you be in a relationship with someone for all those years and all of a sudden decide to step out on them?"

"He tried to make it seem like it was my fault. It made

me wonder if this was the first time." She twisted in her seat. "Was it?"

"Was it what?" Bryson asked, glancing at her before bringing his eyes back to the road.

"Did Cameron see other women when we were in college? You two were lab partners. Surely you talked about stuff—"

She stopped at his emphatic head shake.

"Hell no," Bryson said. "Cameron and I were lab partners, not friends. We were the opposite of friends. He didn't ask about my social life and I sure as shit didn't care about his. And once I discovered that he was dating you?" He shook his head. "I would have thrown myself out the window of the vet med building before I listened to Cameron talk about your relationship. I wanted no part in it."

That made sense. Cameron had never even mentioned Bryson's name to her. He'd always referred to him as his "annoying lab partner" or "the perfectionist." She couldn't really see the two of them shooting the breeze.

"Well, there you have it," Evie said. "That's what happened. A tale as old as time."

And one she knew the beats of all too well.

"I'll say it again—he's an asshole," Bryson said. "A cheating asshole, which is the worst kind." He switched hands on the steering wheel and reached across the console to take her left hand in his. "He never deserved you, Evie. It was obvious to me a decade ago. I'm glad you finally saw it, though I'm sorry you had to find out this way."

She suddenly had a hard time swallowing. "Thank you for saying that," she said.

She feared he would take his hand away, but he didn't. Instead, he held on to her for another seven miles, until they turned off Highway 90. The solace she experienced from his simple touch wrapped around her heart like a warm, welcoming hug.

She couldn't remember the last time she'd felt this way. It exposed more about her previous relationship than she wanted to explore. That was the past. The man holding her hand could be her future if she only allowed it to happen.

Ten minutes later, they pulled up to a beautiful redbrick building.

"Is this your high school?" Evie asked.

Bryson shook his head. "No. I went to a private school in Houma. This is the high school where most of the kids who grew up on this side of Terrebonne Parish go to school."

They got out of the car at the same time and Evie came around to the back of the Jeep just as he was opening it. He pulled out an elongated duffel bag and held it up.

"Brought along a little show-and-tell," he said.

Evie narrowed her eyes. "Is it something gross?"

"Of course," Bryson said. "Well, it depends on the student. Some will think it's gross, and others will think it's cool. I think it's *very* cool."

They entered the school and were greeted by a woman with heavily teased hair like something out of an eighties music video. She introduced herself as Cheryl Anne, no last name.

"We conduct Career Day a little differently these days," Cheryl Ann said. "We now bring the guests to the students instead of the other way around. Those big assemblies were just too much to manage, and this way we can tailor it to each age group." She referred to the electronic tablet in her hands. "It looks like you're speaking to Mrs. Breaux's earth science class and Mr. Douglass's chemistry class."

She looked over at Evie. "You wouldn't happen to write poetry, would you?"

"Um, no," Evie said.

The woman stomped her foot. "The speaker we had for our English classes is embroiled in a plagiarism scandal that broke out on TikTok last night." She lowered her voice. "I wasn't surprised. We graduated together and I was suspicious from the moment I read his first book, because I can remember his essays. There's no way he wrote them."

"Sorry I can't help." Evie hunched her shoulders. "I would be as phony as the plagiarist if I pretended to be a writer."

She waved a hand. "I'll figure out something."

Cheryl Anne showed them to the first classroom. A younger woman with straight brown hair that nearly reached her knees greeted them.

"You must be Dr. Mitchell. I'm Joni Breaux," she said.

Bryson pointed at her. "Did your granddaddy run a vegetable stand along Bayou Blue Road?"

Evie's head jerked back at the difference she heard in Bryson's tone, and in the way he'd dropped the last syllable on some of the words. She fought to hide her grin as she listened to him converse with Mrs. Breaux. It had only taken moments for him to slip into the distinct dialect of the people from this part of the state.

"You can set up right here," Mrs. Breaux said, pointing to a table in front of a whiteboard. "The bell should ring in another five minutes. Most of the students in this class are coming from the gymnasium, so they will trickle in a little late and blame it on the long walk."

"Still a great excuse to be late for class," Bryson said. "I used it a time or two thousand myself."

Mrs. Breaux laughed, and Evie was once again amazed at how quickly he could turn on that charm. She hadn't stood a chance against falling for him eight years ago, and she certainly didn't stand one now. Why was she fooling herself by staving off the inevitable?

A calming wave of relief washed over her, flooding her veins. It was as if her body had been waiting for her brain to accept what her heart already knew. She was ready to give herself a second chance with the only other person who had captured her heart.

An easy smile lifted the corners of her mouth as she followed Bryson to the front of the classroom.

"I had no idea I would get to see this other side of Bryson Mitchell when I agreed to join you," Evie said.

"What side is that?"

"The Cajun side," Evie said.

"I didn't know I had a Cajun side," he said.

"Oh, you absolutely do. The moment Mrs. Breaux greeted you in that thick accent, you took on that same sound."

"You're making fun of me."

"I'm not. I adore the accent. I adore this part of the state. Such unique and colorful culture."

He rolled his eyes. "You really do sound like city folk."

He placed the bag he'd brought with him on the table and unzipped it.

"Whoa. What is this?" Evie asked, pointing at the model dog. "This is way too realistic."

"I know, right?" Bryson said. "It's synthetic. At first I wasn't sure about replacing cadavers—even though I get where the animal rights activists are coming from—but after working with this thing for a few months, I'm sold."

She ran her hand along the canine model's synthetic muscles. The fibers felt like real tendons. It was remarkable.

"What's his name?" Evie asked. When he didn't respond, she looked up to find Bryson staring at her with a confused frown. "You named it, didn't you?"

"I...did not."

Evie pinched her lips together and nodded. "Okay. Got it. You've only spent countless hours gaining knowledge at the expense of the poor synthetic animal. One would think that at least warrants a name, but I guess not."

"Really, Ev?"

"I'm just saying," Evie said. The effort to hold in her laugh was overwhelming.

Bryson tipped his head to the side. "Why does it feel as if we've had this conversation before?"

She couldn't hold it any longer. "The green parakeet," she said with a laugh.

"That's it." Bryson snapped his fingers.

"What did we settle on for a name?" Evie asked. "Was it Skippy?"

"Wait a minute. All the shit you gave me over that bird and you can't even remember the name?"

"It was a long time ago!" She could barely get the words out past her hiccupping laugh.

Bryson shook his head. "There were times when you were annoying as hell back then."

"And yet you still called me in to assist whenever you needed help."

"Even when I didn't need help," he said. He winked. "I just wanted to see you."

She met his grin with one of her own. His warm gaze felt like a caress against her skin.

The bell to change classes rang, and, contrary to what Mrs. Breaux had predicted, within moments students began filing into the classroom. They dropped their bags at their desks and ran to the front of the class, congregating around the table. It was soon evident that far more eighth graders thought synthetic cadaver dogs were cool instead of gross.

As she watched him with the students, Evie understood why Bryson commanded such an impressive speaker fee. He was brilliant at it. He spoke with authority, but also with humility, admitting when he wasn't knowledgeable about something instead of giving the students a bullshit answer.

"What made you want to become a veterinarian?" a young Black boy with blond locs asked.

"That's an easy one," Bryson said. He settled his hip against the table and clasped his hands in front of him. "I had this amazing dog when I was eight years old, a little mutt named Pepper. One day, he got into the trash and ate a chicken bone and got really sick—side note, never feed your pets chicken bones. Anyway, we brought Pepper to the vet and the vet saved him. I still remember how I felt when he walked into the waiting room and told us that Pepper would be okay." He shrugged. "I knew then and there that I wanted to make other families feel that kind of joy."

A soft smile drew across Evie's lips. It shocked her that she had never asked him that question.

"That's not only why I chose to become a vet, but also why I specifically chose to be a veterinary surgeon, but there are different kinds of vets out there." Bryson turned to her and said, "This is Dr. Evie Williams. She's also a veterinarian, and I'm sure she has a lot she could add to this discussion."

Evie froze. No he didn't . . .

"I'm here for emotional support, not for questions," she whispered to Bryson through a clenched smile as she walked up to the table.

"You're the role model they need. Knock 'em dead." He winked.

At first, Evie received more questions about what products she used on her natural curls than about her work, but then one intrepid student with cat-eye glasses asked if it was difficult being a woman veterinarian and the floodgates opened. Evie relished the engagement, watching in real time as the students' faces shifted from indifference to keen interest.

This! This is why the mentorship program at The Sanctuary was so important.

Another student raised her hand.

"Do you have an Insta?" she asked.

"Um, yes, I do," Evie said.

"Can I DM you when it's science project time?"

"I . . . " She looked to the teacher. "I will give Mrs. Breaux my contact information." Because there was no way it was appropriate to have eighth graders sliding into her DMs, even if it was just to ask questions.

Mrs. Breaux walked over from where she'd been waiting near the shelf of model planets.

"Let's give Drs. Mitchell and Williams a huge round of applause," she said. "I'm pretty certain I will see more projects on veterinary medicine at this year's science fair than I ever have before."

"That means we did our jobs," Bryson said.

"Does this mean we can call on both of you to be judges?" Mrs. Breaux asked.

The bell rang just in time, saving them from having to answer.

She and Bryson were ushered to the chemistry class. It took the tenth graders a bit longer to warm up to them, but by the end of the class period, they were working together to answer questions as if they'd practiced it.

Once they were done, Ms. Douglass, who introduced herself as a friend of Bryson's mother, and Cheryl Anne, the Career Day coordinator, thanked them profusely for participating.

"I think we should take this act on the road," Evie said as they made their way to the Jeep. She gestured to the duffel he carried. "Chi Chi, of course, will be the star."

"Chi Chi? There has to be a better name," Bryson said.

"If you wanted a better name, you should have named him."

"Still annoying," he said as he put the duffel in the back of the Jeep.

Evie chuckled as she went around to the passenger side of the car. Bryson started the car the moment she secured her seat belt, but instead of backing out of the parking spot, he let it idle. He draped his wrist over the top of the steering wheel and stared straight ahead.

"Everything okay?" Evie asked.

He looked over at her. After a breath, he asked, "Would you like to come home with me?"

Evie did a double blink.

"Not *my* home," Bryson said quickly. "I mean, not my current home in New Orleans. My childhood home. Here."

She wouldn't deny that she was a little disappointed that his invitation *wasn't* to join him at his home in New Orleans. Now that she'd decided falling back in love with him was inevitable, she wanted to skip straight to the good part. Although, with Bryson, nearly every part had been the good part. This time they would have the chance to make up for the one aspect they'd gotten wrong.

He looked at her expectantly, waiting for her answer.

"I would never pass up the chance to see where you grew up," Evie said. "Let's go."

CHAPTER TWENTY-ONE

The drive from the high school to the turnoff that would take them to his parents' home was about eight minutes, and in that time Bryson had thought up at least a dozen reasons to make a U-turn and head back to New Orleans.

His heart rate rose as they drove along the gravel driveway, an agitated prickle moving across his skin when the massive oak tree he used to climb as a kid came into view. Even in the winter, when its branches were still bare, the trunk was positioned in such a way that it hid the house from view. But the moment they rounded the curve, there would be no more hiding.

You can still turn around.

An unsettling sensation planted itself in the pit of his stomach. Hadn't he decided years ago that he would no longer allow anyone—including himself—to make him feel ashamed of where he'd come from? His parents had worked hard for that house. It may not be a mansion in a gated community with a golf course and private security, but it had kept him safe and secure throughout his childhood. It continued to provide that same safety and security for his parents.

He continued driving.

They made the curve around the tree, and the house came into view. Bryson drove into the spot where his dad usually parked his truck, next to the piece of painted driftwood his mother had repurposed to serve as a border for one of her many flowerbeds.

"This is so charming," Evie said.

He replayed her words, searching for a hint of deceit or feigned sincerity, but there was none.

Had he really expected Evie to belittle his home? She'd proven again and again that she wasn't that type of person, yet for a moment, he'd prepared himself for derision.

He tried to see the house through the eyes of someone who had grown up in a mansion.

The two-bedroom gray clapboard structure with white shutters and a galvanized steel roof was tiny but quaint, with a porch that spanned the front of the house. Bryson had paid for the porch to be reinforced with new pillars, but his dad refused to let them put a railing because then he wouldn't be able to sit on the edge and let his legs dangle off the side, one of his favorite pastimes.

Evie got out of the car and headed straight for his mother's flower garden.

"This garden is sublime," she said. The roses had been pruned and the annuals wouldn't bloom for another few months, but the soft pink witch hazel and deeper pink camellia flowers were showing out. "And how adorable is this!"

She pointed to the old tire that was used as a planter. Painted on it were several scenes of a dog frolicking through the marsh.

"That's Pepper at various ages throughout his life," Bryson said. "My mom painted it years ago."

Evie clasped both hands to her chest. "I *loved* your Pepper story. Was that really the catalyst for you wanting to become a vet?"

"Yep," Bryson said.

"I had a similar incident with one of the strays I rescued as a kid—Humphrey. Unfortunately, the outcome wasn't a good one."

"I'm sorry," Bryson said.

She lifted her shoulders. "I found Sparks two weeks later and kept her until I left for LSU. That's the thing about dogs—you'll likely outlive them, so you take the time you have to spoil them rotten. And when you've done all you can, you find another one to spoil."

"It's what I tell owners when surgeries aren't successful," he said. He plucked a petal from one of the camellias and brought it to her nose. "This scent reminds me of my childhood. My mom has been growing camellias since before I was born."

"It's lovely. This entire garden is like a dream."

He slipped his keys from his pocket and gestured toward the house. "Let's go inside? If we're lucky, she has some satsuma syrup."

"I've never heard of it."

"Because you're city folk," Bryson said.

"Stop it," Evie said.

"I'm only joking," he said as he gestured for her to climb the porch steps ahead of him. "There's a bunch of citrus trees in the backyard. My mom makes this syrup from the satsumas that she mixes with iced tea or lemonade. She would ship it to me in North Carolina."

"Well, now I'm curious."

"Cross your fingers that my brothers haven't cleaned out her stash," he said as he unlocked the door.

"It's funny that you just moved back home and already have a key to your parents' house," she said.

Bryson stopped with his hand on the door. "What do you mean? I've had this key for years."

"I haven't had a key to my parents' house since my freshman year of college. Even now they give me a temporary key code whenever I come over."

"Damn. That's cold," Bryson said.

"It's just how they are."

And to think he envied rich kids.

They entered the house and, as usual, it was spotless, yet cozy.

"Okay, this is so far beyond adorable," Evie said. "I can't imagine growing up here."

No shit. He couldn't imagine her growing up here either. But he hadn't heard any malice in her words. She appeared to be genuinely charmed.

Bryson took in the small living room. The baby blankets his mom crocheted for each of her sons were now draped over the backs of the sofa and matching recliners in the living room. The curtains she'd sewn hung over the windows.

"It took leaving for me to appreciate it," Bryson said.

He directed Evie to the house's lone bathroom, and once she was done, she demanded to see his bedroom.

"My mom changed it to a craft room a long time ago," he said as they stood in the doorway. "I can't complain. At least

I had the bedroom to myself. My two older brothers had to share their entire childhood."

"And they still get along? Me and my brother could never," Evie said.

There wasn't much more to the house other than his parents' room, which he never entered without their express permission—he guessed that was one thing his and Evie's parents had in common—and the covered back porch that had long ago been turned into a bragging room by his parents. His and his brothers' diplomas and degrees, along with every academic and athletic plaque and trophy any of them had ever earned, were on display.

Bryson pointed to the wall. "The degrees on the wall in my office are replicas. My mom insisted on keeping the originals here."

"It's obvious how proud she is of her boys," Evie said. "It's precious." She looked up at him. "I hope you know how lucky you are."

His gaze moved over her entire face. "It's becoming clearer every day."

The faint blush that rushed to her cheeks was both adorable and sexy. It reminded him of those times that long ago summer, and the myriad things he would say and do to bring about this same blush.

"I really want to kiss you right now, Ev," Bryson whispered.

Her eyes shimmered with amusement and a touch of heat. "What's stopping you?"

Bryson lowered his head and skimmed his lips over hers, brushing back and forth in an easy, unhurried dance that had his skin tingling and his mind quickly going to more indecent places. He brought his hand up and cupped the back of her head, holding her steady as he added more pressure to the kiss, parting her lips and slipping his tongue inside.

She tasted like everything that was good in the world. The cinnamon from the candy she'd sucked on as they drove in from the school, and that flavor that was uniquely her.

Bryson brought his other hand to her lower back and pressed her body against his.

Something buzzed against his groin.

Bryson jumped back. "Shit, what was that?"

Evie gazed up at him, her half-lidded eyes awash with arousal. The buzz sounded again.

"Text message," Evie said, pulling her phone from her pocket. Her breaths came out in shallow pants, and her hands shook as she swiped her fingers across the screen.

She read through the message, then stuffed the phone back in her pocket and rolled her eyes.

"This canine carnival is getting out of hand. We've both been shut out of the planning process. Ashanti and her twin sisters have taken over."

Bryson cleared the lust from his throat. Assuaging the ache that kiss had left him with would take more time.

"Does she still think she can pull this off by next Saturday?" he asked.

"Oh, she will pull it off. I have no doubt about it. I'm going over there tomorrow to 'talk strategy,'" she said, making air quotes. "But something tells me Ashanti already has everything planned down to the minute."

"Do you have plans for the rest of this afternoon?" Bryson asked.

She glanced up at him. "No," she said. "We just have to be back by six to pick up the dogs from the daycare. Well,

Ashanti probably won't mind if I'm late, but you're going to get charged for Bella."

"It would be worth it, but I think I can have us back by six." He hooked his thumb toward the front door. "I spotted something outside that I think you should experience before you leave the bayou."

A half hour later, they were standing along the banks of the narrow tributary that ran along the edge of his parents' property. Evie held one of the long fishing poles his dad had fashioned out of sugar cane. She looked so out of place it was hard not to laugh.

"You do realize the fish won't bite you, right?" Bryson said. "The goal is to get them to bite the earthworm I put on the hook."

"Don't remind me about the earthworm," she said, looking as if she was ready to lose the grilled cheese sandwich he'd cooked for her just before they made their way over here.

"City folk." Bryson shook his head, not bothering to hide his smile.

She moved her hand even farther down the pole, until it arched so much it looked on the verge of slipping out of her hand.

"Here," Bryson said. "This is how you hold it."

He walked up behind her and wrapped his arms around her waist. Gripping the pole with his left hand, he took her right hand in his and wrapped her fingers a third of the way up the pole.

"You want there to be some tension," he said in a low voice that had nothing to do with not scaring away the fish.

"There's plenty of that in the air," Evie whispered. She nudged her hips back, tucking her ass against his groin.

His dick swelled with a swiftness he hadn't experienced since freshman year phys ed.

Bryson groaned. "Evie, please."

"You know, erotic fishing wasn't on my bingo card, but I can't say I mind it."

"Fuck the fish," he said, yanking the pole from the water and tossing it to the ground.

Burying his face against her throat, he gripped Evie by the waist, turned, and backed her up against the live oak a few steps away. Bryson settled her against the tree's thick trunk and cradled the back of her head in his left palm. He traced the curve of her jaw with his lips, running them across her soft skin, basking in the low moans rising from her throat.

He flattened his right hand against her stomach, then inched upward, his fingers tingling as they skimmed the underside of her breast. He brushed his index finger across her nipple and sucked in the gasp she released against his mouth.

He plied her with deep, sensual kisses, probing the inside of her mouth with his tongue while his hand became bolder in its exploration, pinching and squeezing and rubbing her through the fabric of her shirt.

He was dying to slip his hand underneath the hem and feel her skin against his fingers, but if that happened, all clothes would be off within a matter of minutes. The first time he made love to Evie would not be under a tree in his parents' backyard.

Which meant he should put an end to this now.

He gave his tongue one last, reluctant swipe inside her mouth before pulling away.

"Okay, I think I like fishing now," Evie said with a breathy laugh.

Bryson tried to reply, but all he could do was smile and concentrate on catching his breath.

"I like your version of fishing even better than the one I grew up doing," he said when he was finally able to speak.

Her gentle laugh rippled across his cheek. "Maybe you can give me a proper fishing lesson the next time," she said.

Bryson drew his head back and gazed down at her. "Already thinking about coming back?"

"You promised to take me out on the boat," she said.

"That I did." He nodded, then chuckled. "You know, up until we got here, I contemplated turning around," Bryson admitted.

"Why?" she asked.

He considered holding back the truth, then decided against it.

"Because you grew up in a house ten times the size of this one. And people who grew up like you always made me feel as small as that pebble right there."

"Really, Bryson? This again?"

He shrugged. "I'm sorry. I know it isn't fair, because *you* never treated me that way, but you have to understand, Ev. From the time I entered high school, I was made to feel like I was less than. Your ex took his share of digs during the three semesters we were lab partners."

"Because he's an asshole," she said. "We already established that."

"There are many assholes like Cameron in this world."

"And you thought I was one of them." It wasn't a question; it was an accusation.

"At first I did," he admitted. "I quickly learned how wrong I was, because you *proved* me wrong. I've learned it's a defense mechanism. That it's my brain's way of protecting itself against those taunts I suffered throughout high school. I've worked hard at not automatically expecting the worst in people, but I still fall short."

"Why did you stay at that high school if it was so bad?" Evie asked. "The school we spoke at this morning seems amazing."

"The school I went to had better opportunities," he said with a shrug. "I don't regret staying there, but I'll admit it took a while for the scars to heal."

Bryson shifted until he was standing beside her, his back flat against the tree.

"For a long time, I didn't want to come back home at all because of what I went through," he said. "In the eight years since I've been gone, I've only returned to this house four times. Today is the first day I've been here since my nephew's high school graduation a year and a half ago."

"But you've been back in Louisiana for a couple of weeks now. Why haven't you visited?"

"Because my parents have been gone nearly the entire time since I've moved back home. They've taken up cruising and I won't be surprised if they become one of those couples who sell their house and live on a cruise ship."

"Let me know if it ever goes up for sale. I'd buy it just for the peace and quiet," Evie said. "You know that swing hanging from the oak tree back at their house? Give me that, a good book, and a cold glass of lemonade, and then leave me be."

Bryson grinned. "You just described Sunday afternoons for my mom when I was growing up. My older brothers would bring me out here to fish, Pop would go help my uncle Rooster work on cars at his shop, and my mom would have the afternoon to herself. We always found her on that swing."

She tipped her head to the side. "Remind me again about your brothers? I know you told me they were older, but it's been a while."

"Jeremy is the oldest. He was a junior in high school when I was born. And Roman is two years younger than him. They were both grown and out of the house before I could get a sense of what it felt like to grow up with two big brothers. We're a lot closer now that I'm older."

"I can never see my brother and I having a close relationship, but that's because Marshall is a dick. Nothing to do with the four-year age gap."

He chuckled. "I'm sure my brothers would be happy to become surrogate brothers for you."

Her brows shot up. "Okay, then. You don't play around, do you?"

Bryson replayed in his mind what he just said to her.

"Shit, that's not what I meant," he said. "Did I just make things weird?"

"I'm teasing you," Evie said with a laugh.

Bryson rolled his eyes. "On second thought, let's get married. You'd fit right in with my family."

"Can we maybe start with an actual date?" Evie asked, peering over at him with an impish grin he couldn't wait to kiss off her face.

He twisted back toward her, positioning her body between his and the tree. Leaning forward, he whispered, "I think we can make that happen," just before connecting his mouth with hers.

CHAPTER TWENTY-TWO

Evie could feel the blood pounding in her ears. She knew what she wanted; she just wasn't sure if she possessed the boldness to go through with it. The ride from Bryson's childhood home had been filled with the same easy banter they always engaged in, but after the kisses they'd shared, there was a level of awareness pulsating between them that couldn't be denied. It clung to the air like perfume, this warm, energized charge that made her skin tingle with anticipation.

The edginess intensified as they turned onto Fontainebleau Drive, en route to her house. If she was going to make this decision, now was the time to do it.

Evie sucked in a slow breath and slid her phone from her pocket. She sent a quick text to Ashanti just as Bryson pulled up to her house.

They spoke at the same time.

"Thanks for—"

"Do you want to—"

Evie released an uneasy laugh. "Of course that happened," she said. "Go ahead."

"I was just going to thank you for joining me," Bryson said. "I had fun today."

"So did I," Evie said. She peered over at him, staring into his eyes so that her meaning could not be misinterpreted. "I was going to invite you in."

"Thank God." His shoulders slumped with relief. "And thank you for not making me beg. I was just about to start." He blew out a shaky breath. "But I need to see about Bella first—"

"Taken care of." She held up her phone. "Barkingham Palace can keep Bella and Waffles overnight. They have to share a suite, but I think they get along well enough that we don't have to worry about them maiming each other."

She watched as he flexed his fingers on the steering wheel, then gripped it tight with both hands.

"Evie," he said.

There was a thread of unease in his voice that made her heart sink to the pit of her stomach.

She frowned. "What's wrong? I assumed by the way you kissed me—"

"I'm not about to turn you down, Ev. Be for real," Bryson said. "Didn't I just say I was on the verge of begging?"

"So what's the problem?" she asked.

"I need to make sure we're going into this with a clear understanding of where we both stand."

He turned his body toward her and rested his left forearm on the steering wheel.

"Remember the night we ate Ethiopian, when I told you

that I would have been willing to settle for any crumbs you threw my way?"

She nodded.

"I've decided I don't want crumbs, Ev. I want more than just your body. I want *all* of you." He reached across the console and brushed his fingers along her cheek. "That being said, I understand if you're not ready to give all of yourself. If you need more time before you can fully share your heart with me, I'm willing to wait for it."

Evie took a moment to collect herself as gratitude threatened to overwhelm her.

"So, what you're saying is that we can be more than just friends, even if I'm not ready to commit to being in a full-fledge relationship?"

He nodded. "That's what I'm saying."

He leaned over and, with a tenderness she hadn't felt in longer than she could remember, captured her mouth in a sweet, gentle kiss. Evie closed her eyes and absorbed it, relishing the feel of his perfect lips skimming over her own.

All her worries seemed to melt away as she lost herself in Bryson's skillful attack upon her senses. His tongue glided along the seam of her lips, briefly breaking past the barrier before retreating much too quickly.

"We can find an in-between," Bryson whispered against her lips. "Whatever resides in that space between friends and wearing matching outfits to Sunday brunch."

Evie laughed against his lips. "For future reference, know that I never want to wear matching outfits to brunch."

"Thank you, God," Bryson said. "Now let's get inside."

They opened their respective car doors at the same time and made their way up the walkway leading to her front door.

The minute they stepped inside, Evie pulled Bryson to her and crushed her lips against his. He captured her face, cupping her cheeks in his palms as his tongue pushed past her lips and into her mouth.

The moan Evie released came from deep within the pit of her belly. Waves of heat flooded her with each swipe of Bryson's tongue against hers. She backed him up until he stood against the door, then went for the waistband of his slacks.

"Hold on." Bryson captured her wrists. "Slow down."

Evie looked up at him, a mixture of confusion, panic, and heat shooting through her.

"What's wrong?"

"Evie Williams, I have been waiting for this moment for nearly a decade. I will not be rushed."

Evie's fingers shook with pent-up need as she brushed her hair behind her ear.

"How long is this going to take?" she asked.

"As long as it takes for me to process that I'm really standing here with you after all this time."

"I'm here, Bryson. I'm not going anywhere."

"Just try," he said, pulling her to him.

He crushed his mouth to hers, his tongue plunging inside with a fierceness that stole Evie's breath. Her skin tingled with the need to feel him against her. She wanted him, no clothes, in her bed. But his drugging kisses were so intoxicating that she couldn't bear to tear her mouth from his long enough to voice her wants.

"I expect a tour of the house when we're done," Bryson said against her lips. "But right now the only room I'm concerned about seeing is your bedroom."

"Finally," Evie said. "Follow me."

She took him by the hand and led him through the living room and to the hallway leading to the back of the house, kicking Waffles's plush toys along the way. For the briefest moment, Evie considered turning left into the guest room, but she refused to allow the memory of Cameron with that nurse to pollute the sanctity of her bedroom any longer. It was time to banish that memory and create new ones.

She and Bryson stood at the foot of the bed and began to undress with a leisure that was both sexy and frustrating. After divesting himself of his pants and sweater, he brought them to the reading chair in the corner and hung them neatly across the arm.

Evie rolled her eyes. Still a stickler for everything being in its proper place.

He walked back to her in a pair of navy-blue boxer briefs that fit him like they had been made exclusively for his body. Perfection. Sheer fucking perfection.

He had always been attractive, but the sight of his lean, contoured muscles, smooth dark brown skin, and those indentions at his waist made it hard for her to remain standing. She kicked the clothes she'd just taken off to the side and put her hands on her hips.

"So," Evie said. "Are we doing this?"

Bryson motioned to her with his chin. "You're wearing more clothes than I am."

Evie looked down at her bra and underwear. She would never forgive herself for not putting on a matching pair, but she'd had no idea this was going to happen when she dressed this morning.

She reached behind her and released the single hook at the center of her back, then let the soft blue cotton bra fall from her shoulders and down her arm. She released the sigh of relief that was automatic whenever she took off her bra, but it was drowned out by Bryson's groan. His eyelids slid closed and his Adam's apple flexed with his deep swallow.

"Do you have any idea how many times I have pictured you naked in my mind over the years?" he asked.

"A thousand?"

He opened his eyes and shot her an incredulous look. "In eight years, Ev? Do I look like a monk?" He huffed. "Multiply that by ten and it's probably still not high enough."

"Well," she said, closing the distance between them and hooking her arms around his neck. "You don't have to just picture it in your head any longer. I'm right here and I would very much appreciate it if you would take those off and get in this bed with me."

The grin that lifted the corner of his mouth was too sexy for words. He hooked his thumbs in the waistband of his boxer briefs and pulled them down his legs.

Evie peered down between them and sucked in a breath.

"Enough looking," Bryson said.

He clamped his hands on her waist and pulled her with him to the side of the bed, picking her up and setting her on the mattress. Evie pulled her very unsexy cotton briefs off and tossed them on the floor with the rest of her discarded clothes.

"There are condoms in the nightstand," she said.

Bryson stood up straight, that incredulous frown once again creasing his forehead.

"Do you really think I would use Cameron Broussard's leftover condoms?"

Evie burst out laughing. "No, I guess you wouldn't want to do that."

"We're not at the condom stage yet anyway," Bryson said. He grabbed her by the ankles and pulled her toward him.

Evie's back hit the mattress with a soft thud. She peered up at him with half-closed eyes as he pressed a kiss to the inside of her right ankle, then the left one. He advanced up her legs, placing gentle kisses on her calves, behind her knees, then up her inner thighs, giving each leg equal attention.

When his head lowered over her center, a sound Evie had never heard before escaped her throat. Her breaths came out in thin pants as pleasure and desire collided in her chest. She buried the back of her head into the mattress and pumped her hips in rhythm to every slow, sensuous lick Bryson plied her with.

Need ignited low in her belly, and all she could think about was how much she wanted this. How much she wanted *him*. How long had she fought the memory of his kiss and the joy he made her feel with a simple smile? No matter how much she'd tried to erase him from her mind, he had always been there.

Evie cried out as he pulled her sensitive flesh between his lips and sucked hard.

"Don't do this, Bryson. Don't make me come like this. I want you inside me."

He didn't listen. Instead, he elevated his sensual play, adding two fingers that toyed with her opening before slipping inside. Evie brought her hands to her breasts and squeezed them. Sensations assaulted her from so many areas of her body that she didn't know where to focus.

Her orgasm hit with barely any warning, crashing through her with the force of a tidal wave.

As her body continued to shiver with pleasure that was

so exquisite it brought tears to her eyes, she felt Bryson move away.

"Where... where are you going?" Evie panted.

He returned a moment later with a condom between his fingers. He opened it and quickly rolled it on; then he moved her so that her head was at the foot of the bed. After climbing in next to her, he lay flat on his back, reached over, and captured her by the waist, then sat her in his lap.

"Evie, you are so fucking beautiful. You don't even seem real," he said. The raw emotion in his voice sent a shock of fiery need racing through her.

He lifted his head high enough to give each nipple a lick, then grabbed her hands and placed them on the rim of the sleigh bed's footboard.

"You ready to ride me?" he asked, and Evie nearly came again.

She pulled her bottom lip between her teeth and nodded. Then she waited as Bryson gripped his erection and guided it inside of her.

She slowly lowered herself onto him, giving herself time to adjust to his size. Bryson's forehead creased with single-minded concentration as he flattened his right palm to her midriff and gripped her waist with his left hand.

"Are you okay?" he asked in a low voice.

"Perfect," Evie breathed just as she took all of him inside of her. She remained motionless for several moments before rocking forward, her fingers digging into the polished mahogany footboard. She tried to hold herself to a slow, even pace, but with every upward thrust of Bryson's hips, her need became more urgent. A primitive longing snaked through her, driving her hunger to something Evie didn't recognize.

She had never felt this way before, this overwhelming demand to possess all of him.

"Bryson," she gasped as she ground her hips against him. Another orgasm was building deep in her belly. Her thighs shook as the sensation began to roll over her, shooting streaks of hot pleasure throughout her body.

Before she had the chance to catch her breath, Bryson flipped them over and plunged deep. He pumped his hips with fevered thrusts that sent another violent orgasm coursing through her.

He caught her scream, taking her mouth in an erotic kiss as he drove harder and deeper.

Finally, with a strangled cry that tore out of him, Evie felt him let go. He climaxed with an agonizing gasp, as if he didn't want to finish but could no longer hold on.

He collapsed onto his back and for several minutes they both just lay there, staring up at the ceiling.

"Did you think it would be this good?" Bryson asked.

Evie shook her head. "I figured it would be good, but not this good. Who would have thought it could be *this* good?"

"Okay," he breathed. "I just wanted to make sure I wasn't alone in this."

He turned onto his side and gathered her against his chest. Evie tried to keep her eyes open, but she could feel herself drifting.

When she woke up, she was still resting against Bryson's chest. She felt his fingers tracing along her jaw, down to her bare shoulder, and then back to her jaw.

"You're awake?" His voice was velvety soft.

"How long was I asleep?" Evie asked.

"Only about nine hours or so?"

"What?" She sprang up. "What time is it?"

"Just after eight in the morning," he said. "I'm due at the hospital by ten but couldn't wake you." His phone dinged with a text message. "That's probably the hospital now," Bryson said.

He reached over and grabbed his phone from the bedside table.

"Oh shit," he said.

Evie's body stiffened. "What's wrong?"

"Shit!" Bryson looked over at her. "It's from Odessa. She said a building inspector and real estate agent just left The Sanctuary. They said they were sent by Stanley Shepard's grandson."

Her stomach dropped. "Did the succession go through?"

"Odessa didn't say, but if he's sending over an inspector, he has to be close to putting the building on the market."

They were running out of time.

CHAPTER TWENTY-THREE

Bryson spotted Evie's gray SUV in the parking lot of the glass building in Metairie. It took him less than ten minutes to get here from the hospital, where he'd left Bella at the employee daycare while he and Evie went on what he was certain was a fool's mission.

But Evie was convinced if they pleaded their case, face-to-face, the same man who had been cut out of his grandfather's will would miraculously have a change of heart and do the decent thing. Bryson had known assholes like this his entire life. He had no doubt Stanley Shepard's grandson would sooner kick a newborn puppy in the ribs than not sell The Sanctuary out from under them.

Evie's goal was to get him to donate the building, which would *never* happen. Even a person whose heart wasn't composed of sulfur and stone wouldn't be that generous.

Bryson pulled into a parking spot two cars down from Evie's. By the time he got out of his Jeep, she was waiting at the end of it.

"Thanks for driving over," she greeted.

"Did you think I would let you do this alone?"

"Well, you said it was a waste of time when I texted my plan."

"I still think it's a waste of time. That doesn't mean I want you facing this guy on your own."

She peered up at him, an incredulous frown creasing her forehead. "I don't think I'm in physical danger, Bryson. He may be a selfish SOB, but I doubt he would touch me."

"I'm more concerned about you laying hands on him, not the other way around. Nobody's got time to bail you out of jail."

She rolled her eyes.

"Let's do this," Bryson said. He put a hand on the small of her back and guided her to the entrance of the building.

Lucas Shepard's law office was on the fourteenth floor. Of course he was an attorney. A personal injury one at that. He probably had more money in the bank than any of them.

"Can I help you?" a receptionist greeted.

"I'm Dr. Evelina Williams and this is Dr. Bryson Mitchell. We're here to see Mr. Shepard. I called earlier."

Bryson's brow shot up. Where had that starched, serious voice come from?

"Give me just a moment. Mr. Shepard is in a meeting with the other partners a floor below us, but it should be wrapping up any minute. I'll check with him." She shot off a message. Seconds later, she nodded. "Yes, he'll be up in just a few minutes. He asked that I show you to his office. Can I get you coffee or water? We have both sparkling and still."

"No thanks," Evie said.

Bryson could use a water, but he didn't want to contradict Dr. Evelina Williams.

The receptionist guided them into a large corner office with expansive windows that provided views of both Lake Pontchartrain and New Orleans's downtown skyline.

Yeah, this dude definitely had more than enough money to live on. Bryson doubted the profit from the sale of The Sanctuary would have a significant effect on his lifestyle, unless he was in the market for a third vacation home and fourth speedboat.

"Ugh, this isn't a good sign," Evie said. She pointed to the wall, where a banner with familiar Greek insignia hung. "That's Cameron's fraternity."

"Yeah, I know," Bryson said.

If there was any question that they were dealing with a prick, he'd just gotten his answer. His hunch was confirmed a moment later when Lucas Shepard burst into the office with an air of such self-importance that it carried a stench. Or maybe it was Shepard's cologne.

"Hello," he greeted. "What can I do for you?"

The fact that he didn't offer them a seat told Bryson that he didn't plan for them to be here very long. Good, because he didn't want to be around this asshole any longer than he had to.

"Hi, Mr. Shepard," Evie started.

"Lucas is fine," he said.

"Lucas," she corrected with a strained, uneasy smile. "I'm Dr. Williams and this is Dr. Mitchell. We're both veterinarians who matriculated from the mentorship program at The Sanctuary, which you know is housed in the building your grandfather owns."

"Owned," Lucas said. "My grandfather died."

"Yes, we know that," Evie said. "As I'm sure *you* know, your grandfather generously donated the building's use to the rescue. His good friend Dr. Fredrick Landry has operated The Sanctuary for years."

"My grandfather was very generous. To some," Lucas said. "But, as we've established, he's dead. His estate is currently going through the arduous testate succession process required by Louisiana—gotta love that Napoleonic code. The property near the river is part of the estate."

He was intentionally telling them shit they already knew, and it was starting to get under Bryson's skin. He spoke up for the first time.

"A building inspector and real estate agent visited The Sanctuary this morning," Bryson said. "When is the building hitting the market, and what will be the asking price?"

Shepard looked over at him with raised brows, as if he'd forgotten Bryson was there. "I'm not planning to put the building on the market," he said.

Bryson blinked in surprise. That wasn't what he'd expected to hear.

"You aren't?" Evie slapped a hand to her chest, releasing a relieved laugh. "Thank goodness."

"You plan on raising the rent, though, don't you?" Bryson asked. His grandfather rented the building to The Sanctuary for a dollar per year. There was no way in hell the man in front of them would continue that practice.

Lucas settled on the edge of his desk, crossing his ankles in front of him.

"You misinterpreted what I meant when I said I'm not

putting the building on the market," Lucas said. "It's not going on the market because I already have a buyer."

Bryson could tell by Lucas Shepard's sardonic smile that he'd purposely misled them. Why was he not surprised the man had turned out to be the kind of asshole he'd expected him to be all along?

He took little comfort in knowing he was right, especially when he looked over at Evie and saw the utter devastation on her face.

"To who?" Evie asked.

Lucas barked out a laugh. "I'm not sharing that information with you so that you can go and harass my buyer." He moved from his perch on the edge of the desk, walking around to the chair behind it. "I have another meeting. I trust you can see your way out?"

Evie just stood there looking shell-shocked.

Bryson wrapped his fingers around her wrist and gave her a gentle tug. He wasn't sure if she was on the verge of crying or going into a rage, but he refused to give Shepard the satisfaction of seeing either.

"Come on, Ev," he encouraged.

Lucas Shepard tapped a pen against his open palm, that smirk still turning up the corner of his mouth. The bastard was getting off on what he probably saw as a power move. It was the epitome of small dick energy.

Bryson's instinct to protect his livelihood and reputation was stronger than his urge to slap that smile off Shepard's lips, but not by much. He needed to get the hell out of here before he did something stupid.

"Ev," Bryson urged again.

She jumped as if he'd startled her, then nodded. Wordlessly, they left the fancy corner office. Bryson was sorry he hadn't brought Bella with him. He would have waited around long enough for her to shit on the carpet.

He had managed to get his anger under control by the time they made it to the parking lot, but he knew if he saw Lucas Shepard again anytime soon, he would have a hard time not punching the smug bastard in the face.

"Well, that went as horribly as it could have," Evie said, folding her arms tight over her chest. "The succession can go through at any moment, Bryson. Just like that." She snapped her fingers. "The Sanctuary can cease to exist, just like that."

Bryson pointed out the obvious. "That has always been the case, Ev."

"I know," she said. She ran a hand through her springy curls. "It's just . . . it seems inevitable now." She pointed to the building. "He looks as if he will enjoy watching The Sanctuary close."

"Scrooge McDuck will probably throw a party when the rescue shuts its doors," Bryson said.

She snorted a defeated laugh. "I should have walked out the moment I saw which fraternity he belonged to," Evie said. "I spent too many years around their kind."

She blew out a sigh. "You will think I'm insane, but I'm not ready to give up. I know you don't believe finding a new place to house The Sanctuary is an option, but I won't be able to sleep at night if I don't at least explore the possibility."

He held his hands up. "Whatever you need to do to sleep at night, Ev. Who knows, there may be something out there."

"I'll start searching tomorrow. Right now, I just want to

hug my dog and forget about the disaster of a meeting we just went through."

Bryson stuck his hands in his pockets and debated the wisdom of speaking the words he was about to say. The afternoon had already turned into a shit show. He figured he didn't have anything to lose.

"Not to sound like a horny, insensitive asshole, but we can always go back to my place and cheer each other up with sex."

He fully expected Evie to call him on his horniness, insensitivity, and assholery. Instead, she nodded and pointed at his car.

"Go get Bella. I'll get Waffles and meet you at your place in an hour."

CHAPTER TWENTY-FOUR

They could not have asked for a more perfect day for a carnival if they had ordered it from a catalog. The sun was shining but not oppressive, and the slight breeze felt like heaven on Evie's skin as she carried a laundry basket filled with purple, yellow, and green plastic balls from her car.

Too bad her stomach was twisted into knots. Despite the pep talk she'd given herself this morning, she couldn't help but feel this was all for nothing.

It's not. You and Bryson will figure something out.

Those knots twisted even tighter at the thought of Bryson. An awareness of how quickly things were moving with him sat in the back of her mind, nudging at her whenever she felt herself getting too comfortable with the thought of jumping headfirst into a legitimate relationship.

Well, except for every night this week, when she found herself more than just comfortable in his new bed with his thousand-thread-count sheets that felt even better than her green ones.

Focus, Evie!

There was too much to be done today. She would not let the memories from last night derail what could be The Sanctuary's best chance of surviving.

She took the walking path that led to the backyard of Barkingham Palace's new location. Her mouth fell open the moment she entered the gate. The outside play area had been transformed into a Mardi Gras–themed wonderland for dogs.

"Evie! Bring those here!"

Evie carried the basket over to where Ashanti stood, stringing balloons onto a balloon arch.

"Kara went back home to get the blow-up pool," Ashanti said. "That's where those will go." She gestured to the yard. "It's looking pretty good out here, huh?"

When Ashanti first suggested the canine carnival, Evie had imagined a few games, maybe a doggy photo booth, and possibly a silly Mardi Gras–themed costume contest. She had not expected a full-blown extravaganza, complete with a doggy Ferris wheel and carousel. The grounds were peppered with over a dozen kiosks and booths offering everything from spa treatments to dog-friendly cupcakes.

"This is a lot more than I anticipated," Evie said.

"You want to raise money, don't you? You have to give people something to spend money on. Now, the food trucks with be here at—"

Evie whipped around. "Food trucks?"

"Of course," Ashanti said. "I have three coming. And each have pledged fifteen percent of their sales to The Sanctuary." She clipped on the last balloon, then held up one end of the arch and handed it to Evie. "Help me bring this over to the photo area. Just wait until you see it!"

The photo area had been designed to look like the dogs were riding on a Mardi Gras float.

"You know that you were only supposed to help with this, and I was supposed to do the heavy lifting, right?" Evie asked.

"And I told you that you would only get in the way. Kara and Kendra are using this as their volunteer hours." She pulled out her phone and tapped something out on the screen. "I just sent you the list of work assignments. Several of the twins' classmates who also need volunteer hours will help run the agility-course apparatuses and operate the booths."

"Is there anything for me to do?" Evie asked jokingly.

Ashanti's forehead crinkled as her mouth dipped with a confused frown. "Um, not really."

"Shanti!" Evie hollered.

"Just messing with you," she said. "Turn the paper over. There's a whole list just for you."

Evie had just finished setting up the Guess the Number of Dog Treats in the Jar booth when she turned and spotted Bryson entering from the side entrance. Her entire body flushed cold and hot at the same time.

He'd spent the past week working fourteen-hour shifts. Two of the surgeons at the hospital came down with stomach bugs, so the others were picking up the slack. Evie had surprised him with lunch on Wednesday, but he'd been called into an emergency surgery after one bite of his shrimp po'boy.

"Hey," he said as he approached her, a fatigued yet alluring smile curving up the corners of his mouth.

"Hey," Evie answered. She wanted to kiss him, but there were way too many eyes around.

She was most concerned with one set of eyes that belonged to her best friend. She knew she couldn't keep this relationship she wasn't ready to call a relationship from Ashanti and Ridley for much longer, but she wasn't ready to discuss it right this minute. She needed to get through this carnival first.

Bryson looked around. "This is . . . something."

"Welcome to Ashanti Wright's world. We're just participants in the production."

"Based on the line of people with their pets waiting to get in, she knows what she's doing."

Evie looked down at her watch. "But the carnival doesn't start for another half hour."

He shrugged. "They're ready." Bryson leaned over until his lips brushed her ear. "By the way, you left your underwear on the floor in my living room. The cleaner put it with my laundry."

Her face turned into an instant campfire. All it would take was a single look from Ashanti, and Evie wouldn't have to tell her anything about her relationship with Bryson.

"Dammit, Evie Williams," Bryson said in a teasing voice. "Why are you so damn cute when you blush?"

She took a step back from him and held up a finger. "Stay back. You go over there somewhere. Today is too important and I will not have anything distracting me, including you."

He lifted both hands in surrender. "You don't even see me. Actually, you won't see me for very long. I have to get back to the hospital in about an hour, but Derrick Coleman will be here to help out."

She wasn't surprised Bryson couldn't stay, but she was still hurt that he would miss so much of the event.

However, once the carnival officially started, Evie didn't

have time to think about Bryson or anyone else. Barkingham Palace went from being a doggy daycare to a madhouse. Evie never anticipated having to turn people away, but they reached capacity within twenty minutes of opening the gates. Ashanti instituted an on-the-spot time limit for each booth and agility apparatus so they would be able to get as many people to come through as possible.

It took another hour for things to calm down enough for Evie to take a bathroom break. When she returned to the Guess the Number of Dog Treats booth, Ashanti and Kendra were waiting for her.

"Ken is going to take over this booth for a few while we chat," Ashanti said. She grabbed the hem of Evie's shirt and dragged her behind the ticket booth. "Okay, are you going to tell me what's going on between you and Bryson, or do I have to bring you to my torture chamber?"

"You don't own a torture chamber," Evie said.

"I will create one for the sole purpose of forcing you to tell me what's going on."

"What makes you think something is going on?" Evie asked.

"That man could not keep his eyes off you the entire time he was here. It was even worse than it was back when we were at LSU."

Oh, goodness. Really, Bryson?

"You've got it all wrong," Evie tried. She didn't sound at all convincing. She was never good at lying.

Ashanti plopped her hands on her hips. "Evelina Williams, how long have I known you? You can't hide anything from me, woman."

Evie blew out a breath. She shouldn't have even tried.

She leaned over and whispered, "What do you *think* is going on?"

Ashanti gasped. "I knew it!" She batted Evie's arm like she was trying to kill a mosquito. "I knew it! I knew it! I knew it! This is phenomenal. This is exactly what *should* have happened eight years ago. Is he good in bed? What am I even asking, of course he's good. I'm so happy for you!"

"Shanti!" Evie grabbed her by the wrist. She dragged her to the narrow alleyway between the house and the fence.

"Really?" Evie said. "You're happy for me? You are supposed to talk sense into me!"

"No, I should have talked sense into you back when we were in school and it was obvious that Bryson was so much better for you than Cameron. I had only known you for a couple of years back then and didn't feel comfortable putting my nose in your business, but here it is," Ashanti said, pointing to her nose. "I've known you long enough to get all up into your business now, and I'm telling you that this is a good thing."

"But what if it isn't?" Evie asked.

"Wait? So the sex isn't good?"

"No!" Evie yelled. She looked around, even though she doubted anyone could hear her above the pandemonium happening around the carnival. "The sex is amazing," she said. "Like the most amazing I've ever had."

Ashanti closed her eyes, a blissful smile breaking out across her face. "I knew it," she said. "You can tell just by looking at him."

"Shanti, would you be serious for even one second? I need advice here."

"About what?"

"About what?" Evie's brows shot up. "About this! About what I'm doing with Bryson."

"Well, Thad and I haven't been together that long, but I can give you some pointers."

Evie groaned up at the sky. "Can you *please* be serious?"

"I would if I thought *you* were being serious. What kind of advice are you looking for me to provide?"

"You can tell me if I'm in over my head," Evie said. "Or if I'm moving too quickly. What if this is just a rebound? I can't possibly be ready to jump into a real relationship so soon after ending such a long one with Cameron, can I?"

"Wait, we're talking relationship? It's not just sex?" Ashanti shook her head. "No, of course it's not just sex. The two of you have always had too much chemistry to do the random hookup thing."

"What do you even know about our chemistry?"

"Um, because I was there, Ev. That summer you were with Bryson was the happiest I've ever seen you." Ashanti's eyes narrowed. "Is there more going on?"

Evie knew she'd made a mistake when she looked away. A quick glance, but that's all it took.

Ashanti pounced. "There is! What are you not telling me?"

"Nothing," Evie said. "And even if there was more, I am not discussing it in the middle of a doggy carnival."

Ashanti leaned in close and whispered, "Torture chamber. Give me the full story or you get the torture chamber. There will be spiders."

"Goodness, you're annoying," Evie said. She blew out a breath. "We'll talk about it tonight at Ridley's."

"Fine," Ashanti said. "It'll help with Rid's salty mood. You know how she gets on her birthday."

"I plan on plying her with liquor and sweets," Evie said.

"The Imperial March" from *Star Wars* started playing.

"That's Kara," Ashanti said, plucking her phone from her back pocket. "Why are you calling me when we're in the same place?" She waited a beat, then said, "Oh shit."

"What's wrong?" Evie asked.

"There's been an incident at the dunk tank." She pointed two fingers at her own eyes, then at Evie. "Remember, I want to know everything."

By the time they arrived at the dunk tank, Thad had taken care of the squabble between two Labrador retrievers and their owners. Evie checked in with Kendra, and once she'd made sure she was good at the Guess the Number of Dog Treats booth, she went to help with the photo booth.

The crowd continued to spend money like it was falling from the sky. By the time the carnival was over, they had taken in nearly eight thousand dollars for The Sanctuary.

"I cannot believe how successful this turned out," Evie said as she connected Waffles's leash to his harness. He'd spent the day in one of the daycare's fancier suites. "I can't wait to tell Bryson how much we raised."

"Mmm," Ashanti said.

"Because he has a stake in what happens with the rescue," Evie clarified. "We've been working together on this for weeks."

"Mmm-hmm," Ashanti said.

Evie rolled her eyes. "Shut up. I'll see you at Rid's in an hour."

"Are you sure you don't want to leave Waffles here?"

"Rid said it's okay to bring him," Evie reminded her.

"Oh, yeah, I forgot about the soft spot she suddenly has for dogs. I'm a little suspect, if I'm being honest."

Evie laughed. "It'll save me a trip back here to the Lower Garden District, so I'm not going to question it. I'll see you over there."

She tried getting in touch with Bryson on her way to the grocery store to pick up Ridley's gift, but he had just begun a gastropexy that would last at least another hour, according to the tech she'd spoken to.

"You are not sad that you can't speak to him for an hour," Evie assured herself, despite the melancholy encroaching on her good mood. She looked at Waffles in the rearview mirror. "Things are getting pretty ridiculous."

Waffles tipped his head to the side, wrenching out a laugh from her.

"Sit tight. I'll only be a minute."

She ran into Whole Foods and picked up what she needed for Ridley's birthday celebration, then headed for her friend's condo.

Evie watched the numbers on the elevator climb as she balanced a container of berries and Chantilly cream cupcakes in one hand while carrying a bottle of Cristal she'd picked up from Total Wine in the one that also held Waffles's leash. It was a splurge, but today was Ridley's thirty-fifth birthday. Her friend didn't handle birthdays well; a mid-milestone birthday like this one would no doubt have her in a salty mood.

The elevator stopped on the twelfth floor of Ridley's downtown high-rise building and Evie headed for her apartment. She used her foot to knock on the door.

"Open up. It's me," she said.

A minute later, Ashanti answered the door. "Oh good, you have cupcakes. I wanted to buy a cake, but I was running late and didn't have the chance to stop."

"Is that Ev?" Evie heard Ridley call.

She deposited the cupcakes and champagne on the entryway table and walked over to where Ridley sat barefoot on the sofa.

"Happy birthday, honey," Evie said, giving her shoulders a squeeze and pressing a kiss to the top of her head.

"Enough with that," Ridley said. "Grab those cupcakes and bubbly. According to that one over there, we have things to discuss."

"Really, Shanti?" Evie said.

"Aht. Don't blame her," Ridley said. "I would have known the minute you walked in. I smell the sex on you."

Evie rolled her eyes. "Let me get Waffles settled in," she said.

"There's a dog crate in the second bedroom," Ridley said.

"A what?" Evie and Ashanti asked in unison. They looked at each other, then took off for Ridley's guest room.

Evie entered the room and came to a sudden stop. "What in the world?" she said.

The crate was at least four feet wide and three feet high, with a gabled roof and an ultra-plush doggy bed inside.

"Do you think she's dying?" Ashanti asked. "This isn't a sign of her trying to buy her way into heaven, is it?"

"I am not dying," Ridley said as she walked up to them carrying a glass of champagne. She shrugged. "The two of you always have your dogs. This way I don't have to worry about fur all over my house."

"Are you sure you aren't dying?" Ashanti asked. She reached over as if to feel her forehead, but Ridley knocked her hand away.

"Stop," she said. She gestured to Evie with her glass. "Lock Pancake up so we can get to eating and chatting, please?"

"His name is Waffles," Evie reminded her.

"Whatever."

Evie secured Waffles in the Ritz-Carlton of crates, then joined the others in the living room. She lifted a square of the fig, prosciutto, and arugula pizza from the array of food spread across Ridley's glass sofa table. There was also a bowl of mixed nuts, a platter of fruit, and the cupcakes she'd brought over.

"Start talking," Ridley said.

"Can we at least sing 'Happy Birthday' before I'm forced to divulge all my secrets?" Evie asked.

Ridley pitched a cashew at her. "Your ass shouldn't be keeping secrets," she said.

Ashanti cleared her throat. "You sure you want to go there?"

Ridley shot her a nasty look. "We're talking about Evie now."

"Can we talk about you after we're done with me?" Evie asked.

"Come on with it, Ev. I'm not getting any younger here."

"Fine." Evie blew out a sigh.

"I'll give you a head start," Ashanti said. "She and Bryson are sleeping together."

"About damn time!" Ridley said. "By the way, I kinda hate you right now, because that man is fine and I just know you are getting the kind of sex I need in my life. Tell me everything. Is he curved? Does he growl or is he a screamer?"

"Ridley!" Evie nearly choked on a chunk of fig. She laughed to the point that tears streamed down her face. "How are you so classy and so crass at the same time?"

"It's an art form." Ridley sipped her champagne and wiggled her fingers at her. "Now back to the basketball player."

While noshing on bougie pizza and expensive champagne,

Evie gave a highlight reel accounting of everything that had happened in the past week.

"You've been in his bed every night?" Ashanti asked.

"That man has you dick-whipped, Ev."

"It's not like that," Evie said.

Although, maybe it was? It was quite possible that she was utterly dick-whipped after one week, if being dick-whipped meant that she thought about the time they'd spent in bed at least a dozen times every hour.

"I still can't believe you waited all these years to sleep with him," Ashanti said.

"I never would have slept with Bryson back then. I had just broken up with Cameron."

"That's why you *should* have banged the basketball player back then," Ridley pointed out.

"Well, I didn't," Evie said. "It started as just a little innocent flirting—teasing and jokes, nothing too serious. As the summer went on, things started to get a bit more serious." She shrugged. "And a little more, and a little more."

"But no sex," Ridley said.

"He did finger-bang me in the supply closet until I had the most intense orgasm I'd ever had up until that point," Evie said.

"Yaaaassss!" Ashanti's hands shot in the air like a referee signaling a touchdown.

"Now that's what the fuck I'm talkin' about!" Ridley said, snapping her fingers.

"He's learned a lot over the years, because the four orgasms he gave me last night were so much better."

"In one night! Oh, bitch, stop playing around and marry this man," Ridley said.

"Can I be single for a few months first?" Evie asked. "It's been a while."

"Being single isn't all it's cracked up to be," Ridley said before tipping her head back and emptying her glass in a single gulp.

Evie looked over at Ashanti, who cocked a brow in unspoken agreement.

"Uh, Rid, I know it's your birthday, and I want to respect that, but don't you think it's time you did a little sharing too?" Evie asked.

"I overshare. Isn't that what you two always tell me?"

"You *used* to," Ashanti said. "But that all changed around the time Thad and Von held the soft opening for The PX. What happened, Rid?"

Ridley's face immediately clouded. She refilled her champagne flute and dropped three raspberries in it. She shrugged and, with obviously forced nonchalance, said, "What makes you think something happened?"

"We're not stupid, Ridley," Ashanti said. "I know you slept with Von."

She set the flute down with a thump. "Did he tell you that?"

"He didn't have to! It was obvious the two of you were into each other from the moment I introduced you, but then you jetted off to London within days of meeting him and Von spent the next two months asking about you every single time I came around. Did he do something to you?"

"No," Ridley said. "Of course not. He just . . . " She shook her head and let out a deep breath. "I don't know. He scares me, okay?"

"Was he violent?" Ashanti screeched. "Because if he was, Thad will kick his ass! *I* will kick his ass!

"Not that type of scary," Ridley deadpanned. She pitched her head back and pinched the bridge of her nose. "Why are we talking about this?"

"Because you aren't acting like yourself. *That's* what's scary," Evie said.

"Fine!" Ridley said. "Fine. Look, you both know me when it comes to men. I'm in their beds for a good time, not a long time. But with Von . . ." Ridley chewed on her bottom lip, then admitted, "I didn't want to leave his bed."

Evie's eyes shot to Ashanti's. They both stared at each other, mouths agape.

"Months later and it still feels like a fairy tale," Ridley continued. "We spent two of the most amazing days and nights in bed together. He was so sweet, and so gentle, and so unlike any man I've ever been with."

Evie slapped her palm to her chest. The soft, vulnerable woman sitting across from her on the sofa didn't even sound like Ridley.

"So why did you leave?" Evie asked.

"Because it scared the living shit out of me," Ridley said. She held up her hands. "First, let's get one thing straight. I did not go to London solely to avoid Von. My career comes first. Always. That special project in London was an opportunity to show my bosses that I'm better at this job than every other executive at my level. The opportunity just so happened to drop into my lap exactly when I needed to get the hell out of New Orleans."

"So, are you done avoiding Von?" Ashanti asked.

"Probably not." She bit into a strawberry, then waved Ashanti off with the fruit stem. "Enough about me and my sex life, which is as dry as the damn Sahara at the moment,"

Ridley said. "That's the other thing. I spent the last few months surrounded by fine European men and felt nothing. I'm still mad about it."

"And you had the nerve to call me dick-whipped?" Evie clucked her tongue.

"Whatever," Ridley said, throwing another cashew at Evie's head. "Back to you. What are you going to do about your new boyfriend?"

"He's not my boyfriend. Oh my God, I sound like a thirteen-year-old," Evie said.

"Yes, you do," Ridley said.

"But Bryson isn't my boyfriend," Evie said. "At least I hadn't thought about him in that way."

"Would it be such a bad thing if you did?"

Evie didn't want to give voice to that feeling she couldn't shake, that thing that hovered at the periphery of her brain, nagging her. But if there was anyone she could share it with, it was these two.

"What if he leaves?" she asked. "He did it once before. What if he leaves again without a word?"

"He wouldn't do that," Ashanti said.

"I didn't think he would the first time," Evie said. "But he did."

"That was different. He switched veterinary programs."

"He could get another job offer somewhere else just as easily as he switched programs as a student," Evie said. "The probability is even higher now. He's an in-demand, world-renowned surgeon. I'm sure he gets offers from around the country on a daily basis."

Silence fell over the room, something that rarely happened

when the three of them were together. Then Ridley said, "Start dropping those tracking devices around his house."

Evie rolled her eyes.

"I'm serious. Just bring one or two with you every time you go to his place, and tuck them in his jacket pockets, suitcase, shoes."

"Shoes?"

"Well, hell, I don't know. I'm trying to help."

"Maybe you need to have this conversation with Bryson," Ashanti said. "Let him know that the way he left is still an issue for you."

"You're probably right," Evie said.

The thing is, she and Bryson had already had that conversation. Yet, something about his explanation for why he'd left didn't sit right with her. It was like Doc Landry's incomplete story about all that was happening with The Sanctuary. Something in her gut told her that Bryson was holding back.

Maybe Ashanti *was* right. Maybe it was time she and Bryson got everything out in the open.

CHAPTER TWENTY-FIVE

Bryson tracked the headlights driving toward him, trying to make out the model of the vehicle. It passed his Jeep and he noticed Evie's mass of curls behind the steering wheel. He watched in his rearview mirror as she turned into the driveway of the house next door, backed out, and came back toward him, pulling up to the curb in front of her own house.

He waited until she opened her door before grabbing Bella and getting out of his Jeep.

She caught sight of him when he was still a couple of yards away.

"Hey! What are you doing here?" Evie asked.

She opened the back door and unleashed Waffles from his car seat. When she set him down, he immediately ran to Bella. The two started their sniffing ritual. It had become a thing that took place no matter how many times they saw each other in a day.

"I thought I would drop by," Bryson answered with a shrug. "I was hoping you wouldn't mind some company for a little while."

"Not at all," she said. She looked him up and down. "I can even be talked into a sleepover."

"Ugh, don't say that," Bryson said, slapping his hand to his chest. "I can't do a sleepover tonight. My parents' flight from Fort Lauderdale gets in just after ten o'clock. They're spending the night at my place and I'm driving them home tomorrow. Dr. Blake is finally well enough to come back to work, so no more fourteen-hour shifts for me. At least for now."

"Thank goodness," Evie said. "I know this has been exhausting for you. And your parents finally get to see your new condo! That's exciting!"

"Yeah, I just have to make sure there isn't any lacy underwear hiding in plain sight."

"Ha ha," she deadpanned.

Bryson tried to smile, but it felt forced. Evie picked up on it right away.

"What's wrong?" she asked.

He decided to come right out with it. She was going to find out sooner or later.

"The succession went through," he said.

Her entire body seemed to deflate. "Nooooo. On a Saturday? How?"

"The judge signed the papers yesterday afternoon. Odessa called me. She has a friend at the courthouse who has been keeping tabs on the succession as it made its way through the system."

"Shit," Evie said. "I was still riding high from the money we made earlier at the carnival, but what good will eight thousand dollars do now?"

"It's a good first step toward a down payment on another building, or the first few months' rent if that's the route we have to go," Bryson said. "We still have options, remember?"

"But are those options realistic?"

"Hey, where's this coming from?" Bryson wrapped an arm around her shoulders and gave her a squeeze. "I'm the one who was ready to give up on The Sanctuary. You're the one who convinced me we still had a chance to save it. Don't give up on me now."

She blew out a weary breath, but then nodded.

"Okay," she said. "I'm going to start searching property sites as soon as I get Waffles settled inside."

"Why don't you wait until tomorrow to do that." Bryson looked at his watch. "I know it's kinda late, but I spotted something on the ride here that I think will cheer you up. Are you hungry?"

Her forehead creased. "I had pizza at Ridley's, but I can use a bite," she said, her voice a mix of caution and curiosity.

"Good. Let's go."

They piled into his Jeep, and a few minutes later, Bryson pulled into the parking lot near Poydras Avenue. There were three food trucks lining the outer perimeter. He parked and pointed to the yellow and red one.

"Does that look familiar to you?"

Evie gasped. "Is that Sally's? When did they get a food truck? The restaurant has been closed since the pandemic."

"I guess they found something that works for them. I would assume a food truck has less overhead," Bryson said. "I just hope they still have that hot roast beef po'boy they used to sell."

The food truck did indeed have the same menu from their days as the brick-and-mortar sandwich shop he and Evie frequented back when they volunteered at The Sanctuary. Bryson opened the tailgate on the Jeep and he and Evie sat inside, their legs dangling from the trunk as they ate their sandwiches. He broke off a piece of the crusty French bread and held it out to Bella.

"Will you question my dog parenting skills if I give this to her?"

"No." Evie shook her head. "I will question your sanity for sharing this delicious sandwich. You can give Waffles a piece, too, because I'm not giving up any of mine."

He laughed as he broke off another piece and slipped it to her dog.

"I had a feeling this would cheer you up," he said.

"Eh, it's more like eating my feelings," Evie said. "I'm trying not to show it, but I'm scared, Bryson. Lucas Shepard can show up tomorrow demanding we shut down The Sanctuary."

"That's a possibility. But it's been a possibility for a while." He shrugged. "What can you do?"

"But I *needed* this!" Evie said. "I know it's selfish, and I know it should be about the animals, but *I* needed this. I wanted to do something big, something significant. I needed to prove to my mother that I'm more than your run-of-the-mill veterinarian. Hell, I wanted to prove it to myself!"

"Ev, why are you buying into this bullshit? There's nothing run-of-the-mill about you or the work you do as a vet."

"Says the hotshot surgeon."

"No, you don't get to do that. I have my role as a surgeon, but you have a role too. Do I have to remind you about the skill it takes to examine an animal you've never encountered before and issue a diagnosis? You've already done the hard part by the time the patients get to me."

"I know, I know," Evie said. "Sorry for taking that cheap shot, especially after you bought me a sandwich."

"A good sandwich," he reminder her.

"The sandwich of all sandwiches," she said with a wry grin. "And you do not have to convince me that domestic animal veterinarians like myself play an important role."

"Then stop downplaying your worth," Bryson said.

Her shoulders drooped. "It's just that I wanted to prove that I could accomplish something without my parents or Cameron holding me up. It sucks that the thing I set out to achieve—saving The Sanctuary—may not happen. It just has me in a mood. I'm sorry."

"Ev, it's not—"

"I know there's still a chance of saving it."

"Then stop talking like all is lost," Bryson said. "Who knows, this could turn out to be the best thing yet for The Sanctuary. We may find a building that's even better to house it."

She slanted an irritated look his way. "Why are you rationalizing everything when I want to wallow in my misery?"

"Because I don't like it when you're miserable," Bryson said. "I take it as my personal responsibility to make sure you are never miserable."

She snapped her head back and let out a crack of laughter.

"That is an undertaking that may be impossible even for the great Dr. Bryson Mitchell."

"Are you challenging my abilities to bring joy and pleasure to your life, Dr. Williams?"

"No," she laughed. "I am underscoring the unavoidable misery I will soon face." Her mouth scrunched up in a frown. "My parents' anniversary party is tomorrow. They will be celebrating forty years of whatever is the opposite of marital bliss. You would never know it by the show my mother will undoubtedly put on for everyone." She looked over at him. "You should come with me to the party."

Bryson drew back, giving his head a slight shake. "I don't know about that, Ev. That's really not my scene."

She shrugged like it wasn't a big deal. "What? It's just a party. An elaborate, over-the-top party, but still just a party."

"Exactly. An elaborate party with your parents and a bunch of people who are like your parents."

"Wait a minute." She held up a hand. "I'm usually the last person to defend them, but just what do you mean by a bunch of people who are like my parents?"

"Rich people, Ev. High-society people. Even though I technically do fit in with that crowd these days, I still don't feel comfortable around them. I doubt I ever will."

Her features softened with understanding. "Don't let that get to you. I'll be there. I promise I will not leave your side for a minute."

She could glue their hands together and it still wouldn't help.

"I'll think about it," Bryson said, although the thought made his stomach hurt. "Speaking of parents," he said. "Do you want to meet mine? You can come with me to pick them up from the airport."

Her brow furrowed. "Um, are you sure we're at that stage? Meeting the parents, I mean?"

"You *just* asked me to come with you to your parents' party."

"Yeah, but you wouldn't even have to meet my parents. They'll be so busy putting on a show for the two hundred people my mother has invited that they probably won't even notice that *I'm* there."

"I want you to meet my mom and dad, Ev," Bryson said, struck by how ardently he meant it.

"Will they like me, or will they judge me for my rich family the way their son did?"

"They will like you," he said. "I'm sorry I ever told you about that."

"I didn't give you a choice," Evie reminded him. Her chest expanded with the deep breath she sucked in. Bryson could tell she was struggling with the decision.

"Come on, Ev. My mother, for one, will love you. I can basically guarantee that."

"Okay." She nodded. "Okay. Let's go."

An hour later, Bryson, Evie, his mom, and his dad, along with Bella and Waffles, sat outside under the covered veranda at Morning Call. The legendary coffee stand had been around since the eighteen hundreds, and in Bryson's opinion, served the best beignets in the city.

"I rarely come here, so this is a real treat," Evie said, biting into a pillowy, powdered-sugar-covered beignet.

Bryson couldn't help but watch as her tongue licked a bit of sugar from the corner of her lip. He had to look away. He could not entertain the thought that rushed into his brain with his parents sitting at the same table.

"I have them every chance I get," his mother said. She took a sip of her decaf café au lait and looked back and forth between Bryson and Evie. "So, you and Bry went to LSU together?"

"Bryson was two years ahead of me, but we were there at the same time. We also volunteered at an animal rescue here in New Orleans one summer."

The fact that she didn't mention Cameron and how he was connected to both of them thrilled Bryson. He wanted Cameron Broussard to stay in the rearview mirror, right where his ass belonged.

As he observed his mother and Evie chatting about an upcoming Broadway show heading to the Saenger Theater, Bryson was even happier that he'd asked her to join them. They got along as if they were old friends instead of strangers who'd known each other for all of an hour.

One of the fire-engine-red Canal Street streetcars made the corner and pulled in next to the coffee stand.

"That is the quintessential New Orleans portrait," Evie said, holding her hands out in front of her as if making a picture frame. "It's even prettier when the azaleas are in bloom. Although, the azaleas aren't nearly as stunning as your camellias."

"You've seen my camellias?" his mother asked.

"I brought Evie with me when I went down to speak at Southwest Terrebonne High," Bryson said.

"You did!" His mother's eyebrows reached her hairline. She smiled. It was that cagey smile, the one that told Bryson her brain was cooking up something. "Well, he needs to bring you back when the rest of the family is there." She bumped his dad with her elbow. "Maybe we can have a crawfish boil, Wallace."

Pop nodded and garbled something that sounded like "yes" as he chomped on his second order of beignets.

"It's been even longer since I had boiled crawfish," Evie said.

"That settles it." His mother slapped the table, and Bryson knew for certain that there would be a crawfish boil in their near future. When Stella Mitchell got that gleam in her eyes, there was nothing stopping her.

"I hate to break this up, but it's getting pretty late," Bryson said. "We need to bring Evie and Waffles home before we get to the condo."

"I hate that you're right, but you are," his mother said. They rose from the table and piled into his Jeep. Once they arrived at Evie's, his mother insisted on getting out of the car to give Evie a hug.

"It was so nice meeting you," his mother said. "You need to come out to the bayou soon."

"I promise I will," Evie said.

Knowing that his mother's questions would come rapid fire if he didn't preempt them, Bryson filled the conversion with talk of this latest cruise. By the time they arrived at his condo, he'd heard about every meal and port of call and knew the names of the cruise director's three children.

His stonewalling lasted until the end of the tour of the condo. The moment they were done, his mother said, "So, Evie is delightful. And gorgeous. She looks creole."

"I didn't ask for her DNA profile, but I'll be sure to do that next time I see her."

"Don't be a smart-ass," his mother said. "How serious is this?"

"Don't start, Ma."

She plopped her hands on her hips. "I absolutely will start. Do you know how many nights I have prayed that you would find someone after you broke up with that Alyssa girl? If I'd known Evie back when you both were in school, I would have been praying for her from the get-go."

Bryson silently acknowledged that if he'd had the

opportunity to introduce her to his parents back when they were in school, he probably wouldn't have. The admission settled in his gut like a bitter pill. He would never forgive himself for hiding his background and his family the way he had.

He walked over to his mother and gave her a kiss on the forehead.

"Evie and I are really good friends. If it develops into something more, you will be the first to know."

In his head and in his heart, they were already a lot more than he was letting on, but that information would be shared on a need-to-know basis, and the only people who needed to know that right now were himself and Evie.

CHAPTER TWENTY-SIX

Bryson had attended his share of ritzy gatherings over the years. One of his colleagues on the team at Tuskegee was renowned for his elaborate dinner parties and department soirees. But as he stood next to a wall of cascading ruby-red roses that flowed into a swimming pool strewn with the same roses, along with heart-shaped floating candles, he felt safe in saying that this was, by far, the ritziest shindig he'd ever attended. A mix of round tables with chairs draped with elegant sashes, red velvet couches, and gold velvet settees occupied the space around the pool and throughout the Williams's backyard.

He'd eaten way more shrimp cocktail and what the server had called lamb chop popsicles than he cared to admit, and he still wasn't done. There was an entire table with various kinds of caviar, freshly shucked oysters, and lobster tail he had yet to visit.

It was obvious the Williamses had spared no expense.

Drinks were flowing faster than Niagara Falls from the open bar, and Bryson was certain he'd seen the live band that was performing tonight on one of the nationally syndicated late-night talk shows. The party was a who's who of New Orleans's most notable residents, including several city council members, prominent business leaders, and a local attorney whose face was plastered on billboards all over the city.

He had never felt more out of place.

None of the guests had done anything in particular to make him feel unwelcome, but he'd come to accept that he would never feel comfortable amongst this set. His tailored tuxedo, the spit-shined shoes, and the expensive cologne he wore were nothing more than a costume. If not for his wanting to be here for Evie, he would be at home with Bella. His meal wouldn't be as fancy, but he would be a helluva lot more relaxed.

Bryson slipped his hand into his pocket and took a sip of the too-sweet cocktail he'd gotten from the bar. As he observed the crowd, he caught sight of Evie weaving her way through the throng, and every drop of discomfort he'd felt dissipated. She had that effect on him.

She was, in a word, stunning.

She'd literally taken his breath away when he'd arrived at her house to pick her up for the party. Her shimmering red gown hugged her subtle curves, leaving just enough to the imagination. Except he didn't have to imagine what was underneath that dress. He'd spent hours upon hours over the past two weeks exploring every inch of her. As exquisite as she looked in that gown, he couldn't wait to peel it off her.

She moved toward him, the gemstones at her neck catching the light of the hundreds of candles that lit up the backyard.

Ruby red was the theme of the night. As he'd learned upon arriving, it was the traditional color to celebrate a couple's fortieth wedding anniversary. His parents had celebrated fifty-four years of marriage late last year, but the most they ever did for their anniversary was a nice dinner at the fanciest steak house in Houma, which was to say, not much.

"Sorry that took so long," Evie said as she approached him. "I promise that is the last time I leave you."

"You don't have to babysit me, Ev. It hasn't been that bad. The most anyone has done is ask if I liked the signature cocktail." He peered at the drink in his hand. "I'm still undecided. What's in this again?"

She hunched her shoulders. "Pomegranate, grapefruit, and rum, I think. The taste doesn't matter. As long as it fits the theme, Constance is happy."

Bryson had been taken aback when she'd referred to her mother by her first name when she'd made introductions earlier this evening. It had to be a rich kid thing. Even the thought of calling his mother Stella made Bryson want to duck for cover. And to say it to her face? He cherished waking up in the morning too much to ever make that mistake.

"Are we supposed to mingle?" Bryson asked Evie.

Her lips scrunched up in a frown. "Do you want to?"

"No," he said quickly. "But I know it's what's done at these types of parties."

"I hate these types of parties," Evie said, looking out at the crowd. "And I hate mingling even more. But this place is crawling with people with deep pockets, and I'll bet half of them have properties around this city that we can potentially use. The ones I've looked into still leave too much to be desired in my opinion." She grabbed his glass, took a sip of his drink, and handed it back to him. "Time to do a little reconnaissance and sweet-talking."

She took him by the hand and together they began making the rounds. Evie introduced him so many times as World-Renowned Veterinary Surgeon Dr. Bryson Mitchell he was certain if he took out his driver's license, he would see the title printed on it.

He understood why she did it—the expressions on people's faces changed the moment they heard the title—but it rubbed him the wrong way that she felt she had to lead with that in order to earn their respect. He didn't give a fuck about earning the respect of anyone at this party. Well, outside of Evie's family. Then again, he didn't care whether they respected him either, so long as they didn't mess up his chances with Evie.

But then something happened that Bryson would have never expected in a million years.

There were people in this crowd who actually knew he existed. In fact, *several* of the people Evie introduced him to had already heard of him. One had even been able to recite some of the findings from the work he did at Tuskegee.

"Told you that you were famous," Evie said with a smirk once the man walked away.

Bryson rolled his eyes. "You're so annoying."

Her smirk deepened. "I think you like that about me."

He fucking loved that about her. The more exasperating, the deeper he fell. It was bizarre and maddening and he wouldn't have it any other way.

Bryson leaned forward and kissed the tip of her nose. "I wouldn't change a thing about you. Except for your dislike of the local cuisine."

"I like the food here!" she laughed.

"Whatever," he said.

"Evie! Evie, is that you?"

They both turned at the sound of her name being called.

"Bianca!" Evie waved. She whispered to Bryson through her smile, "Bianca Taylor. She owns several boutiques on Magazine Street. She also married a man who is the same age as her son, which caused all sorts of drama."

"Love is love. It knows no age," Bryson said.

"But it does know a hefty bank balance."

"Evie, it's so great to see you," Bianca greeted.

The tall, slim redhead, who was dressed in an elaborate gown that seemed more suited for those couture runway shows than for this party, gave Evie air kisses on both cheeks, before holding out a hand to Bryson.

"Bianca Taylor. Pleasure to meet you. That tux is fabulous," she said. "Marks & Spencer, right?"

He hadn't the faintest idea. His sister-in-law had picked it out a few years ago and he'd been rocking it ever since.

"Of course it's Marks & Spencer." She turned to Evie. "I was just talking to your mother about you the other day. You're friends with the owner of that doggy daycare that's been all over the news, aren't you? There was a grand opening for their new place in the Lower Garden District yesterday. My dog has been on the waitlist for months."

"Actually, the official grand opening hasn't happened yet. You're thinking about the canine carnival that was held there. It was a fundraiser for a local animal rescue that I would love to tell you more about."

"Oh, that's okay. I don't need to hear about it," she said. "But I *do* need Misty in that daycare. If you can put in a good word for me, I would appreciate it so much."

"I'll...uh...see what I can do," Evie said.

"You're a doll. Amanda!" Bianca shouted past Evie. "Amanda Chapelle is that you?"

And just as quickly as Bianca Taylor had arrived, she was gone.

"I wonder how much she would be willing to pay to get Misty at Barkingham Palace," Bryson said. "You think Ashanti would mind if we sold access?"

"She would probably be upset that she didn't come up with the idea first," Evie said. "I should call..."

Her words trailed off and a look of pure disdain fell over her face.

"What the fuck," Evie all but growled.

Bryson turned and, for the first time in eight years, laid eyes on his old lab partner.

Cameron Broussard stood just to the right of the five-foot-tall spiraling champagne tower, dressed in a tuxedo that didn't fit him nearly as well as Bryson's fitted him. His sister-in-law would get an extra hug the next time he saw her.

"I cannot believe this," Evie said. "No, actually, I can. I can *totally* believe she would pull this bullshit."

"Ev, it's not a big deal," Bryson said.

"The hell it isn't," she said. "She knows Cameron and I are no longer together."

"But is it worth making a scene over?" he asked. "Especially if you want to get money for The Sanctuary out of these people?"

Evie blew out a breath. "Fine, Mr. Voice of Reason." She lifted a glass of champagne from a passing tray and turned to him. "Do you want to know what Ashanti and Ridley told me? They both said they were hoping I would end up with you instead of Cameron back when we were in school."

"Really?" Bryson's brows arched. He was surprised by the intensity of the gratitude that came over him. "I'm... flattered."

Even her friends had had better sense than he'd shown. He would never forgive his own stupidity. His gullibility.

He'd talked himself out of a life with Evie. He'd allowed Cameron to talk him out of a life with her, believed that asshole when he told him that Evie would never be with someone like him.

"I wish I had known I was a choice for you back then, Ev."

"I wish you had asked instead of making the decision on your own, without bothering to consult me," she said. She hooked her thumb toward her ex. "Look where it got me. He is such a petty bastard for showing up here."

"Cameron's a petty bastard for so many other reasons," Bryson said. He took her hands in his. "Don't let him ruin tonight for you. He's not worth it."

She lifted her face up to his and pressed a fierce kiss to his lips. "No, he isn't."

Bryson was just about to deepen the kiss when a cool, composed voice killed the mood quicker than a bullet to the heart.

"Evelina, look who's joined us."

CHAPTER TWENTY-SEVEN

Evie closed her eyes for the briefest moment before releasing Bryson's lips and turning to face her mother and her ex. She could only hope the smile she offered was convincing enough to conceal the fury building within her. She entwined her fingers with Bryson's and tucked herself against his side.

"Hello, Ev," Cameron said, his gaze squarely on Bryson. He stared at his old classmate with overt contempt in his cool blue eyes.

"Cameron," Evie returned. "It's quite a surprise to see you here."

"It shouldn't be a surprise at all," Constance said, patting Cam's forearm. "We've considered Cameron part of this family for years." She gestured to Bryson. "Cam, this is Brian, a friend of Evelina's."

"Bryson," Evie corrected her.

"Oh, I'm sorry," she said.

"Actually, I knew Cameron before I knew your daughter," Bryson said. He took a step forward and stuck a hand out to Cameron. "We were lab partners at LSU."

"Oh, really!" Constance said. Her surprise was genuine.

Instead of accepting Bryson's hand, Cameron brought his champagne to his lips while sticking his right hand in his pocket.

Evie heard Bryson's low chuckle, but she had no idea how the sound made it past the blood angrily pounding in her ears. She had to count to five to stop herself from unleashing the obscenity-laced tirade that was sitting like rancid bile on the tip of her tongue. She wasn't sure who she wanted to direct it to, her ex-fiancé or her mother.

Tami, the event coordinator, swooped in next to Constance. "Dr. Williams, it's almost time for the toast. Are you changing into the gold?"

"Yes! The toast!" her mother said. "Cam, you will join us on the dais, won't you? It wouldn't feel right not to have you there."

"No, he is *not* joining us. He is not family," Evie said.

Bryson gave her hand a gentle squeeze. Evie knew she should wait until the party was over before addressing the flagrant disrespect her mother showed to her by inviting Cameron, but this felt purposeful. Her mother knew exactly what she was doing.

"I'll be right back," Constance said. "I have a special wardrobe change for the toast."

Evie let go of Bryson's hand. "I'll come with you."

"No, Evelina. I want this to be a surprise."

"I'm coming with you," Evie repeated in a voice that brooked no argument.

Her mother's lips thinned in an irritated smile. "Fine. You can help me change," she said in a calm, controlled voice. She looked to Tami. "My daughter will help with the dress. Why don't you make sure all is in place for the toast?" She turned to Evie. "Well, are you coming?"

Evie could feel her anger rising as she followed her mother into the house and up the stairs. Once Marshall left for college, her mother remodeled his bedroom and the adjoining guest room into a dressing suite that was as large as some studio apartments.

The minute they entered the dressing suite, Constance turned and said, "I don't want to hear your mouth, Evelina. You're here to help me change into my toast dress and that is all we're doing."

"Do you think I give a damn about some toast? Why would you invite Cameron to this party, Mother?"

"Evelina, watch your mouth," she warned in the tone she used whenever Evie got out of line as a teenager, but she was no longer a child.

Evie folded her arms across her chest. "We are not leaving this room until you explain why Cameron is here."

Constance turned and walked to a black garment bag hanging next to the floor-to-ceiling mirrored panel. "Help me with this," she said.

"Why did you invite him?" Evie asked. "Cameron and I are no longer together. I didn't think I would have to expressly tell you that he is no longer invited to family functions."

"Cameron *is* family," her mother said as she unzipped the bag, revealing a metallic gold gown.

"No, he isn't!" Evie screamed as she stomped over to where her mother stood. "Dammit, Mother!" She pointed to her chest. "*I* am your daughter." She pointed in the direction of the backyard. "*He* is the son of a bitch who brought another woman to my bed!"

Constance let go of the garment bag, her hands falling to her sides. She slowly turned, her mouth twisted with grim annoyance.

"*That* is the reason behind your breakup?" her mother asked.

"Yes, Mother. He cheated on me. And I'm pretty certain it wasn't the first time."

"Evelina." The condescension in her voice sent Evie's blood from boiling to scalding. "I cannot believe you ended your engagement over some woman who probably meant nothing to him."

Evie stepped back. She stared at her mother in disbelief.

"Do you hear yourself?" Evie asked. "Do you know what you sound like right now?"

"Like a reasonable adult? Like someone who understands that relationships are complicated and you do not throw away ten years over foolishness?"

"Foolishness!" Evie screeched. She huffed out a laugh. "Yeah, foolishness. I'm the fool. I'm the biggest fool there is for not expecting this exact reaction from you. I should have known better."

"Stop with the dramatics," her mother said.

"You made the decision to put up with Dad's infidelity, but there's no way in hell I was going to sit back and let Cameron do the same thing to me."

"Marriage is not the sunshine and roses it's portrayed to be in the movies, Evelina. Sometimes you have to be willing to accept things that are unpleasant for the sake of the partnership. You and Cameron had the *perfect* partnership, working in the veterinary practice together. You could have helped him grow it into the biggest animal clinic in the city. You should have thought about what you were throwing away before you made such a hasty decision."

She didn't get it. Her mother truly thought it was better to put up with the kind of disrespect she'd dealt with all these years for the sake of what? A job? An image?

"There are certain compromises that I'm not willing to make," Evie said. "Go ahead and toast to your forty-year 'marriage.' I refuse to be a part of this."

"Evelina, you are behaving like a child. Grow up."

Evie stared at the beautiful, intelligent, accomplished woman standing before her and all she could feel for her was pity.

She'd done what she could to please her, especially after the crushing blow of not following in her footsteps and becoming a cardiologist. But over the past few weeks, Evie had come to realize that a large part of the reason she'd continued to go back to Cameron was due to the guilt over not falling in line with her mother's wants. It was like a penance. A sacrifice to win the love and respect she'd lost when she chose to become a vet.

Her penance was over. She would no longer sacrifice her happiness.

"I hope you eventually recognize that you deserve more than the marriage you have settled for all these years," Evie said; then she turned and walked out of the dressing room, swiping at a tear that cascaded down her cheek. She fought the urge to turn around and beg her mother to use this opportunity, while surrounded by the colleagues and friends who'd known about her father's infidelity for years, to finally call him out on it. But Constance Williams would never. It wasn't her way.

"Thank goodness you're not like her," Evie whispered.

And that was the painful, simple truth in all of this. She and her mother were two totally different people. Evie would never agree with the way Constance had chosen to handle her husband's cheating, but it wasn't her place to tell her mother how to live her life, in the same way it wasn't her mother's place to tell Evie how she should live hers.

Evie stopped at the base of the stairs and counted to ten before turning and climbing back up the steps. She took a deep breath just outside the door to the dressing room. When she reentered, her mother was standing in front of the mirror, the back of her gown flapping open.

Their gazes connected in the mirrored wall, but neither spoke as Evie crossed the length of the room and stepped up behind her.

"Will you at least admit that you were wrong in inviting Cameron to this party knowing that the two of us are no longer together?" Evie asked as she clasped the fabric-covered button at the base of her mother's neck. "Just think of how it made Bryson feel to have my ex show up tonight."

"In my defense, you did not tell me you were bringing a date." Constance smoothed the soft metallic material over her hips and turned slightly to look at herself from the side. "However, as I reflect upon it, I can see that it was not the best idea."

"No," Evie said. She stepped around so that her mother faced her instead of the mirror. "I need you to say it. Say that it was wrong and hurtful and disrespectful."

"Evelina—"

"If you want me to come out there and put on a show like we're one big happy family, you will acknowledge what you did."

"We *are* one big happy family," she said. "We are *our* kind of happy, which is just fine as far as I'm concerned."

Evie rolled her eyes. She folded her hands across her chest and said, "I'm waiting."

Constance's nostrils flared with her indignant huff.

"It was disrespectful," she finally said. "I apologize. You were right. You are my daughter and I should have put your feelings above what I thought was proper. Cameron does not belong at this party if you do not want him here. And Brian—"

"Bryson," Evie said. "His name is Bryson Mitchell. *Doctor* Bryson Mitchell."

"Bryson," her mother said. "He should join us for the toast."

When she had just invited Cameron to join them for the toast with Bryson standing right there? Evie refused to insult him by making him feel like a second choice.

"Why don't we stick to the Williamses when it comes to the toast," she said instead.

"That's an even better idea," her mother said. She turned and gave herself a final once-over in the mirror, then said, "We need to get back to the party. I spent a lot of money on this gold dress. It's a nod to the next milestone."

"Next time you should skip the party and spend your fiftieth anniversary in Tahiti, with a nice young cabana boy."

"My goodness, Evelina. You are not allowed to take the mic during the toast."

Evie laughed. As if she would ever.

Once outside, she played the part she was expected to play as she listened to her father expound on the sacredness of a joyous marriage, fighting the urge to chug her glass of champagne the entire time. Cameron hadn't taken the hint to leave, so as soon as the toast ended, Evie took Bryson by the hand and together they weaved their way through the throng of people dancing a second-line and exited her parents' backyard through the side gate.

"Well," Bryson said once behind the wheel of his Jeep. "That was . . . something."

"I'm so sorry about Cam showing up," Evie said. "It never occurred to me that my mother would even consider inviting him. That's all on me, because it *should* have occurred to me that she would do something like this."

He reached over and took her hand.

"I don't care about Cameron showing up, Evie. It's just . . . everything. Tonight was a lot. I can safely say that I have never and would never fit into the world your parents live in." He looked over at her and gave her hand a squeeze. "You want to know what's wild? I realized tonight that *you* don't fit in that world either. You may try to fit in, but you don't, Ev. You're too down-to-earth. I think that's why I first fell in love with you all those years ago."

Evie's heart skipped several beats. "First of all, I know that I don't fit into their world. Black sheep of the family, remember?"

"You're not the black sheep," Bryson said with a grin.

"Odd one out, then," she said. "And secondly, did you just say you are in love with me?"

"I never fell out of love with you," he said softly. His eyes roamed over her face like a caress. "I tried, Ev. I had all but convinced myself that I was over you. But it's always been there."

Her heart swelled to the point that it felt as if it would burst out of her chest.

"I'm not sure I even know what love feels like, Bryson. I never saw it in my parents. I don't know if it's truly what I felt for Cameron all these years. But I know you make me happy. You make me laugh. You make me want to be with you every time I'm not around you, and I can promise you that is something I never experienced when I was with Cameron. I looked forward to 'me' time when Cam and I were together. I haven't given a damn about 'me' time since you came back into my life."

"That sounds like love to me, Ev."

"Good," she said, fighting back tears. "Because I like this feeling."

She leaned over to his side of the Jeep and captured his mouth with her own. If the overwhelming contentment she felt in this moment was indicative of what a person felt when they were in love, Evie wasn't sure if she had *ever* been in love with Cameron. This was different. This was life-affirming.

"Bryson?" she whispered against his lips.

"Yes?" he whispered back.

"Are we going to your place or mine?"

He pulled away slightly and looked into her eyes. "The dogs are with the sitter at my place, remember?"

"That's right," Evie said. "Then why don't we go relieve the dog sitter?"

Bryson straightened himself behind the wheel and started

the Jeep. "The dog sitter ain't the only one getting some relief tonight," he said.

Evie threw her head back and laughed. Out of the corner of her eye, she noticed Cameron walking down the driveway.

Bryson pulled onto the street, and Evie laughed even harder.

CHAPTER TWENTY-EIGHT

As they waited for the first traffic light, Bryson paid the dog sitter through the app he'd used to hire her. At the next light, he sent a text telling her he was almost home and that she could leave. By the time he and Evie arrived at his condo, they found both Bella and Waffles sleeping peacefully in their respective dog beds. Waffles awoke and ran to Evie for a head scratch. Bella lifted her head, looked at the other occupants in the room, then tucked her head under her blanket and went back to sleep.

"I hope he doesn't need a W-A-L-K," Evie said.

Bryson turned his phone to her. "The sitter took them both for a W-A-L-K just before she left. Bella and Waffles will be fine until morning. I, however, will lose my mind if you remain in that red dress a minute longer."

"Impatient much?" Evie laughed. She took him by the arm and tugged him toward his bedroom. Once there, she turned her back to him and swept her thick, natural curls to the side. "Unzip me."

"With pleasure," Bryson said, exposing her light brown flesh as he pulled the zipper down to the small of her back. He unhooked her bra and pushed the dress off her shoulders and down her arms. It slithered onto the floor like a ruby-red waterfall.

She turned to face him and that feeling of disbelief he'd experienced from the very first time he'd taken her to bed swirled through his head. He wasn't sure he would ever get used to being like this with the woman he'd dreamed about for so long. But he sure as hell would have a good time trying.

"This is a really nice tux," Evie said. "But it would look even better over on that chair."

"With"—Bryson tugged the tie at his neck—"pleasure."

She sat on the edge of his bed in black lace panties that matched the bra tangled up in her dress on the floor. Evie braced her arms on either side of her, stretched her legs out, and crossed them at the ankles. She stared at him as if he was performing a striptease for her.

"If you start humming stripper music, I'm putting you out," Bryson said. It was a bald-faced lie, but still.

She threw her head back with a laugh.

"I'd never considered doing such a thing, but now that you've put it in my head."

"Don't do it, Ev," he warned.

"Just get naked and come over here," she said.

Bryson toed his shoes off as he unbuttoned his shirt, then took off his pants. He scooped up Evie's dress and carried everything to the chair in the corner, adding his socks and underwear to the pile.

His sister-in-law would knock him upside the head if she knew how he was handling the tux she'd picked out, but he didn't give a damn about the threads at the moment. The anticipation of climbing into bed with Evie trumped everything.

When he turned, Evie said, "Someone's excited."

Bryson looked down at his erection and then back up at her.

"Not because of that." Evie laughed. "Although that is rather telling. I'm talking about the way you tossed your clothes. You're so particular with everything you do."

"I have been called a perfectionist in the past," Bryson said, stalking toward the bed. "That works in your favor when it comes to what I'm about to do."

He held a hand out to her and she placed her right hand in his. Bryson tugged her up from the bed and took her mouth in a slow, delicious kiss. His skin burned with the need to feel her against him, so he pulled her close, until her body was flush against his. The sensation of her nipples pressing into his chest was almost more than he could withstand. Almost.

"I will never get over the fact that I finally have you to myself," Bryson said. He slipped his tongue in her mouth and nearly lost his mind at how good she tasted. "Eight years is a long time, Ev."

"Well, you don't have to wait any longer, so why are we not in bed?"

He grinned, then pulled her with him to the bed. Bryson's heart jumped into his throat as he stared down at the woman who'd invaded his dreams too many times to count. She was no longer a fantasy; she was here, warm and willing and everything he had ever hoped she would be.

He used his legs to part hers and eased himself inside her. She felt like heaven. Pure heaven.

He began to move with a slow, steady rhythm he knew he wouldn't be able to sustain, not when every fiber in his body was yearning to go faster and deeper and harder.

His instinct was to close his eyes and savor the sensation of driving so deep inside her, but he forced himself to keep them open. He wanted to look at her. He needed to witness the bliss traveling across her face as she reached for him, lifting her hips to meet his every thrust.

He braced his hands on either side of Evie's head and quickened his pace, pushing deeper. He could feel her coming apart underneath him at the same time pressure began to build at the base of his spine. It took only a few more thrusts before pleasure exploded within him, his body shaking violently with the force of his orgasm.

He rolled off Evie and collapsed alongside her, quickly reaching over and pulling her so that she lay on top of him. He doubted five minutes had passed before both he and Evie fell into a deep, exhausted, satisfied sleep.

Bryson heard his phone vibrating on the bedside table. He picked it up and stared at the time: 4:46 a.m. Nothing good could come from a phone call at this time of the morning.

He frowned at the number on the phone, debating whether to even answer, but something in his gut told him that even solicitors wouldn't be calling before five in the morning.

Peering down at Evie, who stirred but didn't wake, Bryson pressed the screen and said, "Hello?" in a low voice.

The shaky voice on the other end made the hair on his neck stand on end.

"Shit!" Bryson said. "Give me twenty minutes. I'll be there with Evie."

"What's wrong?" Evie asked, sitting up in bed.

"Outbreak at The Sanctuary. Odessa thinks it's parvovirus. The dogs started showing symptoms late last night. She said she couldn't sleep so she went in to check on them. It looks bad."

The virus took at least five days to incubate, so they all must have been infected at the same time.

He and Evie both jumped out of bed and started getting dressed. She only had the red gown she'd worn to the party, so Bryson grabbed a pair of drawstring joggers and a sweatshirt from the closet shelf and handed them to Evie. The clothes were at least three sizes too big for her, but she would fit right in with any of the kids he saw hanging at the bus stop wearing oversize hoodies.

"Were the dogs not vaccinated?" Evie asked. "Don't answer that. It was rhetorical. I know you have no idea about the vaccination records. It's just that this—whatever it is—was preventable."

"Let's just get over there so we can see what's going on."

It proved to be as bad as Bryson had imagined. Of the nineteen dogs currently housed at The Sanctuary, eleven were experiencing symptoms of canine parvovirus, some more severe than others.

He learned from Odessa that Doc was visiting his sister in Gulf Shores this weekend.

"There's no need to disturb him on vacation," Bryson said. "It would take at least three hours for him to get here. If we don't have things under control by then, there won't be anything Doc can do."

Evie gave Odessa her phone. "Go to my contacts and search for Cameron Broussard. Let him know what's going on and that he's needed here."

"Really?" Bryson asked, pulling a stethoscope from the table of supplies and handing another to Evie.

"He's a good vet," she said, taking the stethoscope. "This is bigger than my feelings or your ego. It's about the dogs."

She was right. He fucking hated that she was right, but she was.

He and Evie started with the assessments. It was clear that two of the dogs—two puppies, which were the most vulnerable to the highly contagious virus—were in need of immediate attention. Their tiny bodies jerked violently.

"I'm not sure monoclonal antibodies will be enough for them," Evie said. "They need a plasma transfusion."

"I need to get them to the animal hospital," Bryson said.

"I can't handle all these dogs by myself," Evie said. "Odessa," she called over her shoulder. "Can you find Ashanti Wright in my contacts and tell her I need her here asap."

Five minutes later, Ridley came through the door.

Evie's voice rose in clear surprise. "Ridley?"

"Ashanti sent me to pick up sick puppies?" she said. "What? She said it was an emergency and I was two blocks away."

"It's not even six a.m. What are you even doing out at this time of the morning?"

"Get out of my business and give me the damn dogs," Ridley said. "Where am I bringing them?"

Bryson rattled off the address of the animal hospital, which she typed into her phone. They secured the puppies in two small crates that Ridley carried out, one in each hand.

"You have no idea how weird that was," Evie said. "It feels like I'm in the Upside Down."

Cameron came in about twenty minutes later, his hair mussed and sweatshirt stained and wrinkled. He looked as if he'd rolled out of bed and threw on the first thing he picked up from the hamper.

He didn't greet anyone, just set a black insulated cooler on the steel table where Bryson was inserting an IV into a Chihuahua mix.

"I brought all the monoclonal antibodies we had at the clinic, but it's only eight doses," Cameron said.

"Every bit helps," Evie said. She gestured to her right. "Start with those over there."

They worked for two hours, administering antibodies and fluids and examining the other dogs in the rescue to make sure they were not showing any symptoms of the virus. Either by a miracle, or just damn fine veterinary skill, they managed to save each and every dog. Bryson called the hospital to get an update on the puppies Ridley had brought in. Relief weakened his muscles at the news that the puppies would make it.

All of the dogs that had been infected would have to undergo weeks of treatment; whether they would have a roof over their heads throughout that treatment remained to be seen.

Cameron left The Sanctuary as stone-faced as he'd arrived, barely speaking to anyone on his way out. Bryson, Evie, and Odessa retreated to the break room.

Evie stood with her back against the wall. She'd put her hair in a ponytail using a thick rubber band.

"Well, if we didn't already know The Sanctuary was truly done for, this was our biggest sign yet." She pressed the heels of her hands to her eyes and let out a sigh. "All the money we raised at Barkingham Palace will need to be used for treatment."

Bryson had come to the same conclusion.

"This never should have happened," Odessa said, shaking her head. "All because of a power outage."

While the doctors were busting their asses trying to save the dogs, Odessa had been trying to figure out how they got sick in the first place. All the dogs had been vaccinated for parvo. After some digging, she discovered the vaccines they were given had been stored in a refrigerator that was not hooked up to the generator. During one of the city's frequent power outages, the medicine, which must be kept below a certain temperature, had sat for hours with no power. The dogs had all been vaccinated with a vaccine that had gone bad.

"Look at it this way," Odessa said. "At least you all got to save the dogs one last time."

Bryson knew she was right. They had been able to pull off a miracle. But that didn't make this any easier, not when he knew how much Evie's ultimate goal of saving the rescue meant to her.

Sometimes the wins they had to settle for were a far cry from the wins they originally set out for. It looked as if that would be the case with The Sanctuary.

CHAPTER TWENTY-NINE

Evie's entire body ached as she climbed out of Bryson's Jeep and followed him to his building's elevator. But the ache in her neck and back didn't hold a candle to the one in her chest. Every dose of the monoclonal antibodies she'd administered this morning had felt like a shot to her own heart, because she knew with every dose, significant, expensive follow-up care would be needed. Care the rescue could not provide without more funds.

They entered the condo and Evie burst into a jumbled mess of laughter and tears, the sight of Bella and Waffles sending her overwrought emotions past the breaking point.

"Hey, hey," Bryson said, pulling her into a hug. "It's okay, Ev."

"Don't mind me," Evie said, swiping at her nose with her sleeve—his sleeve. "I've been on the verge of losing it for at least an hour. Something about seeing those two together sent me over the edge." She pointed to the dogs. "I mean, just look at them."

Bryson's dog lay on Waffles's back as if he were a pillow put there expressly for her.

Bryson huffed a laugh. "We're lucky they get along so well."

"We are." Evie cocked her head to the side. "But they don't seem like they're boyfriend and girlfriend the way Ashanti and Thad's dogs are. They get along more like siblings."

"Bella is absolutely the frustrated older sister that tolerates the younger brother following her around."

Evie held the sweatshirt out in front of her. "Do you have another one of these I can borrow? We can't go near the dogs in these contaminated clothes."

"I'll grab a trash bag from the kitchen," Bryson said. "Leave the clothes on the floor in my bedroom, and I'll have another pair of joggers and sweatshirt for you when you get out of the shower."

Evie took a quick shower. She was too exhausted to go through her normal washday routine, but she wasn't willing to go near Waffles or Bella without washing her hair. She lathered twice and rinsed, then when in front of the mirror, towel dried it as best she could. She scooped her hair into a messy bun and secured it with the rubber band she'd grabbed at The Sanctuary. She wrapped the towel around her chest and exited the bathroom.

Bryson stood at the foot of the bed, his chest bare.

"The shower's all yours," she said.

"I guess I wasn't quick enough," he said as he shucked off his pants and added them to the trash bag at his feet. He winked as he walked past her on his way to the en suite bathroom. "Next time, I'm joining you in the shower."

"You're always invited," she called to him before he closed the door.

Evie spotted the jogger set folded on the edge of the bed. Sitting on top of it was the panties that Bryson's house cleaner had found and added to his laundry. She slipped on the panties and the joggers, and heard the bathroom door opening as she pulled the sweatshirt over her head.

"That is so unfair," Evie said to Bryson.

"What?"

"That you can shower in three minutes."

"If you had been in there with me it would have taken me longer," he said.

"I would hope so," she said, unable to stop her smile. Evie blew out a sigh. "But now that I'm clean, I need to hug my dog."

She went back into the living room and sat on the floor next to Waffles and Bella.

"How are they?" Bryson called from the bedroom.

"Still resting," Evie called back. She rubbed Waffles on the head, not wanting to disturb Bella, who was still using her dog as a pillow.

"And looking as spoiled as ever," Bryson said as he came into the room.

"In a way, I feel both grateful and guilty. I was able to rescue this one, but it just seems so unfair to all the other dogs I left at the rescue."

Bryson sat opposite her. He lifted Bella from Waffles's back and sat her in his lap.

"You can't adopt them all, Ev," Bryson said. "I know today was hard, but look at all the dogs we saved. We didn't lose a single one. That counts for something."

She sighed. "I know. I just wish I could have done more. I

wish I could save their home. What's the good in saving them this morning if they have to be shipped out to a kill shelter in a few days?"

"That won't happen. I will personally knock on strangers' doors and beg them to take the dogs first."

"Oh, that's a feasible plan," she said with a sardonic laugh.

"I'll offer free vet care for the first year of their lives. House calls."

"Oh, really? World-renowned veterinary surgeon Dr. Bryson Mitchell turned mobile vet. You can ask Sally's for the name of the guy who built their food truck."

"That's not a bad idea. The world needs more mobile vets," Bryson said, leaning forward and kissing her.

"If that's the case, maybe *I* should go talk to Sally's," Evie said. "Operation Rescue the Rescue was my excuse for not looking for a new job."

"I have no doubt that someone will scoop you up as soon as word gets out that you're looking to join a new practice," Bryson said. "I knew you were going to be a great veterinarian back when we volunteered together, but seeing you in action today confirmed it. You are damn good at your job. Whatever you decide to do once this business with The Sanctuary is done, you're going to be amazing at it, Ev."

A fresh set of tears trailed down her face. Evie didn't realize how much she needed to hear those words. She didn't realize how long it had been since she'd received praise from someone other than Ashanti for the work she did.

Bryson leaned forward and used his thumbs to wipe at the tears on her cheeks.

"Will everything make you cry today?" he asked.

"Not everything, but when you say something like that, what do you expect?"

He grinned. "It'll all be okay, Ev."

She gave Waffles a kiss on the head, then stood. "It'll be even better once I've changed into clothes that actually fit me. Not that I don't appreciate yours, but . . ."

"I think you look cute," Bryson said. "But maybe I just like seeing you in my clothes."

She tipped her head to the side. "What about *out* of your clothes?"

The flash of heat that entered his eyes said it all. Evie felt it on her skin.

He stood and walked over to her, clamping his palms on her hips.

"If I didn't have patients to check on at the hospital, I would show you just how much I like seeing you out of my clothes." He gave her a swift but deep kiss. "Why don't I bring you and the dogs to your place? You can nap while I go to the hospital. Then we can go out for breakfast." He looked at his watch and grimaced. "Lunch."

"That sounds perfect," Evie said.

When they arrived at her house, Evie headed straight for her bed. She'd been running on adrenaline all morning, but now that the parvo crisis was over, she was exhausted. She took off Bryson's clothes and slipped under the covers in only her underwear.

She woke two hours later. Bryson had sent a message an hour ago, letting her know that the puppies were doing well but that an emergency ruptured gallbladder had come in. He'd sent another text telling her that he was done with the surgery and would be back at her place by one. She'd slept through them all.

Evie grabbed Bryson's sweatshirt from the floor and pulled it over her head. She then dragged herself to the bathroom so she could tackle her hair. But first she allowed herself to have the good, cleansing cry she'd been wanting to have all morning. Knowing she wouldn't be able to save The Sanctuary ate away at her very soul. She wanted it so bad. She *needed* it. Those animals needed it.

When she thought about the tens of thousands of dollars her mother spent on that party last night—something that lasted a few hours and was now over—it made her physically sick. The people who were there last night could save The Sanctuary with the change found between the cushions of their Italian leather sofas.

"Maybe we should give the rescue a cute name like Barkingham Palace. People like Bianca Taylor would throw money at it."

She froze.

"Don't get too excited," Evie warned.

She'd gotten herself worked up over ideas before, only for them to fall flat. Or worse, to have some catastrophe ruin everything. Granted, none of those past ideas were *this* good.

But could she pull this off in such a short amount of time? Bryson would think she'd lost her mind.

"Fuck it. I'll do it myself if I have to."

But she wouldn't have to. Bryson would not sit back while she did this alone. He'd stuck by her side throughout this entire process when others would have told her The Sanctuary was a lost cause.

She heard her phone ringing. She turned off her flat iron—

her hair would have to wait—and went into the bedroom to answer it.

It was Bryson.

"Hey," Evie answered.

"Hey, I'm at the door. Wanna let me in?"

"I'm not fully dressed," Evie said. "Give me two minutes."

She quickly put on a bra and threw on the cotton T-shirt dress she kept on a hook behind the closet door.

Waffles and Bella both followed her to the front door.

Bryson was smiling when she opened it, but his smile quickly dropped.

"What's wrong?" Evie asked, sticking out her leg to prevent Waffles from escaping.

"You said you weren't dressed." He gestured to her. "I was hoping you'd answer the door wearing less clothes."

"Oh, sure, because my neighbors totally want to see me answering the door half naked," she said.

"I'm sure they dream about it on the daily."

She rolled her eyes. "Get in here."

As he told her about the emergency surgery he'd had to perform, Evie thought about the best way to approach him with her plan. She decided feeding him first was a better idea. People were always more agreeable on a full stomach.

"Are you ready for some food?" Evie asked. "There's a little café not too far from here that serves sandwiches and salads. Why don't you let me buy you lunch?"

And convince you to help me pull off the most outrageous fundraiser ever.

While she changed into jeans and a sweater, Bryson let the dogs into the backyard for a few minutes to handle their business. They then got into her SUV and headed to the Garden District. There weren't any tables available at The Chicory House when they arrived, so they spent some time browsing the shelves at the Garden District Book Shop, one of her favorite bookstores.

"This place has a bar," Bryson said. "How can you not love New Orleans?"

"Books and booze, always a winning combination," Evie said.

After purchasing the latest Rachel Howzell Hall novel and convincing Bryson to try Maurice Carlos Ruffin, they managed to snag a table at the café. They ordered two chopped salads and two fresh-squeezed lemonades.

"Okay," Evie said. "I already know what you're going to say, but I'm going to tell you my plans anyway."

"Oh shit," Bryson said, setting down his fork. He ran a hand down his face. "What are you up to now?"

"Is that really fair?" Evie asked.

He stared at her with an arched brow.

"I'm doing it anyway," Evie said. "But I wanted to give you the option to join me in helping to save The Sanctuary."

"Is this Groundhog Day, because I'm pretty sure you've said those exact words to me before."

"And I'm saying them again. I know we've made several attempts to save the rescue already. But—"

"But there comes a point when we have to accept that it cannot be saved. I know you don't want to hear this—I hate even having to say it, Ev, but we reached that point this morning. We're going to save those dogs, but The Sanctuary is beyond saving."

"I think there's still a chance," she said.

He dropped his head back and sighed. "Does this involve buying a shit ton of lottery tickets, because that's the only thing I can think of that would raise the kind of money that's needed."

"I have something better," Evie said. She put her elbow on the table and rested her chin on her fist. "I think we should throw a gala."

Bryson's brow arched. "A gala?"

"A puppy gala! Something grand, on the scale of the party my mom threw last night. We invite the same crowd, and we convince them to give tens of thousands of dollars to save The Sanctuary."

Evie was prepared to argue her point, but she didn't have to.

"This is as good an idea as anything else we could come up with," Bryson said. "Rich people love to throw money around at stuff like this." He lifted his shoulders. "I say we go for it."

"Really? So, you're on board?"

"Why the hell not? It's a Hail Mary pass, but the reason teams take them is because they sometimes work."

"Exactly!" Evie said. "Imagine how much we could raise if we did a silent auction that included a stay at Barkingham Palace? I know Ashanti would be all for it." Evie clapped. "Okay, we have to get going on this like yesterday. But I really think we can pull it off. Ridley has this friend in public relations, Dominique. She's amazing. A little bit scary, but amazing." She pulled her phone from her pocket. "I'll text Rid right now so she can get the ball rolling."

Evie could barely contain her excitement as she and Bryson left The Chicory House. They were going to do this. Whether they could raise enough to buy a new building remained to be seen, but knowing the crowd her mother associated with, she could almost guarantee they would raise enough to cover rent on one of the places she'd scoped out on her property search.

She and Bryson had just walked out onto Prytania Street and crossed at Washington Avenue, heading back to her car, when Evie heard, "Three times in less than twenty-four hours? Who would have thought?"

She turned to find Cameron and a slim blond woman—not the one he'd had in her bed—walking toward them. He was carrying foil in the shape of a swan, a signature of how leftovers were packaged at Commander's Palace, one of the most famous restaurants in the city.

"One would think New Orleans was big enough to avoid these chance encounters," Cameron said.

"Well, my parents' anniversary party wasn't really a chance encounter, was it?" Evie said. "You were an asshole for showing up there last night."

"I was invited," Cameron said. "But you're right, it wasn't a chance encounter. Neither was this morning. You're welcome, by the way."

"You took an oath to use your veterinary skills for the betterment of society," Evie reminded him. "That's what this morning was about."

"Ev, let's just go," Bryson said, taking her by the wrist and giving her a gentle tug.

"It only took you eight years to finally scrape up my sloppy seconds, huh, partner?" Cameron asked.

"Excuse me—" Evie said.

"I knew you wanted to fuck her since we were back at LSU. At least you finally got your chance."

That son of a bitch! Evie's hand balled into a fist of its own accord.

"You're just pissed that I won," Bryson said.

Evie jerked her head back and looked up at him, but Bryson's gaze was focused solely on Cameron. The piercing hatred in his eyes was unlike anything she'd seen in him.

"You won what I no longer wanted," Cameron said.

"No," Bryson sneered. He took a step closer. "I won everything, Cam. I have a more successful career than you have. I have more accolades than you have. And I have Evie. The only thing I don't have is your daddy's money, and I don't need that because I have my own.

"I know it's hard to imagine a scholarship kid from the bayou coming out on top, but that's what happened. Do a comparison in any category, and I win them all."

Cameron's pale ivory skin had turned red. He didn't speak, just spun around and walked away, not even bothering to see if the woman he was with had followed him.

Evie stared until he turned the corner, then looked up at Bryson, who was still glowering in Cameron's direction. He finally looked at her.

"I don't know how you stayed with that asshole for so long, Ev. Let's get back to the dogs."

Evie nodded, folded her arms across her chest, and continued on to her car.

CHAPTER THIRTY

Is there a reason you're so quiet?" Bryson asked from behind the wheel as they waited for the light to change at Napoleon and South Claiborne Avenues.

Evie shook her head, not bothering to look up from her phone. She knew if she tried to speak, her voice would shake with the violent fury she was working with all her might to suppress.

"Forget about what Cameron said," Bryson continued. "That guy has always been an asshole and he'll continue to be one. It's probably in his DNA."

Evie nodded. The rage still wouldn't let her say a single word.

The moment he pulled up to the curb in front of her house, she hopped out of the Jeep and went inside. She went straight for the dogs, guiding them both to the backyard. She heard the door leading to the backyard open a few minutes later, but didn't turn.

Bryson came up behind her and put his hands on her shoulders. Evie flinched before she could stop herself.

She felt Bryson grow still.

"Ev?" he said, his voice a mix of confusion and concern. "Are you okay?"

"No." She shook off his hands and took a couple of steps, putting distance between them. Evie pulled in a deep breath, then turned to face him.

"What did you mean by 'you won'?" Evie asked.

He frowned. "What?"

"You told Cameron that you won everything, including me." She tilted her head to the side and stared up at him. "Is that what this has been about all this time, Bryson? Has this been some twisted game of one-upmanship you've been playing to get back at your old rival?"

Hurt flashed across his face. "Is that what you think?"

"That's what it sounded like to me. 'I have a more successful career. I have the accolades. I have Evie.' As if I'm just an item on a scorecard you've been keeping."

A nerve ticked in his jaw. "You know that's not the case."

"So you're not in competition with Cameron? Explain it to me, Bryson."

"Look, you wouldn't understand."

"Oh, I wouldn't?"

"No, Ev, you wouldn't! How would you understand what it's like to have to deal with people like Cameron day after day when you *are* a person like Cameron?"

"Excuse me? Didn't you just tell me last night that I'm *not* like the people who were at my parents' party?"

"It's what I told myself." He shook his head and huffed out a humorless laugh. "But we both know it isn't true. Go out and ask the average unemployed person on the street if they can just decide not to look for a new job because they'd rather work on a little pet project in order to feel better about themselves. People who are not like you and Cameron have to work for a living. We don't get to just play at it when the mood hits us."

The anguish that struck her was sharp and debilitating, rendering her momentarily speechless. She had to swallow several times before she could speak.

"You can leave," she told him. "Now."

Bryson's eyes slid closed. He brought his hand behind his head and kneaded the back of his neck.

"Ev."

"I don't want to hear anything else you have to say, Bryson. You convinced yourself a long time ago that we could never be together because we're from two different worlds, and you were not going to stop until you proved it. Congratulations. You proved it."

"Evie."

She pointed to the back door. "Just go."

He stared at her, his eyes a storm of hurt, despair, and disbelief. But he didn't say anything. He went over to where Bella and Waffles sniffed at a pile of leaves, scooped his dog into his arms, and walked right past her.

Evie wrapped her arms around her middle and pulled her trembling bottom lip between her teeth. The pain in the back of her throat made it difficult to swallow, but the pain in her chest made it difficult to breathe.

Where was the numbness? She needed the numbness now!

"No." She shook her head.

She was not going through this again. She would not

spend the next two days spiraling, watching breakup scenes from her favorite rom-coms on the couch while the rest of the world passed her by. She had a gala to produce.

Two hours later, Evie sat on Ridley's sofa, cradling a glass of wine and massaging Waffles's back with her bare toes. Ashanti sat on the floor with Duchess, feeding her blueberries from the carton she'd brought with her.

Ridley came in from the kitchen, carrying a mug. "The dogs have their own room. Why are they not in it?" she asked.

"Because Waffles really likes your rug," Evie said. "He keeps rubbing his belly against it."

Ridley pointed at Waffles. "Don't get fresh with my rug, dog. I just had it cleaned."

She sat on the other side of the sofa and brought her mug to her lips.

"Are you drinking tea again?" Evie asked.

"I like it." She shrugged as she took a sip. She nodded at Evie. "So, the fine basketball player from LSU turned out to be just a man like all the rest of them, huh?"

"I guess he did," Evie said, a fresh stab of misery piercing her chest. "Surprised the hell out of me." She kneaded her left temple with her thumb and forefinger, still working to overcome the shock of what happened today. "I really thought Bryson was different."

Ashanti raised her hand. "Uh, I know I don't have to point out that it's not all men."

"You are not about to 'not all men' her," Ridley said.

"But it's true."

"Nah-uh." Ridley wagged a finger. "Happily coupled people do not get to participate in the bitching fest. Go back to feeding your dog her blueberries."

Ashanti stuck her tongue out at her before popping a blueberry into her own mouth.

"I don't want this to turn into a bitching fest either," Evie said with a heavy sigh. "It's my fault I didn't sense Bryson's resentment."

"Ev, I saw the way that man looked at you," Ashanti said. "I didn't notice any resentment. He looked infatuated with you."

"Well, it didn't sound like there was any infatuation once he finally got everything off his chest," Evie said. "I think he's been resenting me this entire time and was just stringing me along until he got the chance to rub his success in Cameron's face. It was an added bonus that he could tell Cam that he was also screwing his fiancée."

"You're Cameron's ex-fiancée, so why the hell should he care?" Ridley asked. "And at least the sex with Bryson was good, so you got something out of it."

Evie huffed out a laugh. "You always know how to find the bright side, Rid."

"It's my gift," Ridley said.

"Enough about Bryson," Evie said. "I have a puppy gala to pull off, and I want to earn enough to buy a new building outright. I've already found a few options. I even looked at a few outside of the city that aren't as expensive. But I'm getting ahead of myself. What I need to focus on right now is getting the word out about the gala." She turned to Ridley. "Have you talked to Dom?"

Ridley held up her cell phone. "You are lucky as fuck. Her latest client had to cancel, so her schedule just opened up. And when I say you are lucky, I truly mean that you are *lucky*! Because Dom said she will do this pro bono. You all have turned her into a dog person too."

"That's fantastic!" Evie clapped her hands.

"And you don't have to look for a venue, because she has already pulled in a favor and secured the Audubon Tea Room."

The Audubon Tea Room, along with the gorgeous grounds surrounding it, would be the perfect location.

Evie was afraid to feel too hopeful, too soon, but she couldn't fight the excitement that began building in her bloodstream.

"I'm going to pull this off," Evie whispered.

"Damn right you will," Ridley said.

She would. But Evie knew there was another person whose help she needed in order to make this gala the success the rescue deserved. It was time to swallow her pride and do what was best for The Sanctuary.

She called her mother and learned that she was at the hospital today, which was located downtown, not even ten minutes from Ridley's condo. Ashanti offered to take Waffles to the dog park where she and Duchess were meeting up with Thad and Puddin'.

When Evie arrived at her mother's office, she was told Dr. Williams was consulting in the Cardiac Care Unit. Evie opted for the stairs since it was only one flight up and found her mother standing at the nurses' station, surrounded by six people in white coats.

Even though she couldn't hear what was being said, the respect on the younger doctors' faces as they listened to her mother filled Evie's chest with a level of pride she wouldn't even try to deny. The group broke apart a minute later and her mother, who hadn't shown any indication that she'd noticed Evie, headed straight for her.

"What's so urgent, Evelina?" Constance greeted. "Your call made it sound as if the world was on fire."

"Not *the* world," Evie said. "Just *my* world. And I've put the fire out, for the most part, but I'm not above asking for help when I need it. And I need your help."

"Oh?" Constance's brow arched. "It must be important if you're willing to come to the hospital to get it. I know how you feel about this place."

"It is important," Evie said. "It is one of the most important things I have ever attempted, and I want to see it through. Can we go to your office?"

"I don't want to leave the CCU," Constance said. Her mother tapped the old school pager on her hip. She was one of a surprising number of doctors at the hospital who still used them. "I have two post-op patients I'm monitoring and don't want to be too far away if I'm needed. We can use one of the consult rooms. Follow me."

They started down the hallway. Once again, Evie noticed the deference being paid to her mother by everyone who passed them. There was outright hero worship on the faces of some of the younger doctors wearing the shorter white coats. Just before they reached the consult room, they had to move aside for a patient on a gurney being wheeled to their room.

Constance held the door open for Evie to go in ahead of her.

"You know, every time you're here, I realize how much you don't fit in," her mother said.

Evie narrowed her eyes. "I'm not sure if I should take that as an insult or as the truth."

"It's not an insult, Evelina." Her mother perched against the arm of the standard-issue upholstered chair. "I have been thinking about our... discussion, if you will... last night." She released a breath. "You will rarely hear me say this, but it's probably a good thing you didn't listen to your mother and become a cardiologist. Both you and your patients would have suffered for it."

"Wait a minute." Evie put her hands up. "Did you just feel the earth shake underneath your feet?"

Her mother rolled her eyes. "Always with the dramatics." But then her expression softened. "I do not always say it, but you do know that I am proud of you, don't you?"

Evie stiffened with shock. The emotion that welled in her throat was instantaneous and abundant enough to choke on.

"Sort of," she managed to say. Then she shook her head. "No. Actually, I did not know that. I have *never* doubted your love for me, but pride?" She shook her head again. "It has always been a struggle for me to decide what meant more: my happiness or earning your respect and approval. It's something I still struggle with, if I'm being honest."

"That's my fault," Constance said.

"It is," Evie said with a hiccupping laugh. "But mine too. I should have spoken up a long time ago."

She studied her mother's face, wondering how they had arrived here. She'd come to ask for her mother's assistance in planning the gala. But now that they were finally having this conversation, Evie decided to go all the way.

"I never should have gotten back together with Cameron after the first time I broke up with him," Evie said. "I continued to go back to him because I thought becoming a veterinarian was my little act of defiance, and I owed you something for not choosing the career you wanted for me. But it's my life. And I'm grateful for what you and Dad have provided, but it should not come at the cost of my happiness or my dignity."

Constance stood and reached for Evie's hands. She took them in hers and gave them a reassuring squeeze.

"I never want you to compromise your happiness for anyone, even me. It is no secret that I have made compromises and sacrifices for things that I think are important, but you are your own person, Evelina."

Evie was overwhelmed by the gratitude that filled her chest. It wasn't as if she hadn't known hearing these words from Constance would affect her; she just had not realized *how much* it would mean to finally have her mother see and accept her for who she was.

"Thank you," Evie said. It's all she could think to say. It's all that needed to be said.

Well, that wasn't *all* that needed to be said.

Evie let out a cleansing breath. "Okay. Now that we've established that I am my own person who can accomplish anything on my own, I need my mommy's help."

Constance's face lit up in a rare smile.

"Oh, you do?" she asked, amusement brightening her brown eyes, which looked so much like Evie's that it felt as if she were staring into a mirror. "And just what do you need my help in accomplishing?"

"You know that fabulous, over-the-top party you threw last night? How about a repeat, but on an even grander scale?"

CHAPTER THIRTY-ONE

Right there. There's another mass."

Bryson used the tip of a ballpoint pen to point out the kidney-shaped mass on the X-ray of a Yorkshire terrier's spleen.

"Dammit," Bryson cursed in a low whisper. He hated this part of his job. "We can't go through with this surgery. It would be different if we were dealing with the one tumor, or a younger patient. But we're up to four tumors on a thirteen-year-old dog. It's too much."

"That's not the news Mrs. Cane will want to hear," the surgical tech said. "She'll be heartbroken if you tell her that she has to put Pinky down."

"I wish I had better news," Bryson said.

"She will tell you that money is no object."

"It's not about the money. It's about what's best for this dog. Money can't solve every problem." He snatched the X-ray from the lighted view box. "Which consultation room is she in?"

"Room three," the tech said.

Bryson slipped the pen back into the pocket of his white coat and started for consultation room 3. He really, *really* hated this part of the job.

The lab tech had been right in her prediction. Mrs. Cane was devastated by the news Bryson had the unfortunate duty of imparting. She took a credit card from her wallet and threw it at his chest, begging him to go through with the surgery. It wasn't until Bryson explained the trauma such a complicated procedure would cause to her dog's body that she finally acquiesced.

He held her hand as she suffered through the most loving act a pet owner could carry out for their cherished companion. Then Bryson held Mrs. Cane as she cried in his arms for a solid ten minutes.

By the time he handed the woman over to her son, who had been called to drive her home, his emotions were shot.

This afternoon fit right in with the hellish week he'd endured. It had been eight days since he'd left Evie standing in her backyard. Bryson had lost count of the number of times he'd picked up his phone to call her, but being unsure of what to say if she answered made him put the phone down every single time.

At first, he had been so angered by Evie's accusations that he could barely see straight. For her to think he'd been stringing her along this entire time just so that he could stick it to his old lab partner? It was absurd. It was more than just absurd—it was insulting.

It wasn't until he'd played back that confrontation with Cameron and saw it from her perspective that Bryson realized just how she had come to the conclusion that this had been some sick game on his part. Then he thought back to what he'd said to her—accusing her of being just like Cameron when nothing could be further from the truth.

That's the part that was inexcusable.

He wanted to kick himself for taking his ex–lab partner's bait. All these years later and he still allowed that asshole to get into his head.

This time it may have cost him more than he could stomach losing.

Bryson massaged the back of his neck as he made his way down the hallway. He stopped into the daycare to check on Bella, who gave him a quick lick on the hand before running off to play with the other dogs. She'd spent the first three nights this week sniffing around the doggy bed where Waffles slept when Evie came over. Bryson had been forced to lock the bed in a closet.

He left the daycare and went into his office. The moment he sat behind the desk, his cell phone rang. He dropped it twice in his haste to answer it.

It was his mother.

"Hey, Ma," Bryson answered, trying not to let his disappointment come through his voice. Apparently, he failed.

"Well, excuse me for breathing," his mother replied.

Bryson frowned. "What?"

"You tell me. I call my son, and he answers the phone like he's at a funeral."

"I'm sorry, Ma." Bryson blew out a tired breath. "I'm just having a rough day at the surgical hospital."

"Oh, I'm sorry," she said. "I didn't mean to call at such a bad time."

"It's okay," Bryson said. "What did you need?"

"Well, I was just calling because your nephew is coming

home from college in a couple of weeks and he has requested a barbecue and crawfish boil."

"Hmm," Bryson said. "When I was growing up, I either got a barbecue *or* a crawfish boil, not both."

"My grandchildren don't have to choose. Will you bring Evie with you?" his mother asked. "Wait, let me rephrase that. You *will* bring Evie with you. It isn't a question."

Shit. Bryson ran a hand down his face. "Um, yeah, about me and Evie."

"Bryson David Mitchell, you better not finish that statement if you're going to tell me that you and Evie are no longer together."

"To be fair, we technically were not together when you met her," he said.

But Bryson wasn't sure if that was true or not. When had he and Evie officially become a couple? Did it ever get to that stage?

"What did you do?" his mother asked.

"Wait, why do you think it's my fault?"

"Fine. What did *she* do?"

He blew out a breath. "No one did anything, Ma. It just . . . " He swallowed. "It just didn't work out."

"This is not the news I wanted to hear when I called you."

"Yeah, well, it's not the news I wanted to give you," he said. He couldn't do this. Not right now. "Ma, I've got another surgery in a few minutes," he lied. "I'll be there for the barbecue. Just make sure you and Pop don't book a cruise between now and then."

"I can't make that promise," she said.

Bryson ended the call and dropped his head to his desk. He hated lying to his mother, but the thought of answering any more of her questions about what happened with Evie made his head hurt. He needed at least another month... year... lifetime... before he could talk about losing Evie.

If he'd ever had her.

That's just the thing. He *had* had her. He'd managed to do the impossible, win Evie back after losing her eight years ago. No, he didn't lose her back then; he'd thrown away what they could have had together.

And like a fool, he'd allowed those same insecurities that sent him running the first time to creep back into his head. He'd allowed Cameron fucking Broussard to creep back into his head.

After everything he'd accomplished in his life, the fact that he still could not see himself as anything but that scholarship kid from the bayou was something he needed to talk over with a professional. It was beyond anything he could work through on his own; that was evident after what happened last weekend.

He guessed what they said was true, that the first step was admitting you have a problem.

Bryson leaned back in his chair and stared up at the ceiling.

Now he needed to figure out a solution to his other problem—convincing Evie he was worthy of yet another chance.

CHAPTER THIRTY-TWO

Evie thought Constance had gone overboard for her fortieth wedding anniversary, but it was nothing compared to what had been accomplished at tonight's puppy gala. Her mother, along with Ashanti and her twin sisters, and the team of designers and vendors Dom and Ridley had strong-armed into donating their time and services, had turned the Audubon Tea Room into a puppy-filled extravaganza.

There were various activities happening throughout the event space and the grounds all night long, but the fashion show currently taking place was one of the highlights of the gala. Participants paid a thousand dollars to have their fur baby take to the stage. Not only had Evie cajoled her father into paying Waffles's fee, but she'd also convinced him that his ear, nose, and throat practice should sponsor the dessert buffet, which everyone was now devouring as they enjoyed the puppies parading in their snazzy outfits. The dogs were definitely the stars tonight.

Evie waited with Waffles, who looked dashing in his puppy tuxedo, if she did say so herself. Of course, he refused to wear the accompanying top hat, but he was behaving so well tonight that she couldn't hold it against him. She just hoped that all didn't change once it was his turn to take his stroll. She'd learned over this past month that her new dog was a bit of a loose cannon. She'd marked it on her calendar to sign him up for obedience classes once the gala was behind them.

"I'm not sure how Waffles will do in front of this crowd," Evie said to Ashanti, who stood next to her with a dolled-up Duchess.

"He'll do fine. He's friendly. The friendly ones always feed off the crowd."

Ashanti motioned with her head. "Now go. You two are up."

Evie took a deep breath, then started on the runway that had been constructed down the center of the Audubon Tea Room. She could admit that she was probably more nervous than Waffles, but she had a lot riding on this night.

Everything was riding on it.

Lucas Shepard's real estate agent had contacted The Sanctuary yesterday, informing them that the new owner would be taking over the building soon. The owner appeared to have a softer heart than Lucas because he was giving them until the end of next month to vacate the property and find a new home for the remaining animals.

Evie refused to allow that home to be an already overcrowded animal shelter. She needed to raise enough money tonight to put a hefty down payment on one of the buildings she'd found in her search. None were ideal, but there were several contenders that would suffice.

She and Waffles finished their fashion walk, making way for the two stars everyone had come to see tonight. The crowd erupted into cheers when Kara, who was serving as the emcee for the fashion show, announced Duchess the Frenchie, and her faithful companion, Puddin' the Poodle.

Thad wore a tux to match Puddin's. It included a vest peppered with pictures of Duchess's face. Ashanti wore a pink gown that complemented Duchess's frilly outfit. They were such cute couples that it made Evie want to throw up.

She immediately felt guilty. It wasn't Ashanti and Thad's or Duchess and Puddin's fault that even the thought of romantic relationships of any kind—including of the canine persuasion—annoyed her.

She wasn't thinking about that tonight. She'd made a vow to evict all thoughts of Bryson as soon as they popped into her head. She would direct all her attention to the gala. She'd done a remarkable job of it, throwing herself into every aspect of the planning for tonight. But she feared what would happen when she no longer had the gala or The Sanctuary to focus on. She had no idea how she would prevent Bryson from creeping into every part of her psyche.

Worry about that if—when, you know it's unavoidable—*it happens.*

Ridley walked over to her and propped her arm on Evie's shoulder.

"You would think nothing would surprise me after the way people lost their minds over Duchess and Puddin' last year, but here I am, surprised as hell. Do you see the kind of money they're shelling out here tonight?"

"Everyone loves cute dogs," Evie said with a shrug. She playfully elbowed Ridley in the side. "Even you, although you don't want to admit it."

"Because it is false," she said. "I tolerate dogs, and only yours and Ashanti's, and *only* on occasion." She crossed her arms over her chest. "I am glad things are going well tonight. You deserve it after the way you've busted your ass these last two weeks."

"I, in every respect, could not have done this without all of you," Evie said.

"Well, of course not," Ridley immediately returned. Then she grinned. "Still, I'm happy for you." She gave Evie a kiss on the cheek. "You've inspired me to one day use my evil for good. Not today. But someday."

She shook her head. Ridley would never change, and Evie was just fine with that. She'd had enough trouble adjusting to the tiny changes she'd witnessed in her friend since she returned from London. She wasn't sure if she could handle a more drastic change.

The fashion show came to an end, which meant the costume contest was up next. Evie had opted to keep Waffles out of this event after seeing some of the elaborate outfits many of the dogs wore. No need to give her baby an inferiority complex.

"Ev! Evie!" She turned to find Ashanti moving quickly toward her. "Hey, have you checked the number on the silent auction lately?"

"Not since before the fashion show," Evie said, pulling her

phone from her pocket. Goodness, how she loved a dress with pockets.

She logged into the app that patrons were told to use to submit their bids. There was a table set up with QR codes attached to auction items ranging from puppy dates with Duchess and Puddin'—for both canines and humans—to dinner at several of the city's finest restaurants. Multiple dog groomers had donated their services. The biggest draw, by far, was a full year of doggy daycare at Barkingham Palace's new Lower Garden District location, along with a year's worth of Duchess Delights Dog Treats.

"Holy shit!" Evie said when she pulled up the page for the Barkingham Palace auction. The bid for that one item alone was already at over thirty thousand dollars.

"*You* are saving The Sanctuary tonight," Evie told Ashanti.

"Duchess and Puddin' are," Ashanti corrected her. She pointed to the photo setup where the two dogs sat on a cream-colored velvet settee. "I can't believe how many people are willing to pay two hundred and fifty bucks for a picture with those two."

Evie couldn't believe it either, but she was damn happy about it. She looked around for Ridley. She could only imagine what she would have to say about these numbers.

"Hey, any idea where Ridley went? I was just talking to her a minute ago."

"She's probably somewhere avoiding Von," Ashanti said. "He showed up about five minutes ago."

Evie shook her head in disbelief. "What could that man have possibly done to have her so shook?"

"I don't know, but it must have been damn good."

"And Von hasn't said anything to Thad?"

Ashanti shook her head. "Thad's just as stumped as I am. More so, because he said Von usually can't wait to talk about the women he's slept with."

They both rolled their eyes. Men.

Then again, Ridley was the same way. Evie had heard more about her friend's sex life over the years than she cared to recall. Yet, she knew barely anything about what happened between her and Von.

"It's so weird to see Rid like this," Evie said.

Ashanti grinned. "Yeah, but you gotta admit it's also kinda fun."

Evie held her thumb and index finger together. "Just a bit."

While the costume party was still going on, Evie and Waffles began making the rounds. Her dog may not be as popular as Thad and Ashanti's, but Waffles was getting a fair amount of love from the crowd. She went over to where her parents and several of their friends sat at one of the round tables, enjoying the offerings from the dessert buffet that had cost her dad a fortune.

There had been an unmistakable shift in her relationship with her mother in the short time since their heart-to-heart at the hospital. There was a lightness to their exchanges now. Her mother had even joked about dog sitting her grandpup. She quickly assured Evie that it was a joke and that Waffles was still relegated to the sunroom, and only when Evie was at the house, but it was still funny at the time.

Her mother's relationship with her father, unfortunately, remained the same. Not that Evie truly expected a change. As much as she loathed it, their partnership worked for them.

"I don't know, Dr. Williams," Evie said as she sidled up to

their table. "You may be this world-renowned cardiologist, but I think a second career as an event planner is on the horizon."

"I do have a knack for it, don't I?" Constance said.

Evie giggled at her cheekiness. It was so unlike her mother. She wouldn't mind seeing this side of her more often.

"Don't forget to bid on the silent auction items," Evie said, giving both her parents a kiss on the cheek. "Doc Landry's sister donated a week at her beach house in Gulf Shores. It will make for a nice vacation spot."

Evie was on her way to check in with the caterer when she was stopped by a kind-faced woman with tight silver curls. She wore a beautiful pink dress that reminded her of Duchess's outfit.

"Excuse me, but are you Dr. Evie Williams? The person who put on this party?"

"I am," Evie said.

"I'm so happy I found you," the woman said with a relieved smile. "Every time someone pointed me in your direction, you left before I could reach you."

"I'm so sorry for that," Evie said. "I've been so busy this evening."

"I understand. This event is lovely. I wish my baby was still here to enjoy it, but she recently joined her brother on the other side of the rainbow bridge."

"Oh, I'm so sorry," Evie said. "I've been there. I think we all have. It's one of the hardest parts of being a pet owner. You know they can't live forever, so you enjoy them while they're here and just keep a place in your heart for them once they're gone."

"Well, I want to do more than just keep a place in my heart for my sweet girl," the woman said. "I was told the animal rescue that tonight's gala is supporting is in need of a new home."

"Um, yes, it is," Evie said.

The woman smiled. "I own a warehouse in Irish Channel. You know where that is, don't you?"

"Of course," Evie said. The neighborhood, known for its rich Irish heritage, was only a few miles downriver from where they were now.

"Well, my building has been sitting there unused since the last tenant vacated it during the COVID shutdown. I would like to donate it to the rescue on behalf of my Pinky," she said. "If the rescue can be renamed in her honor."

Evie's mouth dropped open. Did she just hear what she thought she heard?

"Um, Ms.—"

"Cane. Evelina Cane," she said.

"Evelina!" Evie perked up. "That's my name."

The woman's face brightened. "I wondered if that Evie stood for something else. Well, Dr. Evelina, I will have my people call your people on Monday." She leaned forward and, in a softer voice, said, "My people is just my son, Ryan. He handles my finances. I told him what I wanted to do."

"And he's okay with it?"

Mrs. Cane looked at Evie as if she had just hurled the nastiest insult known to man at her. "It is *my* building and my money, dear. He doesn't have a say in how I spend it; his job is to invest it so that it continues to grow." She tapped Evie on the arm. "We'll be in touch."

Evie was too shocked to move. She could barely breathe.

Excitement, disbelief, and the suspicious feeling that she

was in the middle of a dream and would soon wake up rolled around in her head.

She needed to find Ashanti and Ridley! She had to tell them what had just happened. She needed to call Bry—

Her excitement deflated, along with her shoulders.

Dammit!

She wanted to enjoy this. She *deserved* to enjoy it. She'd worked hard to save The Sanctuary.

But she had not done it alone. Celebrating without the man who'd been by her side through most of this fight just didn't feel right.

"Ma'am?"

Evie turned to find one of the servers holding a folded piece of paper.

"This is for you," the server said.

"What is it?" Evie asked, taking the note.

He hunched his shoulder. "I was told to give it to the woman in green."

She flipped it open and read it.

> Go to the table of Duchess Delights and find the one that isn't like the others.

"What the—" Evie said. She gave Waffles's leash a tug. "Come on, boy."

She walked over to the table covered with treats Ashanti had persuaded Fido Foods, the company that bought her doggy treat business for millions, to donate to the gala. There were three designs: a Mardi Gras king cake, the Muses of Comedy and Drama masks that were usually displayed everywhere during carnival season, and a purple, gold, and green king's crown. Evie shuffled the treats around, searching for one that was different. She noticed a speck of red peeking through two of the masks. She moved one to the side and saw the heart-shaped cookie.

A curious smile curved up the side of her mouth as she picked up the cookie and turned it over.

You can ride me up and down St. Charles Avenue all day long, but tonight you can find me in the basket of toys.

Evie laughed. She knew exactly what this clue was referring to. She'd bought all the plushies from Southern Paws Pet Boutique. The one resembling the iconic St. Charles Streetcar was her favorite.

She looked around, trying to spot Ashanti and Ridley. Those two had to be the ones behind this. They'd both told her she was stressing too much about the gala and needed to unwind.

As she approached the huge wicker basket brimming with plush toys, another woman swooped in and picked up the streetcar.

"Uh, wait!" Evie called. "I think that's for me. Can you turn it over and tell me if there's a note?"

The woman turned it over, and sure enough, there was a yellow note attached.

"Do you mind?" Evie held out her hand. "I promise I'll find you once I'm done with this"—whatever this was—"and you can have the streetcar."

"Take it." She handed Evie the plushy. "I was trying to decide between the streetcar and the Cafe du Monde beignet mix anyway. You just made my choice easier."

Evie read the note on the back of the streetcar.

> There are hundreds just like me all over the city. We're tall, and stately, and the birds love us. The people do too. Step outside and you'll find me.

Definitely the oak trees. There were literally hundreds sprinkled throughout New Orleans.

This was perfect timing. She'd been meaning to make the rounds outside to see how things were going. She tugged on Waffles's leash and started for the exit that would lead to the grounds. There were nearly as many people out here as there were inside. Once this week's forecast confirmed there would be good weather, they had set up tables and chairs all around the lawn, along with a dance floor. A deejay—yet another one of Ridley's contacts—handled the outside entertainment.

Evie peered around the various trees, looking for her next clue.

She froze as she caught sight of a figure standing underneath a huge oak tree. He was cast in shadow by the tree's arching branches, but she would recognize him anywhere.

The adorable papillon at his feet was a dead giveaway.

He wore the same tux he'd worn to her parents' party, and it looked just as amazing on him right now as it had that night. Evie steeled herself against the onslaught of emotions threatening to overwhelm her. She could do this. Whether she could do it without causing a scene was another matter.

You can.

She walked the final few yards, stopping when she was still three feet away. The moment Waffles was within cuddling distance of Bella, he began to prance around her.

Evie held up the streetcar plushy.

Bryson hunched his shoulders. "You never got to hold your scavenger hunt."

Evie fought against the wave of tenderness that washed over her. Her heart pounded against the walls of her chest, but just because her body reacted in this frustratingly predictable way didn't mean her head had to.

She stooped down and gave Bella a scratch behind the ears, giving herself the chance to get her emotions under control. When she stood up again, she had to look away to avoid Bryson's eyes. The torment she'd glimpsed in them made her feel bad for him, and she wasn't ready to feel bad for him.

He gestured to the grounds. "This looks amazing, Ev."

"Thank you," she said. "It wasn't just me. I had a lot of help."

"I talked to Thad in the parking lot. He said you've raised no less than a hundred grand tonight."

"I'm sure it'll be more than that once we're all done." She hesitated for only a second before deciding to tell him about the conversation she'd just had with Evelina Cane. She couldn't hold it in any longer. "But that's not the best news of the night. We may have another location for The Sanctuary. I was approached by a woman who wants to donate a building she owns in honor of the dog she just lost."

"Mrs. Cane," Bryson said.

Evie's head jerked back. "How . . . ?"

"I was supposed to perform surgery on her Yorkie, but it would have been too risky. Mrs. Cane was devastated, of course, but she was a trouper. She held Pinky in her arms through the entire euthanasia. She mentioned that she wanted to do something to honor Pinky's life, and that's when I told her about The Sanctuary."

Evie's jaw went slack, her eyes growing wider with disbelief as Bryson continued.

"I thought maybe she would give a nice donation," Bryson said with a shrug of his broad shoulders. "But when I told her about the issue with the building, she said she would look into doing something more meaningful. Something that could keep Pinky's memory alive forever."

Evie put a hand up to her throat. She could scarcely believe what she was hearing.

"Bryson—"

"Ev, I'm sorry," he said in an aching whisper. His voice had grown instantly hoarse with emotion. Remorse and regret saturated his earnest gaze as his eyes locked in on her.

He took a step forward.

"I am *so* sorry for the things I said to you. They were awful and they were untrue. You have to know that Cameron had *nothing* to do with what has grown between us since I came back home. I never cared about seeking any type of revenge against him, and I . . . I don't know why I said those things, Ev." He ran a hand down his face. "Actually, I *do* know why."

Evie had to clear her throat before asking in the most indifferent voice she could muster, "Why?"

"It's because I still struggle with my own insecurities," Bryson answered. "It doesn't matter how many speeches I give, or awards I receive, it never feels like enough. Cameron knows that, and he preyed upon my lack of self-confidence that day outside the restaurant."

"Cameron did that," Evie said. "So why did you say such awful things to *me*?"

He looked up at her, his eyes teeming with guilt. "You were an easy target."

Evie bit her trembling lower lip. She cursed the emotions trying to take hold of her, but a lifetime of feeling as if she didn't measure up to the rest of her family wouldn't allow her to close the door on the empathy welling within her chest.

"I know it's asking a lot for you to forgive me," Bryson said. "But I hope you can, Evie. I promise to never hurt you again. All I'm asking for is one more chance to prove that I'm worthy of your love."

Evie's heart hammered against her chest as the longing she'd tried to stanch since she last saw him rushed over her.

She felt several tears roll down her cheeks as she closed the distance between them.

"Is this yes?" Bryson whispered.

She couldn't speak. The most she could manage was a nod.

Evie felt him shudder against her. Bryson captured her jaw between his palms and brushed at her tears with his thumbs. He pressed the gentlest, sweetest kisses to the spots he'd just wiped.

"I am *so* sorry," he said again.

He moved to her lips, skimming them with his, then leaned his forehead against hers.

"I swear, if it takes the rest of my lifetime, I will make this up to you."

"I don't want you to spend the rest of your life making anything up to me, Bryson." She took his hands in hers, the leashes they both held rubbing her palm. "I want you to spend the rest of your life *loving* me. That would be enough."

"You've owned my heart for nearly a decade already, Evie." He brought their clasped hands to his lips and kissed the backs of her fingers. "It's yours. Forever."

EPILOGUE

Ev. Evie!"

Evie heard her name being called over the din of the crowd crammed on The PX's main floor. She looked toward where the voice had come from and spotted Ashanti and Thad sitting at the bar that spanned the majority of the downstairs space.

"Over here!" Ashanti waved them over.

She took Bryson by the hand and led him past the high-top tables and stools packed with people. At least thirty screens of various sizes were positioned throughout the sports bar, eight of which comprised the wall behind the bar.

"Sorry we're late," Evie greeted as they approached where their friends sat.

"It's my fault," Bryson said. "I was called into surgery early this morning."

"And I didn't want to leave without him," Evie said. She

turned to Bryson. "I thought we said we weren't going to do that thing where we finish each other's sentences."

He held up his hands. "You did it, not me."

"You're supposed to point out when I do it," Evie said.

He leaned forward and kissed the tip of her nose. "I promise to point it out next time," he said. "Although, for the record, I think it's cute."

Evie looked over to find Ashanti and Thad staring with matching incredulous expressions.

"What?" Evie asked.

Thad just shook his head as he slid off the stool. "Take this one," he said. "I need to check on the dogs."

Evie climbed onto the stool Thad had just vacated. Bryson's focus was already on the basketball game that dominated every screen in the bar.

"That was weird, but I'm in my 'no judging' era, so I won't comment," Ashanti said. "Where are Waffles and Bella? Why didn't you bring them?"

"Because Bryson's mom and dad are dog sitting before they leave for their cruise. They're going for two weeks, through the Panama Canal."

"Jealous," Ashanti said.

"Same," Evie said. "But Bryson and I are too busy to even consider going on a vacation anytime soon."

"That's right, Businesswoman. You have a business to get off the ground." Ashanti beamed. "Are you excited? I'm excited for you."

"I'm very excited," Evie said. "Nervous, but excited."

Thad returned with Puddin', who wore his rhinestone collar. Evie reached down and gave him a head scratch.

"Where's Duchess?" Ashanti asked.

"Still taking pictures," Thad said.

"Did you have any idea when you came up with the idea for The PX that Puddin' would be one of the main reasons everyone wanted to visit?" Evie asked him.

"Uh, if you can recall, I didn't want anything to do with Puddin' when I moved back to New Orleans," Thad said. "I'm still undecided."

"You are not." Ashanti playfully kicked at his shin. "I think Puddin' is the perfect mascot for this place. He softens it up."

"I'm just glad to finally fully open this place," Thad said.

Thad and Von's estimate of a few more weeks until their official grand opening had been off by about another month thanks to a broken water main that took the city longer than anticipated to fix. Yet, the timing could not have been more perfect.

Because of the delay, The PX's grand opening coincided with a significant NBA game featuring New Orleans's franchise. Evie was pretty certain she was the only person here *not* wearing a Pelicans jersey. That included the dogs.

"Look at that one," Thad muttered, gesturing with his chin.

Evie looked to her right and caught sight of Von Montgomery stalking toward them. Make that two people not sporting Pelicans regalia. Von wore an army-green T-shirt with The PX's official logo across the chest. He had a bar towel slung over his shoulder and a determined look on his face. His expression softened when he noticed Evie and Bryson.

"Hey," Von said, kissing Evie on the cheek and catching Bryson's palm in a firm shake. "Glad you two could make it."

"As if we would miss out on the celebration," Evie said. "This has been a long time coming."

He nodded. "I still can't believe it's finally here."

"Yes, it is finally here," Thad said. "So why don't you take a minute to enjoy it instead of running around like a mother hen?"

"Someone has to run this place," Von said. He took his phone out of his back pocket. "Okay, Evie, you said the mobile vet truck will be ready to roll by June, right? I've got you down for the third Thursday of every month."

"Yes." She nodded. "Discounted vaccinations and free exams for service animals. I'll have a link for customers to schedule their services as soon as Kara finishes my website."

"Good," Von said. A loud clang came from the vicinity of the kitchen.

"I'll go see what that's about," Thad said.

"I've got it," Von said. He stuffed his phone back in his pocket. "This place is going to fall down around us before the day is over."

Bryson hooked a thumb in Von's direction. "Does he seem a bit high-strung to anyone else?"

"He's wound tighter than a fucking guitar string," Thad said. "I'll give him until the end of the week to get it out of his system, then I'm intervening." He settled his elbows back on the bar. "By the way, the mobile vet thing is a genius idea, Evie."

"You're welcome," Bryson said, grabbing a handful of peanuts from the bowl on the bar.

Evie rolled her eyes. "Yes, it was his idea, but I designed the interior space. It's the perfect mobile clinic."

Evie already had a host of businesses that had shown interest in her upcoming mobile vet clinic visiting, including several in small towns along the bayou where Bryson grew up. The ability to bring quality veterinary care to smaller, underserved communities was a bonus she hadn't anticipated when she decided to act upon what had first been a joke between her and Bryson.

She planned to continue working at Barkingham Palace, but the rest of her time would go to her new venture. It felt as if she'd finally found her calling.

"The only thing she's missing is a name," Bryson said.

"You haven't decided?" Ashanti asked.

"Nothing fits." Evie shrugged. "I wanted to name it after Waffles, but every name I come up with sounds more like a food truck than a veterinary clinic."

"Well, I still think you should go with Crescent City Mobile Clinic," Ashanti said. "An ode to New Orleans is always a safe bet."

Evie scrunched up her nose. "Half the businesses in this town are named Crescent City something or other."

"Which should tell you something. It's a good name."

"Pugs and Kisses Veterinary Clinic," Ridley said as she crossed Evie and took the seat next to her. She'd come from out of nowhere.

The four of them stared at her in complete silence.

"What?" Ridley asked with a shrug. "She owns a pug. Well, at least he's part pug, right? Pugs and Kisses. You can cover the outside of the truck with pink kiss marks. People will love it."

Thad's head jerked back. "Who *are* you?"

"Weird, right?" Ashanti said.

"Weird, but brilliant," Evie said. "I love Pugs and Kisses."

Ridley grinned and winked. "Told you I would start doing good. This place looks really nice," she said to Thad. "It's not my usual scene, but I get the appeal."

Von chose that moment to return. He stopped at the sight of Ridley.

Evie's heart squeezed at the intense longing that played across his face. Ridley did a better job at masking her feelings, but Evie noticed the shaky breath her friend sucked in.

"Ridley," Von said. "Thanks for coming."

"Yeah, well, I know how important today is to all of you. I wanted to show my face." She scooted off the stool she'd just climbed on. "I need to get going."

"But you just got here," Ashanti said.

"I've got a presentation I need to finish up before tomorrow," she said. "And, like I said, this isn't really my scene." She nodded at Evie. "You can thank me for the name with pastries from that new Black-owned bakery in Central City. Get in line early. They tend to sell out of the chocolate croissants before noon."

"Um . . . okay," Evie said.

To Thad, she said, "Good luck with"—Ridley glanced in Von's direction—"everything."

"So weird," Evie and Ashanti said in unison as they watched their friend stroll out of The PX.

Ashanti tapped Evie with her elbow. "But, hey, it sounds as if your mobile vet business has a name."

"It sure does," Evie said. She held her hands out, as if pointing at a marquee. "Pugs and Kisses to the Rescue."

ACKNOWLEDGMENTS

It has been nearly twenty years since that fateful day I summoned the courage to send a one-page query letter to one of my dream literary agents. It remains the best decision I've ever made in my career. Thank you, Evan Marshall, for guiding me through these sometimes treacherous publishing waters. Your steadiness is something I've come to rely on.

ABOUT THE AUTHOR

Farrah Rochon is the *New York Times* and *USA Today* bestselling author of forty-plus adult romance and young adult novels, novellas, and short stories, including the popular *Boyfriend Project* series from Forever Romance. When she is not writing in her favorite coffee shop, Farrah spends most of her time reading, traveling the world, visiting Walt Disney World, and catching her favorite Broadway shows.

You can learn more at:

FarrahRochon.com
Instagram @FarrahRochon
Facebook.com/FarrahRochonAuthor
TikTok @FarrahRochon
X @FarrahRochon